GW00857785

Dennis Talbot was born
walk with his wife Paulir
ty of Derbyshire.

Dennis wrote his first novel 'A Small Price to Pay, Sir'
at the age of 70. With his lifelong love of the novels of
PG Wodehouse, this was bound to be a humorous offering. It reached the finals of 'The People's Book Prize'
2016. Two further novels featuring the same characters,
Josh & Ellingham followed.

During a spellbinding holiday in America and Canada,
the seeds of a detective story set in the 1930's began to
take shape.

The Killing of Cristobel Tranter the first in the *Whitecross Yard Murders* series was the result.

Introducing PC Will Dexter the main character

Will was born in 1908, the third child of George and El-
len, and the only boy. His sisters Edith and Florence
(Flossie) fussed around him like two extra mothers but
George made sure that Will was a well-adjusted young
man.
Will was an apprentice at Lomas Engineering, where he
met his future wife Alice. Although he enjoyed his time
working in the electrical department of the firm, his real
dream was to join the Police Force.
Within a few weeks of gaining a position as a probation-
ary constable, he found himself in at the deep end.
As the tale unravels, Will became involved in the investigation of what turned out to be a serial killing.

THE WHITECROSS YARD MURDERS

The Killing of Cristobel Tranter

First published March 2018
Reprinted June 2018

If you are looking for a great historical fiction or crime mystery then Dennis Talbot's, *The Killing of Cristobel Tranter,* is for you! I was immediately drawn into the book because the main character, Will Dexter, has a great history and a fascinating job. He's a police constable who right off the bat finds the dead body of a woman. The novel expertly mixes Dexter's home life, past, and the thrilling police work necessary to find the killer! One of the things I found most impressive about this novel was the dialogue. Dialogue can make or break a book, and Talbot did a wonderful job of making it feel authentic. I enjoyed the quirky slang and period appropriate wording. It really helped in character building because it created dynamic characters.

On Line Book Club Reviewer Britt 13

What readers have said:

An outstanding and gripping novel that is a MUST READ!
J McBride

This is a historical detective novel with a cracking story, couldn't put it down!
R Nauen

A brilliant story that captures the era so well, more please!
Dr Peter Meakin (Creative Director)

Dedication

Once again to my wife Pauline

Acknowledgements

Posthumous thanks must go to my Grandfather who was a humble bobby in the 1930's. As a young teenager, I remember we talked for ages of the camaraderie among the ranks and about the seemingly basic methods of policing used then; at the time of course they were cutting edge.

Also by Dennis Talbot
THE WHITECROSS YARD MURDERS

The Killing of Cristobel Tranter

Death in the Back Row

*

THE JOSH AND ELLNGHAM NOVELS

A Small Price to Pay, Sir

Best Foot Forward, Ellingham

Look Lively Ellingham

Death in the Back Row

Dennis Talbot

1

The August afternoon had been hot and sultry, making patrolling Crammingdon marketplace a bit too warm for comfort. The sky was cloudless blue and at midday the sun made the open space near unbearable in full uniform. Eventually I took the highly unacceptable step of loosening my tie and undoing the top button of my shirt, not that it made a huge difference, and I found myself still seeking what little shade was available.

The shouts and laughter of a group of kids filled the air. Supervised by mams and big sisters, they were having a high old time leaping in and out of the pool alongside Alderman Watson's drinking fountain. I had been called in from north division to cover a shortage of officers, mainly due to holiday entitlement and a summer flu epidemic depleting central division staff. I looked at my pocket watch as I passed, for the umpteenth time, the little merry-go-round and swing-boats that had been set up for the school summer holidays. Four-thirty-five, I glanced over at the Town Hall clock, it was still three minutes ahead of time, as I knew it would be. I noticed the people exiting the little cinema next to Lloyds Bank. Not surprisingly, the afternoon matinee had only attracted a small audience. I remember thinking that even the latest Laurel & Hardy "talkie" double bill, wouldn't

1

make me go into a stuffy cinema this afternoon and the "Magnificent Cinema" was stuffy even in the winter. It had the reputation of being a "fleapit" since it was common knowledge that the usherettes went around between houses with spray disinfectant, which did nothing to reduce the stuffiness of the atmosphere. My orders were, patrol until the place was clear enough to no longer present a target for pickpockets and villains, I decided to do just one more lap of the marketplace before signing off at Crammingdon Constabulary HQ Whitecross Yard.

Mothers and toddlers were already drifting away, heading home to get dad's evening meal ready I supposed, and that seemed an excellent time to call it a day. Nothing exciting had happened, the most memorable parts of the afternoon was helping a lost little girl find her mam, who presented me with an ice-cream cornet a few minutes later, by way of thanks. An hour or so later I was swinging a skipping rope, tied to one of the lampposts, for six youngsters amid yells and shouts of several skipping songs; songs I remembered from my own childhood. A dad appeared after ten minutes or so and took over the rope swinging and I continued my wanderings. On afternoons like this, I often found myself thinking, as I was now, that Gilbert & Sullivan had made a mistake; a policeman's lot, can be a very happy one at times!

Something caught the corner of my eye, the blue light was flashing on the police-box outside the town hall. Smartening my step, I hurried to answer the call. I was amazed that the emergency was at the cinema I had just seen emptying. Turning I saw a man in a blue suit whom I recognised as the cinema manager, trotting towards me waving his arms.

'Hurry up! He's in the back row,' he shouted, and I followed him into the tiny cinema.

The building had once been a small music hall. Known back then as the Trans-Atlantic Vaudeville, it had managed to attract a number of first-rate artistes. Unfortunately, the small size of the auditorium meant that it often failed to make a profit. The stage had been removed and a screen installed allowing for another three rows of seats. What set the Magnificent Cinema apart from its rivals was the back row. The seating there was always in big demand in the evening because instead of single seats, it comprised of twelve double seats, small sofas; locals called them courting couches. The show had been a matinee for the kids, and the man causing the manager concern sat in the middle of one of the sofas. He was massively overweight. The confines of a standard cinema seat would have been of little use to him.

There was no need to have hurried, the man was dead and I guessed for at least an hour. I'm no expert of course, but a part of my job is dealing with people who have died. Sadly, this is often elderly people who have no relatives or friends and it can sometimes be several days before they are found. A quick examination of the seats around him suggested that this was just a death by natural causes. I guessed that his weight alone must have put a great strain on his heart.

'Do you know who he is?' I asked the manager getting my notebook out.

'He's a regular matinee customer, that's all I know. Phyllis might know. She runs the box office,' he said.

'Could I have a word with her?'

3

'Not at the moment she's gone to the bank with this afternoon and last night's takings. She should be back any time,' the manager said looking at his wrist-watch.

'Have you sent for a doctor, Mr…?'

'Worthy. Edward Worthy. Yes, he's on his way.'

'Thank you Mr Worthy, I'm going to search his pockets in the meantime, to try to establish who he is,' I said and the manager nodded.

I emptied his pockets, and laid their contents on the seat beside him, though there was nothing to give a clue to his identity. A bunch of assorted keys contained what seemed to be a car ignition key, together with a handkerchief, a wallet containing a pound note and a ten-shilling note and a business card for a local garage. Four shillings and sixpence in loose change was in an-other pocket. An ashtray fixed to the back of the seat in front of him, contained two chocolate bar wrappers, screwed up and stuffed into it, I pulled them out and straightened them, and placed them on the seat alongside the contents of the man's pockets. I had to smile the two bars were from a locally made range. **"Mrs Longdon's Homemade Confections"**, they were both favourites of Alice my wife. On the back of the wrapper of every product was a sort of pedigree.

*"In 1884 Mrs Millicent Longdon began making sweets and chocolate to help the family finances. Originally sold from her cottage door, they quickly gained a repu-tation for quality and taste. When it became clear that demand was becoming greater than she could cope with, we, **Barrington Bros,** offered to produce them for her to her own recipes. That was in 1891. We now produce and*

4

supply her delicious range to the four corners of the world." One was a half-pound fudge bar, the other a large size "Turkish Delight" bar, both of them chocolate coated. Barrington Bros products were always a little more expensive than other products but they were really good.

The doctor arrived as I looked under the seat and generally around the floor for anything that might be helpful.

'Is there no more light than this?' the doctor snapped. The auditorium lighting was subdued to say the least.

'I can turn it up a bit,' the manager said.

'Then kindly do so, can't see a bloody thing in here!' the doctor snapped and the manager hurried off.

'Are those his?' the doctor asked nodding at the chocolate wrappers.

'They were in this ashtray, so I imagine so, unless they are from last night,' I suggested.

'The older I get the more I think people really are their own worst enemy. Look at the size of this chap, the last thing he needs is a mountain of pure sugar!' he snapped.

A few seconds later the light increased, but even so, it was nowhere near as bright as the foyer.

'Is that it?' the doctor asked, as the manager returned.

'That's it but I've brought you a flashlight.'

'Like working in a bloody coalmine!' the doctor said, grabbing the light.

Phyllis, the box office girl had returned from her trip to the bank and, seeking the manager came through into the auditorium. As her eyes fell upon the man I had

5

to smile. She let out a gasp and clutched her mouth in a very "silver-screen" sort of way and slumped into a double seat the other side of the central aisle. I went to the aisle and crouched beside her.

'I'm sorry to have to ask you questions, miss. I can see that this has upset you but I need to find the identity of the gentleman,' I said, nodding in the deceased's direction.

'I don't know his name, but he comes here once a week, always in the afternoon, for the matinee,' she sniffed.

'Never in the evening?' I asked.

'No. Never, he needs a big seat you see, and the back row is always filled with young couples in the evening!'

'I see, what else can you tell me about him?'

'He always arrives good and early, polite he is, always puffing and panting, seems to have difficulty walking, as though his feet hurt him, all that weight I suppose,' Phyllis said, with a sniffle.

'Does he have a car do you know?' I asked.

'I wouldn't know; I doubt he walks very far though, sir. Even climbing the three steps at the front door has him struggling for breath!'

'I found two chocolate bar wrappers in the ashtray in front of him. Would they be his?'

'Yes I served him, myself. He has a half-pound bar of fudge and a large "Turkish Delight". It's always the same, every time he comes in. Very keen on his fudge and "Turkish Delight" the gentleman is... Was!' she said and a tear rolled down her cheek.

'You always serve him?' I asked.

'There's only me in the box office for the mat-

6

inees, it's not so busy in the afternoon so I have to serve the snacks as well.'

'Well, well, well, look what I've found!' the doctor said holding a hip flask at arms-length and waving it around. 'Rum, from the smell of it.'

'I missed that,' I admitted.

'In his back pocket, found it when we rolled him over. You'd better have this as well,' he said holding up a tiny leather bound diary.

The manager's call to Whitecross Yard, had set things in motion. The duty sergeant had switched on the police box light that had alerted me, and informed the CID department. On the arrival of DC George Harrington I made him aware of the situation, and handed over to him, carrying out his request to search the immediate area.   Within the hour, much to the manager's relief, the body of the unknown man had been removed via a fire exit at the side of the cinema, and taken to the pathology department at Crammingdon Hospital. I then, returned to Police HQ at Whitecross Yard to make a written report and then back to my own station in north division.

It wasn't until three or four days later that I learned the man's death was being treated as suspicious. DI Brierly, the head of Crammingdon CID had called me in to Whitecross Yard late one afternoon.

'You found the body, is that right Dexter?' he asked.

'The Cinema manager found him. I was first officer on the scene, yes sir.'

'Tell me your first impressions of the scene.'

'Well sir, the place was hot and stuffy, but then

7

it normally is. As I followed the manager into the auditorium, I saw a big man; I estimated his weight at twenty to twenty-five stone, sir. He had slithered forward until his knees were pushed against the seat in front, and he was lolling back in the seat with his head to one side, sir.'

'The pathologist made him, twenty-six stone, and initially put his demise down to that fact alone. Today he informed me that the chap had actually been very cleverly poisoned or had committed suicide,' the DI grinned.

'Poisoned chocolate bars, sir?' I smiled.

'Maybe! The pathologist is still looking into that.'

'If he bought the bars at the box office, then it's purely chance that it was our chap that was poisoned. It could have been any customer,' I pointed out.

'We will possibly know more once we find out who he is and where he lives. The only real clue we have, is a business card for a local garage, but they reckon they don't know him. A twenty-six stone man is hard to miss so I guess it's just by chance that he happens to have their card in his wallet. That's why I've brought you in, you were first on the scene and you're an observant sort of chap; is there anything that you think we've overlooked?' the DI asked.

'I'm sure there was nothing else at the scene, I had a good look round, sir. I did miss the fact that the chap had a hip flask; the doctor found it in his back pocket when he moved him,' I admitted.

'Not up to you to move the man, so don't let that worry you. Did you search all of his pockets?'

'Yes, sir, there was nothing other than what

8

you're already aware of sir,' I said but added, 'I wonder where he picked up the garage card, sir?'

'We'll never know that.'

'Often businesses put their cards in places where lots of people go, libraries, barbers' shops, post offices that sort of thing. Is it worth asking the garage where they display their cards, sir?' I asked.

'Can't do any harm, I'll get my lads on it first thing in the morning. Thank you PC Dexter, if you think of anything else, let me know!' the DI grinned.

'Of course, sir,' I agreed, and set off home, anxious to see my two-year- old twin boys and Alice my wife, the light of my life.

My route home takes me directly past the shop of Cyril Turner, my own barber, and I decided to drop in to see if he displayed the cards of E M Jenkins, Motor Engineer, the name on the card in the dead man's wallet. I didn't think he did, I couldn't remember seeing them, and such was in fact the case. I made a small detour to call in on Benjamin Wooley a barber a couple of streets away, again without success. The post office is only a few hundred yards from my home, but I didn't even bother to call in, I was sure the murder victim, if that was what he really was, would have been known to me if he lived local enough to use that post office. He was after all a very memorable man!

The boys are growing fast, becoming quite a handful and Alice was glad to pass them over to me when I arrived home at about six o'clock. George, the younger by about half an hour, looks like being the natural leader, with Will happy to play second fiddle. I commented on this after a few minutes of playing wooden bricks with them.

'Do you think so? I've been watching them for days, and they seem to take it in turns to be ringleader. It seems to alternate as they get tired. They had their first little fight this afternoon, about "Wonky Bear",' she laughed.

'They've each got a bear, what was the problem?' I smiled.

'Somehow they both love "Wonky". Let's face it, he has more character!' she laughed.

It was true that although both bears had started out as near identical as we could get them, one of them had been through the wars. "Wonky" had a lop-sided ear and an arm that hung a bit awkwardly no matter how Alice tried to stitch it on straight making him, or her, a bear of distinction!

The boys had eaten and I washed them and put them to bed with a story. We sat in the kitchen by the range, and passed a pleasant evening in our own company.

2

Alice had become great friends with a young mother a few doors away, Nelly Williams, a woman about Alice's age, a happy-go luck person with auburn hair worn in the slightly old-fashioned earphones style. They gave each other a break from their respective kids a couple of times a week. Nelly would be having the boys for a couple of hours this morning to allow Alice to do a bit of shopping. Things, of course, don't always turn out as arranged. I was about to set off to sign in at North Division station in Hartlepool Street when there was a knock at the back door and Nelly burst in dragging her two girls.

'Alice, Alice, can you have the girls? Dick has just been knocked off his bike!' she blurted out, worry showing in her eyes.

'Yes, of course. Is he alright?' we said together.

'I don't know. I want to go with him in the ambulance, can I leave the girls?' she asked, leaving the bewildered girls and racing back down the entry.

'Will you be okay? I'd better follow Nelly, see if there's anything I can do,' I said, quickly tying my boots and grabbing my helmet.

'Yes, I'll be okay, the girls are no trouble,' she said as the pair began to cry and cling to Alice.

The ambulance was at the end of the road, a

hundred and fifty yards away, strangely we hadn't heard its bell. A small crowd had gathered behind it. Nelly was just climbing in the back as I arrived on the scene. A Bedford delivery van stood partially on the pavement and I guessed it was the vehicle which had collided with Dick Williams. A man in an old but clean red and blue checked shirt with rolled-up sleeves, that I took to be the driver, was perched on a front doorstep with his head in his hands. I crouched down beside him and began gently questioning him.

'Good morning, sir. Are you the driver of the van?'

'Yes, er… he just came from nowhere. Suddenly he was there. There was nothin' about and I just glanced at me sheet to check me next delivery, I looked up, only a moment later and he was there in front of me! I'd hit him before I could get me brakes on. Oh my God! Oh bloody hell!' the driver said standing up and beginning to punch and kick the wall at the side of him. He drew his head back and was clearly about to head-butt the wall. I quickly grabbed him by the shoulders and although I was unable to stop him doing so, I drastically reduced the impact.

'Don't do that, sir!' I said, trying to restrain him.

'Oh, God! Say he's not dead! Say he's not dead!' he said, fighting me off and continuing to punch the wall making a mess of his hands.

'Here, tell him to get this down him,' said a neighbour offering a mug of tea, whilst her husband carried a kitchen chair. The driver took a swipe at the mug, spilling about half of the hot tea and making the woman shout with pain. The fact that he had hurt the woman calmed him and he muttered an apology.

'Sit down sir, have this cuppa!' I said gently but firmly lowering him into the chair.

He took one sip of the tea, and burst into tears.

'Dear God, please don't let him die! What have I bloody done?'

'Have another sip of tea and tell me your name, then tell me exactly what happened,' I said taking out my notebook and leaning closer to see if I could detect any trace of alcohol on his breath.

'Joseph Sanford, I'd just done me drop at the greengrocer's shop back there, and heading for me next one. I'm new to the area, so I had to look at me sheet to find where it is. The boss always says, "Look-up yer next drop before yer start movin'," but yer always know best, don't yer? Save a couple of seconds by doin' it on the move. He'll bloody sack me for this, and right too. I always was too bloody clever for meself. The missus is always telling me to stop buzzin' round like a blue-arsed fly. "You'll come unstuck one day forever racin' around," she was right, eh?' he said and started picking at his damaged hands.

The neighbour, who had brought the tea, returned a couple of minutes later, with some soothing cream and bandages and tried to dress his hands. He shook her away.

'Come on love. No use hurtin' yerself. I know you feel bad but this doesn't help does it.' she said resting a hand on his shoulder and calming the chap. He slumped in the chair, shivering and sweating at the same time, but allowing her to gently apply the cream and bandage as I continued to question him.

'How fast were you going Mr Sanford?' I asked.

'Not fast, it was only me second drop so I'm still

13

heavy laden, I was still in second gear. Eighteen – twenty perhaps.'

'You say the cyclist appeared from nowhere?'

''Sright, I looked up and there he was! I hit him and he shot up in the air, hit me bonnet and rolled onto the other side of the road. If anythin' 'ad 'ave been comin' the other way…!'

A police traffic car, PV2 raced up, bell ringing, driven by my old mate "Bong", an ex-Australian copper.

'Hi, Will! What's happened?' he asked, as his mate Bob inspected the cycle.

'Yer too late, it's more or less sorted. This is Joseph Sanford, the driver of that van; knocked my neighbour off his bike twenty minutes ago. He's on his way the City Hospital, and his wife has gone with him in the ambulance,' I said, quickly putting him wise to the state of things. 'I think it's a case of driving without due care and attention, Mr Sanford admits to being distracted whilst looking up his next delivery!'

'We'd have been here earlier but we were dealing with DC Harrington.'

'Dealing with him; how do you mean – dealing with him?' I asked.

'He was stabbed this morning, whilst making an arrest.'

'Oh! Is he okay?' I gasped.

'Not so good I'd say. I'm no expert of course, but he's lost a lot of blood,' Bong said shaking his head.

'What happened?'

'DC Harrington and a uniform, go to make an arrest of a chap they know is stealing stuff from Burton's Foundry. They know he's a nasty character so me and Bob here, go as motorised back up to take him back in

14

the car! Harrington goes round the back of the house and the copper knocks on the front door. There's a scuffle round the back and Harrington, screams and shouts, "He's done me, he's got a knife!". The suspect comes flying down the side of the house and unfortunately trips over the uniform's foot, at the same time as accidentally coming into contact with my truncheon!'

'Twice!' Bob coughed.

'Oh yes, accidentally coming into contact with my truncheon, twice!' Bong grinned. 'Bob slips the cuffs on him and I go to see how Harrington is. He's on the ground clutching the top of his arm and blood's pumping out between his fingers! I've got a little first aid kit in the car and Bob nips to phone an ambulance while I put on a tourniquet and bandaged him as best I can, but I can only slow it down. The ambulance is there double quick. And they do a better job then take him to the City, same as your chap,' Bong said.

DC George Harrington was part of DI Brierly's handpicked team together with DS Whittington. I had worked with them on a case a couple of years back as an acting DC. I was sorry to hear he had been injured, we'd always worked well together and although I'm not a religious man I found myself offering a little prayer for his safe keeping, and of course for the husband of our friend! I left Bong making arrangements for the owners of the van to get it unloaded and sent to our vehicle compound at Central Division for examination, and went back home to get my lunchtime sandwiches and my bike, then off to sign on at North Division.

Having made a report of the incident, I went out on my normal patrol. Things were as quiet as usual

15

midweek. A group of kids had tied a rope to a lamppost and stretched it across the road. 'Hey, mister, swing the rope for us again,' yelled a ragged trousered lad I remembered from the market place.

'Sorry lad, I'm late already,' I laughed.

'Go on mister, five minutes,' they all shouted together. I took out my watch and made a great play of looking at it and making a decision as they stood around with pleading eyes. 'Five minutes, not a second more.'

'Yes!' they all yelled, as I grabbed the rope. This was my type of policing! I felt sure that being the kind of copper who was part of the community, a friendly face but ready to act where things went wrong, was much better than being over pompous and hated. Unfortunately, not all of my colleagues felt the same.

The morning passed off with nothing to report and I returned to the station to grab a cup of tea and eat my packed lunch.

'DI Brierly has requested you to report at Whitecross Yard again Dexter!' the duty sergeant said, as I walked through the door.

'Right, Sarge.'

'I've said you'll be there about two o'clock, so get yer grub first.'

'Thanks,' I nodded.

A brisk ride, wondering all the time what this latest summons was about, brought me to Whitecross Yard with a couple of minutes to spare and I slipped my bike in the shed in the rear yard. I removed my cycle clips, straightened my tie and climbed the steps.

'Good afternoon, PC Dexter, the DI's ready for you. Go straight up, you know where it is?'

'Yes, thank you Sarge. Any idea what this is

about?' I asked.

'Relax! You're not on the mat,' he grinned.

I climbed the stairs to the CID office and tapped on the door.

'Come in,' yelled a voice I recognised as DI Brierly.

'Good afternoon, sir; you wanted to see me?'

'Sit down, Dexter.'

'Thank you, sir,' I replied with a smart salute.

'I guess you've heard about DC Harrington?'

'Yes, sir. Is there any news, sir?'

'The last I heard, about ten minutes ago, is that he's had two blood transfusions, the injury itself isn't normally life threatening but he lost a lot of blood. It's too early to say for sure but they think his chances of a full recovery are good. However he is likely to be laid-up for at least a couple of months,' the DI said.

'That is encouraging news, sir.'

'It is, and it brings me to the point of asking you here. As you can imagine this unfortunate incident leaves me a man short. I've been in touch with the Chief Constable and asked him for a temporary replacement. I particularly asked for you, remembering the sterling work you did on the Cristobel Tranter case a couple of years ago. I brought that to his attention and he agreed to let me second you to CID for the duration,' he grinned.

'Thank you, sir. I'd like that very much,' I said.

'Start in the morning at eight o'clock, I'm running a briefing on this chap who died in the cinema. We've still got no bloody idea who the hell he is,' he said shaking his head. 'The blasted man's a complete mystery.'

'I've been thinking about that, sir,' I nodded.

'Now why doesn't that surprise me!' he grinned. 'Let's have it.'

'He must travel quite a way to go to that particular cinema, but why?'

'You're thinking as we are, that the man is, was, instantly recognisable so unlikely to be a local,' the DI nodded.

'Yes sir. Though why that cinema? There are dozens of cinemas; every town has three or more.'

'We pondered that, and we looked over your initial report last night. Here, read what you put!' he grinned.

It didn't take many seconds to read, it was short-and-sweet to say the least. However, seven or eight words jumped out at me, *the deceased was occupying one of the double seats at the rear...* 'He needed the extra room!' I nodded.

'We've done a bit of research and guess what?'

'Not many cinemas have courting couches, sir,' I smiled.

'The nearest one we could find is the Kings Cinema in Ilkeston, but they don't do matinees. The next one is in the middle of Stafford. You know what that means Dexter?'

'Our chap could come from anywhere within thirty miles, sir.'

'Hopefully not quite that far, but who knows? Still want to be involved?' he chuckled.

'Oh yes, sir. Oh yes, very much, sir!' I nodded.

Alice was over the moon at the thought of me being again included in our little CID department.

'I'm only there until DC Harrington is back in

18

harness, my sweet,' I pointed out. 'Tomorrow is Friday; it will probably mean working the weekend.'

'But it was you he asked for. Don't you see my love; he recognises your special talent,' she said grabbing and squeezing my hand.

'Or perhaps, like the last time, I was the first bobby on the scene,' I grinned.

'I know you don't believe that. I can tell. Your look, when you came in just now, like the cat that got the cream! Deny it William Dexter; go on deny it!' she said kissing my cheek.

'You're right love. I am very pleased with myself,' I admitted.

'I can take the smile off your face; I've had Nelly's girls all day, so there's a pile of washing up needs doing!' she grinned.

With the boys in bed, we again spent the evening quietly in our own company. Alice had me help her winding some wool, then I looked at the evening edition of the *Argus*. The front-page story was about a very disturbing incident in the village of Potempa, in Upper Silesia, a part of Germany. A communist miner had, so the story stated, been killed in front of his family for no other reason than his political beliefs. A group of five young men, had been arrested soon afterwards, not attempting to hide their identities, and admitting to being part of a new movement called the Brown Shirts, under one Adolf Hitler, a name I'd never heard before.

I entered the CID office, dressed in plain clothes, at eight o'clock next morning as instructed. DS Whittington was already there but there was no sign of the DI.

'Good morning Will,' the DS said.

'Good morning, Sarge.'

'The DI should be here any minute, he's generally a couple of minutes late!' he grinned.

'Is there any more news on George?' I asked.

'I rang the hospital at seven-thirty. All they would say is that he'd had a comfortable night. Talk about trying to get blood out of a stone!'

'At least he's no worse.'

'Gordon Hemmings, the chap they arrested has been transferred to the same hospital. It seems he passed out during his interview, suspected delayed concussion. I understand he tripped as he tried to escape hitting his head on a concrete path!' the DS said. I didn't mention the fact that Bong's truncheon might also have been a contributory factor.

'I hope they're not in the same ward!' I smiled.

'I have it on good authority that Harrington is lauding it in a private ward. Running the nurses ragged I shouldn't wonder,' he grinned.

'Who's paying for that?'

'Police Benevolent Fund I should think.'

Our discussion was cut short by the sound of the DI climbing the stairs.

'Good morning, sir,' we both said as he opened the door, instinctively I added a salute.

'Good morning, my merry band. By the way we don't salute in CID, remember?'

'Sorry sir, force of habit,' I grinned.

'Right Dexter welcome to the fold, even if it is on a temporary basis. Your first duty each morning will be the ritual of the kettle. I'm sure I needn't stress the importance of this task' he grinned.

'Right, sir,' I said and set about the time-honoured ceremony.

'Our cinema victim is still very much a mystery. We can't keep calling him our cinema victim or the deceased, what shall we call him until we actually learn his name?' the DI asked.

'How about Mr Big!' the DS chuckled.

'Makes him sound like an American gangster,' the DI said shaking his head.

'I was referring to his size, sir.'

'Mm, yes, tongue in cheek, Mr Big, then,' the DI nodded.

There was a knock on the door and the duty sergeant poked his head into the office. 'Letter, just delivered by hand, sir,' he said handing it to DS Whittington.

'Thank you, sergeant,' the DI said as DS Whittington passed the envelope across. 'This is the long awaited pathology report,' the DI said as he tore it open.

'As usual there's lots of medical jargon, but as always the good doctor has summarised it for we mere mortals. It seems that our victim... sorry Mr Big, died due to a massive sugar overdose!' the DI said a few moments later.

'Sugar overdose!' we both said together.

'Can you die of a sugar overdose?' I asked.

'According to this, Mr Big, was a diabetic. A close examination revealed needle marks. The chap was injecting insulin, though his blood showed a dangerously high level of sugar.'

'I've heard of that. Surely isn't insulin intended to counteract sugar in your food?' I asked.

'I can't pretend to understand it, but I think that's how it works. Perhaps a chat with Dr Armstrong would clarify the matter,' the DI nodded. 'A nice little job for you, Dexter. Once you've sorted the tea out!'

'Yes, sir.'

I'd been to the pathology department of our local hospital before, so was well aware of the smells I was likely to experience. Once again, the day was hot and sultry and the expected aromas seemed to be greatly intensified. DI Brierly had phoned ahead and arranged my little chat with Dr Armstrong.

'You must be DC Dexter, newly promoted I understand,' said the doctor.

'Only an acting DC, sir,' I admitted.

'I'm sure most of police work is *only acting*, young man!' he chuckled.

'So I'm told, sir,' I smiled.

'Now, I believe you've some questions for me, swift as you can please I'm rather busy this morning.

'I've read your report, and you are suggesting that our victim was either murdered or committed suicide.'

'I can't tell which, but your man is definitely an insulin user. He has all of the symptoms I'd expect to see in the advanced stages of diabetes. His toes show the first stages of gangrene. Diabetics have to be most careful about their feet and toes. His fingers look okay at the moment but there could have been some difficulty manipulating small objects, though clearly not a knife and fork!' he chuckled. 'His heart could have given out at any time. People don't realise the amount of extra stress even a few pounds over-weight puts on the poor-old ticker! As I said in my report, there are needle marks ranging in age, the newest being only hours before death I would imagine. Strangely there is no corresponding evidence of insulin!'

'Are you saying that although he had injected himself there was no insulin in his body?' I asked.

'Nowhere near what I'd expect!'

'How could that be?'

'Many people are averse to sticking needles in themselves and get a wife of relative to do it, whilst they look away!' he grinned. 'It's surprising just how many people are scared of needles.'

'That would mean whoever injected Mr Big only stuck the needle in and pretended to inject the insulin!' I suggested.

'That would certainly be one explanation,' he nodded. 'Do you now have a name for the victim?'

'We've decided to call him that until we have an actual name, sir.'

'I see, not exactly over-imaginative, though it fits the bill I suppose.'

'Yes, sir.'

'His stomach contents shows a strange mix swishing about and pretty near pure sugar, even allowing for the percentage that had already entered his blood stream. It's in that jar over there,' he said pointing to a glass jar large enough to hold about a gallon, and close to full. It was a dirty brown colour with a heavy sediment at the bottom.

'I suspect he had eaten two large confectionary bars, sir. The wrappers and silver paper were in the ashtray on the seat in front of him.'

'I'm guessing, and it's only a guess, that your Mr Big had consumed a hefty lunch, at least one cup of

23

tea, probably heavily sugared, the two chocolate coated bars you mentioned and two or three tots of rum. I suspect the man was in his forties, and, of course, massively overweight; that alone could have killed him at any time. I'd say the man was well to do, his suit was made to measure, but then you'd not get anything in his size off the peg, his shirt and underwear are good quality cotton, again I would imagine that they were made to measure,' the doctor said.

'Could I look at his clothes please?' I asked.

'If you are thinking of checking the labels, I'm sorry to disappoint you; they have all been cut out! That's not as unusual as it might seem, overweight people, though it's generally women, tend to cut the labels from clothing, why I have no idea, though my assistant Mr Green, claims to remove them from his own underwear since they tend to irritate, in warm weather,' he grinned.

'Could I take a look all the same, sir?' I asked.

'Of course, be my guest, I've done with them. They are parcelled up in my storeroom, sign a receipt and they are yours,' he nodded. 'The undertaker might need them.'

'I'll take them then, thanks. Can I just recap for my own mind? Mr Big was a diabetic, balancing insulin with his food intake, is that right?' I asked. He nodded and after a moment's thought, said.

'If he intended consuming what we know he consumed he would have injected a considerable dose of insulin. That in itself is dangerous, if for some reason he was unable to obtain the things he intended to consume, his blood sugar would plunge and he would go into a coma! It's a very fine balancing act, play about with it at your peril!' he again nodded.

'Then if he had, as you suspect, injected a dose he thought correct for his estimated sugar intake but then didn't consume it; that could kill him?' I asked.

'Correct; as I said from the state of his heart, his toes and his weight, he'd go into a coma, and the shock to his already weekened heart and pop, out go the lights! At the back of a darkened room with noise and laughter, no one would even suspect he had a problem,' the doctor nodded.

'If he didn't inject himself but then ate the things we know he ate what then?' I asked.

'Then he would be very stupid indeed! As I said, play around with it at your peril! The medical profession is still learning but as I understand it at the moment there are two known types of Diabetes, in one, the body has stopped making insulin and the patient needs to inject it. I suspect that was the case with your Mr Big. In the other, the body makes insulin but it seems that it can't use it properly. The fact that Mr Big was injecting suggests the first type. Unfortunately, ongoing research suggests that there aren't such clear-cut divisions. It's a subject that I only see second-hand, if you see what I mean!' he grinned.

'You suggested earlier that patients often get someone else to do the injection, and I suggested that perhaps that person only pretended to inject, how soon after failing to have the injection would problems occur?'

'Now you're asking me to guess, it would depend on how much insulin was washing about in his body at the time of eating his lunch. He could be feeling a bit tired, as the insulin wore off. That would probably suggest to him that he needed to eat fairly quickly and once seated in the cinema, he might well have scoffed the lot in one massive binge. If, as I can prove he had virtually no insulin the massive sugar overdose Hyperglycaemia, could cause nausea, vomiting, and in his case, due to his huge weight problem, a heart attack *before* the other symptoms! Speculation – not really; he died of a heart attack – fact. Natural or brought on by Hyperglycaemia, sorry, can't say!' he shrugged.

'Thank you doctor, if I could sign for his clothes!'

'Of course.'

By the time I reached the CID office, I was aware how much weight, in clothes alone, Mr Big was carrying around. The parcel of clothes was wrapped in brown paper and tied with string. Even though I had swapped it from hand to hand as I walked the mile or so to Whitecross Yard, the string was cutting into my hand so that I was glad to drop it on my desk.

'What have you got there, Dexter?' the DI asked.

'Mr Big's clothes, sir!'

'I think you'll find they're a bit on the large side, you'll need to get them taken in a bit,' he grinned.

'Dr Armstrong has done with them and I thought we might find something useful from them, sir.'

'Who made them, you mean?'

'Yes sir, but according to him the labels have been removed!'

'That's a bit strange, isn't it?'

'No sir! He says, it's not all that unusual, people can find them an irritation next to the skin, especially in warm weather, sir.'

'Okay, chuck 'em in the corner, we'll have a look at some point. Knowing the pathology department, they'd have ended up in the incinerator so better that we've got them. We'll dump them if they start to smell.'

'Right, sir.'

'We've been informed of a car that seems to be abandoned. DS Whittington and I have been discussing it,' the DI said and Whittington nodded. 'Go and see what the pair of you can find out about it.'

'I've got the bunch of keys you found on Mr Big, let's go and see if they fit,' DS Whittington said.

I dumped the parcel of clothes in the cupboard under our little sink, closed the door and followed DS Whittington down the stairs. The car, a large dark blue Bentley with mid-blue wire wheels, was parked in a little cul-de-sac about three streets from the cinema.

'The chap who owns the printing factory at the end of the road complained because a delivery lorry couldn't get down to his loading bay,' the DS said, as we turned into the road.

The street, little more than a wide alley, was lined on both sides with virtually blank walls; back entrances to shops and small factories, which I suppose was the reason the car was not reported before. As we approached the vehicle it was clear the driver's door had been forced open at some point and although it still closed, the lock was damaged.

'I can't see Mr Big as a car thief, the door is a bit on the small side for a big man. I think this is just a stolen car, but who knows it could have something to do with him,' the DS said.

The ignition key found on Mr Big didn't fit the lock on

27

the dashboard.

'Whoever abandoned this car had an ignition key. There's no sign that it's been tampered with,' I said, looking at the little key. 'There's a number stamped on Mr Big's key, how easily can spare keys be obtained?'

'Car main dealers and some garages have a selection of spare keys in stock, no problem if you know the number. Locksmiths will cut a new one at a price, if you have the original.'

'That must make it pretty easy to steal a car,' I suggested.

'It does, if you know the key number, yes. Car manufacturers don't seem to see a problem; as far as I can see they just keep fitting the same range of keys and locks at random from the range and think that's enough. There's about five thousand numbers in the range to choose from, and once you know the number, the rest is easy.'

'So, do we think our Mr Big is a car thief?' I said.

'Somehow, I don't think this is Mr Big's car,' Whittington said and I nodded my agreement. 'I think we need a word with "Sonny Jim" Belton.'

'Never heard of him,' I admitted.

'Then for your information and education, James "Sonny Jim" Belton is Crammingdon's resident car thief,' the DS, smiled.

'I didn't know we had one,' I said with a shrug, though I was aware that the DS seemed to be the one who generally investigated car thefts.

'Believe it, car theft and thefts from cars will be a major crime in a few years; especially as cars get older and owners less careful. Mr Belton is likely to have a finger in this one, mark my words!' he grinned.

'Do you know where to find him?' I asked.

'Not at the moment, but in about an hour he'll either be in the Dog & Duck in Thirsk Lane, The Green Man in Liversage Street or the Magpie on the Market Place,' he grinned.

'A creature of habit?' I suggested.

'You could say that! The man's as bent as a butcher's hook, always got money to burn, never done an honest day's work in his life and always clean as a whistle whenever I think I have a case against him. Write that registration number down Will, this motor has been nicked from somewhere, probably miles away.'

'Right, Sarge,' I said getting out my notebook.

"Sonny Jim" Belton was nowhere to be seen, he wasn't in any of his usual haunts and the customers and landlords were adamant that they hadn't seen him for days. A trawl of all the town centre pubs brought the same reply. "Sonny Jim" had disappeared off the face of the earth, or at least that bit of it covered by the fair town of Crammingdon.

A check with local forces turned up the fact that the Bentley had been stolen from Nottingham racecourse on the day before Mr Big was found in the Magnificent Cinema in Crammingdon. Because Mr Big's death was now considered a murder enquiry, Nottingham City Constabulary had allowed us free access to their patch, provided we carried out the usual formality and inform them when we entered and left, as a matter of courtesy. We sat discussing the best way to deal with the stolen car since it might possibly provide an insight on Mr Big's demise.

'The car belongs to one Alfred Tatton, a bookmaker often at Nottingham and Doncaster race courses. The car was stolen at a Nottingham race meeting, as we know, whilst he was operating quite legally, however it seems that Mr Tatton also makes a book on race meetings around the country, taking off-course bets. He is well known in Nottingham, and has been arrested and charged on several occasions. We have been given permission to interview him this afternoon. It seems he has again been arrested on a charge of receiving off-course bets,' the DI chuckled.

'I know it goes on, but how exactly does it work?' I asked innocently.

'Have you never placed a bet, Dexter?' the DI asked.

'No, sir. I know you can place a bet on a horse actually at the race meeting, quite legally, but what exactly is off-course betting?' I continued. The DI and Whittington looked at each other and burst out laughing.

'Dexter you're a copper. Have you never chased a bookies runner?' the DI asked.

'No, sir,' I admitted.

Then a vital part of your education has been missed! It is illegal to *take* bets other than on a racecourse; illegal even to *place* bets other than on a racecourse. In other words, if you fancy a quick flutter on the favourite in the two-thirty but you can't afford the racecourse admission, or can't get there because you are working at the mill, hard luck! They don't call it the sport of kings for nothing! Well, your friendly bookmaker sees it as his duty to extend his much needed services to those poor devils unable to be at the meeting,' the DI grinned.

'I know that sir, but how does the bet, get to the

bookmaker?'

'This is where personal enterprise kicks in. The bookmaker has a gang of trusted "acquaintances" who accept bets on his behalf, settling-up at the end of the day when the bookie returns to base. The bookie allows his runners a percentage of the bets he brings in, and the punter is expected to treat the runner out of any winnings he might manage to make. In effect, the runner is a sort of sub-agent, issuing betting slips and dealing with the winnings, then, as I said he settles up with the bookmaker at the end of the day and takes a cut of the profits,' the DI said.

'I see, sir, and Mr Tatton has been caught out,' I nodded.

'Nobbled for illegal bookmaking, *and* had his car nicked! Life's so unfair, don't you think Dexter!' he grinned, whilst sadly shaking his head.

'Yes, sir.'

'I'll arrange for a car to take you and DC Whittington to Nottingham central nick. Have a word with Mr Tatton, see what he knows about our Mr Big.'

'Right, sir,' we both nodded, and within ten minutes we were being whisked on our way to Nottingham.

Alfred Tatton proved to be another of life's big men, nowhere near as large as our nameless Mr Big, but a good three or four stones overweight. His round and ruddy face held piggy eyes behind the sort of spectacles that always seem to me to have been made from the bottom of a bottle.

'They tell me you've found my car,' he snapped as we walked into the interview room at Nottingham

31

police station.

'We have found a dark blue Bentley motorcar registered in your name, yes.'

'And I know who nicked it.'

'Who would that be, sir?' asked DS Whittington.

'Jim Belton, "Sonny Jim" Belton, they call him, he'll be sonny bloody Jim if I catch him. Owes me a lot of money, does James Belton. The dear chap has been helping himself to the takings!'

'To your illegal betting money?' the DS grinned, and Tatton grudgingly nodded.

'Is that why you think he stole your car?' I asked.

'He was seen doing it. Off like a rocket before anyone could stop him, The car was broken into a week or so before and an expensive camera nicked. I'd not had chance to get the door repaired, so he got in easy enough, somehow he must have got a duplicate ignition key.'

The DS explained why the car had taken so long to find, then asked it Mr Tatton had any contact with our twenty-six stone man.

'There's a couple of blokes that might fit that description, big punters in both ways. Never bet less than a fiver! Luckily neither of 'em is very good at picking winners so that's a nice little boost to the days taking, if yer follow me,' he laughed, 'though, I wouldn't have put either of them as heavy as you say.'

'Have you got a name for either of them?'

'They always bet on course, I write a slip, they watch the race, they bring it back if they've won and I pay out. It's a business, if I buy a pair of shoes, they don't ask my name,' he said, making the time honoured

32

open-handed gesture.

'You said they bet on course, which race-course?' I asked.

'Both of 'em at Doncaster. No one that big at Nottingham; not that I've seen anyway. When can I have my car back?' he snapped.

'It's being fingerprinted, then you can arrange collection, we'll contact Nottingham police as soon as we've done with it,' the DS said.

'You do that,' he shrugged.

'You've no idea where we might find James Belton?' I asked.

'Don't worry, I'll find him.'

'I must advise you not to do him any harm, Mr Tatton,' the DS warned.

'Of course not, Detective Sergeant,' he smiled. 'My car; soon as you like.'

We left Nottingham nick, having informed the duty sergeant that we were finished with Mr Tatton, and made our way back to Whitecross Yard.

'Well that was a waste of time,' I said as we settled in for the half hour drive.

'At least we know the car and both Tatton and Belton are nothing to do with Mr Big,' DS Whittington pointed out. 'Though, I can see why our Mr James "Sonny Jim" Belton is in hiding. Mr Tatton is likely to make sure he meets with a nasty accident.'

'Would he do that?' I asked in my innocence.

'Mr Tatton won't, but he'll have a group of local gorilla's that will gladly remodel "Sonny Jim's" face or legs or both for a couple of quid. We won't see him for a long while,' Whittington shrugged.

'He must have helped himself to a goodly dollop

33

of cash to warrant that,' I suggested.

'Not necessarily, Tatton will use what happens to "Sonny Jim" as a warning to his other runners to play by the rules!'

Mr Tatton collected his car the next day and that was the end of the matter; except that a ring around the local hospitals, located "Sonny Jim" Belton laid-up in Ripley general, with a broken leg, and three broken fingers on his right hand. When asked what had happened he stated that he had had a bit too much to drink and fallen down the stairs at home, a story he continued to stick to despite being found by a Ripley bobby at the back of a pub on the main street. None of which forwarded our search for an identity for Mr Big.

DC George Harrington called into the CID office a few days later, with his arm in a sling. We all asked how he was feeling and when he'd be back at work.

'Doctor's given me at least another three weeks off, but I'm getting bored, can't wait to be back in harness,' he moaned.

'They predict a full recovery, then?' the DI asked.

'Yes, it was a bad slash, nineteen stitches, aches and itches like bloody hell but should be okay in a month or so,' he nodded.

'Put the kettle on Dexter,' the DI said, 'least we can do is to offer our fallen comrade a cup of tea.'

'I can't drink tea sir doctor's orders. Unless there's a little tot of the hard stuff in it, sir!' he grinned.

'It's not affected your bloody cheek then, I see,'

the DI laughed.

We discussed the Mr Big case, which of course DC Harrington knew a little about, having taken charge at the cinema, a few days before he was injured.

'The trouble is, we've no idea where he comes from,' the DI pointed out.

'And, without a name, you can't check on driving licences, car ownership or housing rates. Your only chance is if he used a taxi a driver is sure to remember a twenty-six stone man dropped at the cinema,' Harrington stated.

'Dexter has tried that, with no luck so far. We're still waiting for several of the companies to get back to us.' the DI said.

'Should I chase them up again, sir?'

'Can't do any harm. Yes, get on with that, Dexter.'

'Right, sir.'

I spent the rest of the morning phoning the five taxi firms that had not answered our original call. They were all companies with multiple vehicles and drivers, and all of them apologised for not being in touch; all but one had surveyed their drivers with no positive identification. It seemed that since they had nothing to report they hadn't bothered replying. That left Derby & Nottingham Cab Company, the largest company of all, with a depot in Crammingdon. I rang the Crammingdon office.

'We run forty-seven cabs, with just over eighty drivers,' the phone receptionist pointed out. 'Not all of our drivers are full time. Lots of them just do a few hours a week.'

'Is it possible to find out who was on duty in

Crammingdon on a particular day?' I asked.

'Tell me the day and the rough time and I'll try again,' she said.

I gave her the information from my notebook and she agreed to give me an answer before five o'clock that day.

The call came just as I was considering calling again.

'Fifteen drivers were on that afternoon. The driver you want is on holiday, his last shift was on the afternoon you mentioned. He finished at three o'clock, leaving instructions that a Mr Bloor was to be picked up from Crammingdon marketplace. The replacement driver waited but the man didn't present himself; he gave it fifteen minutes, then moved to the taxi rank by the bridge. That's normal practise to cut losses from hanging around.'

'The man's name was Bloor; you're sure of that?' I asked, hoping we had a lead at last.

'Yes, Bloor, definitely.'

'The holidaying driver, when is he back?' I asked.

'Should be back this afternoon, on duty again two o'clock tomorrow; would you like me to get him to give you a ring?' she asked.

'If you'd do that please,' I said and replaced the phone.

'Mr Big is now Mr Bloor,' I grinned.

'A twenty-six stone diabetic named Mr Bloor. He shouldn't be too hard to track down!' the DI nodded. 'Well done, Dexter.'

'Thank you, sir.'

Alice was in the midst of preparing a meal, there's nothing unusual in that, except that the quantities she was preparing seemed larger than normal.

'Henry and Flossie are coming for dinner,' she grinned. Alice, orphaned when very young, was taken in by a distant aunt and uncle, who used her as unpaid help. When they died within a few days of each other, she inherited fifty pounds and at the age of sixteen or seventeen had to make her way in the world. I knew that she now considered my sister Flossie and her husband Henry to be her family, and they doted on our twin boys.

'That's a nice surprise, what brings them?' I asked.

'Flossie has had a letter from Edith; they want to show it to us,' she smiled. 'They are picking your Mam and Dad up on the way!'

Edith is the older of my two sisters; she married Joe a railroad engineer in Canada. They visited us for Christmas 1929. We agreed to keep in touch and this would be the eighth or ninth letter from Edith since they went back.

'The boys have had an afternoon nap so they will be fresh for our guests,' Alice said.

'Where are they?' I asked.

'Nelly is looking after them. I had her girls this morning whilst she fetched Dick from the hospital.'

'Dick is home again?'

'He's got his right leg in plaster and his left arm in a sling, and feeling very sorry for himself,' she grinned.

'I'll have a quick wash and nip and get them,' I said.

'No hurry, I said it would be about half past six.'

'Yes but I want a word with Dick, to see what happened.'

'Oh, that will suit him down to the ground. I know how you men love to be the centre of attention!' she giggled.

'I don't know *what* you mean,' I said, heading up the stairs.

Dick sat by the fire in their kitchen as Nelly let me in.

'Hi, Dick, been in the wars?' I asked.

'Mm! Hurts like hell, especially my shoulder when I use that crutch,' he said pointing to it standing by the parlour door. 'I can get about reasonably with the thing under my right arm but that sort of twists my shoulders and puts pressure on my bad one,' he scowled.

'Any idea when they'll sign you off?'

'Six weeks at least and he's bored stiff already,' Nelly snapped.

'I hate just sitting around. I've read everything in the house. I've even read last Sunday's News of the World from cover to cover, twice. One of the nurses in hospital lent me a book by one of them war poets, Wilfrid Owen; thought it might cheer me up! Have you ever read his stuff?'

'No, can't say I have,' I admitted.

'It's deep and very clever, but full of death and lament. It did make me realise how lucky I'd been. I bet there's not many people get knocked off their bike and live to tell the tale,' he shrugged, and instantly rubbed his shoulder with a grimace.

'It could have been a lot worse,' I agreed. 'What

38

exactly happened?'

'I remember putting me boots on, next thing I know I wake up in hospital with a pretty young nurse fussing around me,' he winked. 'Really upsetting that was!'

'I saw her, she was fifty if she was a day, and would have made three of me,' Nelly grinned.

'That was the one you saw. There were others,' Dick said with another wink.

'You've no idea what actually happened, then?'

'None. The van driver came in to see me yesterday, all apologies; said he was distracted looking at his load sheet. Seemed a nice enough chap; his boss has suspended him for a fortnight for disobeying company rules. He said he was lucky he didn't lose his job,' Dick said.

'He thought he'd killed you when they took you away in the ambulance, kept punching and kicking, even head-butted the wall,' I nodded.

'Is that why his hands were all bandaged up? I didn't like to ask.'

'It was. He made a nasty mess of them, split his knuckles really badly!' I nodded.

'I suppose I'm lucky, if you can call this luck, the boss is holding my job for me and paying me half pay. It means we'll struggle but I've still got a job,' he shrugged and instantly grimaced again. 'I'm going to have to learn not to do that,' he grinned.

'Daddy, daddy,' the boys shouted as they came in from the parlour, followed by the two girls of the house.

At two, the boys were at what I call that interesting stage, into everything, eager to learn.

'We've been making… er?' George said.

'Pastry! Special, grey pastry,' Nelly smiled. 'It's in that bag!' she said pointing to a brown paper bag on the table.

'According to the News of the World gardening column, pastry rockeries are becoming quite fashionable!' Dick grinned.

'Eat it Daddy,' Will said.

'Later, I'm too full now,' I said.

'Coward!' Dick and Nelly said together.

Henry's car was standing at the front door as we walked home. Flossie and Henry were first on the scene to grab the boys as we walked in through the kitchen door. Once they had finished hugging and kissing the pair it was the turn of my Mam and Dad. Mamma and Gandad, was the best the boys could manage but no doubt it would change as they grew older, but for now, it sufficed. Once the evening meal was out of the way, Flossie opened her handbag and took out Edith's letter, more a small parcel. 'Edith has asked me to read a message to you all!' she said, clearing her throat.

"Dear Everyone, I know I normally send you each a letter, and I get three in return, but this time because I've enclosed so many photographs I decided to send just this one and ask Flossie to read it out to you all. Well, where to start? Joe had been put on short time because the railroad was running so smoothly. The directors considered the regular maintenance routine he had developed to be a waste of money. That was in January, I didn't mention it at the time, as I didn't want to worry you all. In any case, Joe is well paid so we had money set aside and he said they would soon see their mistake. Well things ran well until the middle of March,

40

then came the first major breakdown. Nearly all the track in both directions from Kamloops is single line. An overnight freight train shed a wheel bearing halfway between Cherry Creek and Savona, closing the track for over a day as the train was dragged back to Kamloops. Suddenly Joe was back on full time for the track clearing and repair of the loco. A second breakdown between Kamloops and Calgary closed the line for three days. In both cases, Joe was able to show that the locos were due for and because of the new system had missed their scheduled maintenance. He even predicted the next loco to fail. It didn't come to that; the directors had been shown in the most effective way that their idea was un-workable, on the profit and loss sheet. Now Joe is on full time, trying to catch up with his schedules. All of this meant that for nearly three months, whilst Joe was on short time, January to the end of March, we had the chance to take the boys out of school occasionally and go off into the mountains; the photos show you a little of what we got up to. I particularly like the ones of the boys with their eight feet high snowman and Joe falling off the sledge. We took the boys to the Banff Springs Hotel; we honeymooned there if you remember. Well…

There was much more of that as you can imag- ine and Mam got very nostalgic and emotional about her eldest daughter, the things that she remembered from Edith's childhood. It was an evening that passed all too quickly. It was agreed that Henry would get the photos bound into an album, and we all agreed it should live at Mam and Dad's so that we could all look at it and add any future photos.

Mam and Dad left in Henry's car, they were go- ing to spend the night at 'Red Cedars' Flossie and Henry's house. As they left, they reminded me not to be late home the next night, as it was Flossie and Henry's Wedding Anniversary; they had been married for five years – how time flies!

3

Next morning, as I settled myself at the desk I shared with DS Whittington, the phone on the DI's desk rang. The DI wasn't expected in until nearly lunchtime so I answered it. It was the girl from the Derby & Nottingham Cab Company.

'The driver who drove Mr Bloor rang in late last night to say he was home and available for duty this afternoon. I hope I've done right, I've asked him to drop into the police station at about ten o'clock and ask for you,' she said.

'That's a real help, thank you. Could you give me his name then the front desk will let me know the moment he arrives?'

'Of course, Gilbert Lennox, I've told him it's about Mr Bloor, I hope that's okay?' she replied.

'That's fine, and thank you for your cooperation.'

DS Whittington was called away to investigate a shop break-in leaving me to do the interview with Mr Lennox. I had started ringing around all of the doctor's surgeries I could find in the telephone directories, looking for a possible lead on the man I now knew as Bloor. I had worked through to the letter J, Dr M J Jenkins, without getting anything in the way of a positive recognition of Mr Bloor, when Mr Lennox arrived and the duty sergeant escorted him up the stairs.

'Mr Lennox, thank you for taking the time to call in, please sit down.'

'Thank you, sorry I'm late I couldn't find the keys to the cab,' he grinned.

'Don't worry; I'm only too pleased you've come. Are you in your cab, then?' I asked.

'Yes, I've had it all week. It's more or less my cab, I have to clean it and keep it topped up with oil and water; in return I can use it for taking the wife and kids on holiday once a year. I have to pay for the petrol, of course, but it saves a dollop of cash.' he grinned.

'I bet it does; that's very reasonable of your employer,' I nodded. 'You said you've had the cab all week, but it will be a fortnight tomorrow since you last worked.'

'We were at Skeggy, Skegness, for a week, Saturday to Saturday, but I had some extra holiday days due to me and we spent a couple of days each end with the wife's sister and her husband in Grantham,' he scowled.

'And the firm let you have the cab all that time?' I asked.

'Good firm, one of the best! But Muriel said you were asking about my customer, Mr Bloor.'

'How much did she tell you?'

'Only that you had been asking about him and it was important,' he shrugged.

'As I understand it, you dropped Mr Bloor at the cinema on the afternoon you went off on holiday, leaving instructions that he was to be picked up by another cab,' I suggested.

'That's right. Although, I didn't know he went to the pictures. I always dropped him in the corner of the market place and picked him up there at the time he said, always about four-thirty, give or take a couple of minutes, then drop him off at Ripley Market place, always there!' Mr Lennox said.

'I see! On the afternoon, you dropped him off he went to the Magnificent Cinema, and died in his seat, not being found until the end of the performance by the cinema manager!'

'Oh, I'm sorry to hear that. Nice chap always gave me a shilling tip. Can't say I'm really surprised. He was massive, well overweight, I think he was one of them, what's the name, when you have to keep injecting yerself?'

'We know that Mr Bloor was a diabetic, is that what you mean?' I asked.

'That's it, a diabetic. He used to get into the cab, ask me to wait while he injected himself, then off we'd go to Crammingdon market place.'

'Where did you pick him up?' I asked, sensing a possible lead.

'All over the place; most common, Eastwood or Ripley, but Alfreton a couple of times, always to Crammingdon market place,' he shrugged.

'Didn't that seem odd?' I said.

'A bit but in this game yer never surprised by what some people want! I've got one bloke, I pick up in Canal Bank, take him out towards Sheffield, turn round and bring him back,' he said shaking his head!'

'He gets you to wait for him?'

'No! He never gets out, as far as Yorkshire Bridge, turn round and come back to Canal Bank.'

'That's very odd!' I said. 'Don't you ask why?'

'Monday evening, every week, regular as

45

clockwork. He pays one pound ten shillings and sixpence fare and a tanner tip. Don't rock the boat, that' my
motto!' he said shaking his head and I nodded.

'You say that Mr Bloor injected himself before
you moved off,' I asked.

'Always the first thing he did, when he got in the
cab, wherever I picked him up.'

'That must mean he had a kit with him, Hypo-
dermic needle, a bottle of insulin, and such like?'

'Yes, really neat little case, black leather about
the size of two reading glasses cases side by side.'

'You saw it?'

'Yes, every time. It's quite a little rigmarole they
have to go through. He'd fill the needle thing, open his
shirt at his belly, stick the thing in him, makes me shud-
der to think of it, but if it's life and death; anyway when
he'd done he'd put it all back in the little case, slip it in
his pocket and says to drive on.'

'He let you watch him?'

'Oh, no! I've a mirror that lets me keep an eye
on what the passengers are getting up to, discreet like.
I've noticed in that.'

'We know, as I said, that he was injecting, but
we didn't find his kit,' I said. '

'Can't help you; I didn't really watch him, just a
glimpse in me mirror as far as I know he always slipped
it in his jacket pocket!' Lennox said.

'Are you sure he injected that afternoon?'

'Positive! It was such a part of our Journey, I'd
have noticed if he hadn't.'

'Did you clean your cab, before you set off on
holiday?'

'No need, I clean it every morning before I start.

Two short fares before Mr Bloor, then I'm done, bung the wife and kids in and off we go.'

'You didn't find his little kit?'

'Sorry, no.'

'I think that's all Mr Lennox, if you find his kit, or think of anything else, please give me a call,' I said giving him the DI's card.

'There is one odd thing!'

'Anything, it could be just the thing we are looking for.'

'Well, it's probably nothing, but I'm in Ripley one Saturday a few months back, with the missus shopping; it's a good market and we go every so often! Anyway, in the distance, I sees Mr Bloor and waves, but he's looking the other way. "Who yer waving at?" asks the missus. "Mr Bloor one of my fares" I said. "What that fat chap?" she said. "Yes", I said. Then she shakes her head. "His names not Bloor, can't think of what it is but it's definitely not Bloor," she said.'

'She didn't think that was his name?'

'He's on my sheet as Bloor, he rings the office as Bloor, I call him Mr Bloor; as far as I'm concerned, he's Mr bloody Bloor! But, it's no use arguing with my better half, if she says it's not, then I shut up. Saves a lot of blood pressure problems,' he grinned.

'Could you ask her if she's remembered his name? Just in case she's right, I asked.

'I'll do that and let you know. But take it from me, he's Mr Bloor,'

'Thank you Mr Lennox, I might need to talk to you again,' I said.

'I can see why you'd need to find out who he is, so that you can let his family know; but, is there more to it than that?' he asked as he got to the door.

'We think Mr Bloor died in suspicious circum-stances.'

'Blimey! I don't suppose you can say anymore.'

'Sorry Mr Lennox, it's pure speculation, I'm afraid, but the more we learn the stranger the circum-stances become,' I admitted.

'I'll ask her ladyship, when I get home tonight, and keep my ear to the ground. He was a nice polite old chap, I'm sorry to hear he's gone,' he nodded and closed the door.

Having found a name for Mr Big; to have it pos-sibly whisked away again inside twenty-four hours set me wondering if we would ever know his identity. In the past we have run a newspaper appeal for information, using their artist to create a line drawing of the person in question if we had no photograph, and ask if readers can identify the person. I felt sure that the DI would approve the idea, perhaps even be thinking along those lines. I grabbed a notepad and started to produce a rough word-ing.

Crammingdon police urgently need to identify this man. He is --- tall, well spoken, and weighs roughly thirty-six stone. He is believed to be between 40 & 50 years of age, has mid-grey running to silver, hair, slicked back and parted in the middle. When last seen he was wearing a dark-grey suit and black bowler hat. If you can identify this man, please contact DI Brierly at Crammingdon CID.

I had just put my pencil down as the DI entered the office.

'Ah! Dexter, any news from your taxi driver?' he said as he sat down.

'He wasn't aware that Mr Bloor went to the cinema …

…His wife reckons she knows the man and his names not Bloor, though she can't remember what it actually is,' I concluded, having given him a full rundown of my interview with Mr Lennox.

'Are you saying that we are back to calling him Mr Big?' the DI said shaking his head.

'Mr Lennox was pretty sure that his name is Bloor, but there is just a chance that his wife is right, sir.'

'Where did he say he picked up Mr Bloor?'

'Ripley, Eastwood, occasionally Alfreton,' I said referring again to my interview notes. 'Then always drops him at Crammingdon marketplace.'

'Sounds like we're back to square one.'

'Do we need to ask help from the local newspapers, sir?' I asked handing him the piece of paper with the appeal I had jotted down.

'I can't see any alternative, especially if his name isn't Bloor after all. I'll nip and have a word with Tom Greatorix at the *Argus*! Get their artist to pop down to the morgue and do a drawing, he'll enjoy that!' he grinned. 'I'll take this with me,' he said, tearing the sheet from the pad and disappearing down the stairs.

I went back to ringing around the medical practices drawing a blank in every case. The problem with trying to get information from doctors and hospitals is their reluctance to divulge their patients' personal details, needing long explanations before they will admit that they don't have anyone fitting that description! I finished the Crammingdon and district directory about three o'clock, the task being further delayed by incoming calls every time I replaced the phone, and collected the Ripley and Alfreton directories from the front desk to continue my search, as the DI came in.

'I'll say one thing for Tom Greatorix, he keeps a bloody good malt whisky! Shame he spoils it in tea!' he grinned. 'Cast your eyes over that, Dexter,' he added passing me a line drawing.

'Wow, that was quick and, from memory, not a bad likeness!' I admitted.

'Poor bloke must have worked like the wind in the mortuary, he was back with the finished drawing in less than an hour!' he chuckled as the door opened and DS Whittington walked in.

'One shop break-in all cleared up, sir.'

'News to me, what shop break-in?' the DI asked.

'Early this morning the manager of Dawson's off-licence reported an overnight break-in. I left Dexter ringing around the local doctors, anyway, he had an interview with his taxi driver, as you know, and went to investigate. I've been there all day. However, as I said it's all sorted out!'

'You've got a culprit?'

'Oh yes, sir!'

'Anyone we know?'

'The shop manager, sir,' he grinned.

'He broke into his own shop! What was it, a fraudulent insurance claim?'

'It seemed genuine when I first arrived. The chap was dancing around like a scalded cat, wringing his hands, biting his nails, almost in tears. Moaning about the company auditor being due at any second and him with stock that had been stolen!'

'A worried chap as you'd expect,' the DI nodded. 'Did he ring for the auditor or was it a scheduled visit?'

'He was notified, late yesterday evening that a spot check was being carried out around the shop chain and he was due a visit eleven o'clock today, sir.'

'And he's covering for missing stock?'

'Correct, sir! I'd taken his statement, done a quick look around and arranged for the fingerprint lads. They'd just done when the auditor arrived and I left him talking to the manager as I went door to door to see if anyone had seen anything. A woman three doors down across the road is an insomniac; she couldn't sleep last night, complaining of the heat. I have to admit the missus and me had both bedroom windows open. Anyway, she'd got her window open and was standing behind the net curtain when she sees someone walk down the side of the off-licence, out onto the street, carrying what she called an iron bar, a jemmy at a guess from the marks on the shop doorframe. This person looks around, "furtive-like", she said. Then carefully he cracks open the door, he's ever so quiet so it takes a while. All the time she's trying to get a proper look at the chaps face. There's quite a little cracking sound as the door breaks open and he looks around to see if he's roused anybody.'

'And she sees his face?' the DI suggested.

'She did, and recognised him as the shop manager,' Whittington nodded.

'A reliable witness, do you reckon?'

'I confronted the manager with her statement, didn't mention who it was, and he broke down in tears! Admitted, he'd been fiddling the till and was sacked on the spot.'

'Is the company pressing charges?' the DI

asked.

'I'm not sure, there's not all that much missing. Er... twelve bottles of assorted beers, a couple of bottles of port, half bottle of rum and a bottle of whisky!' he said looking at his notes.

'About a fiver all told?'

'Yes, sir, I reckon he could have claimed that as breakages and a bit of pilfering; he'd have had it stopped out of his wages, but still have had a job,' the DS said shaking his head. 'There is of course the damage he did to the shop. I can't see his employer turning a blind eye to that one, so, watch this space as the saying goes.'

'The more I see of folk, the more I think they are their own worst enemy!' the DI shrugged. 'Changing the subject, Dexter's taxi driver's wife reckons our Mr Bloor isn't.'

'Isn't what?' the DS asked.

'Isn't Mr Bloor,' the DI replied,

'Oh, dear!'

'Oh dear! We're back to square one, and all you can say is, "oh dear"!'

'Sorry sir, we've got to have a newspaper appeal, that's the only thing I can think of, sir.'

'Already sorted out, Tom Greatorix is running Dexter's piece with their artist's drawing in tonight's edition and passing it on to the other local papers, extending the area, for tomorrow's editions,' he said, passing DS Whittington the slip from the notepad.

'You'd think a man of that size, would stand out like a sore thumb!' the DS said, shaking his head.

'Am I to carry on ringing around the doctors' surgeries, sir?' I said pointing to the directories on my desk.

'No luck from the Crammingdon book?'

'No results, so far, sir!'

'No, let's wait and see what the newspaper bit brings in. Why are we stumbling in the dark on this one? We are looking for a man who is memorable to say the least, who would almost certainly be remembered by anyone who sees him, and instantly recognised if seen again. Yet it seems that other than the people we know about, the man is invisible. I just don't understand it!' the DI shrugged.

The *Argus* comes out at four-thirty and Tom Greatorix made sure one of the first copies arrived on the DI's desk as soon as the presses rolled into action. The normal agreement between him and DI Brierly was that as soon as there was anything we can release, the *Argus* gets it first. The artist had given his masterpiece a little more work, making it look more lifelike and less like a corpse. I hadn't seen the man in life of course, but I felt sure that the drawing would be instantly recognisable to anyone who knew or had met him. By five o'clock, we had the first phone call. It was from Phyllis, the girl in the Magnificent Cinema box office.

'You spoke to the girl in the box office, Dexter,' the DI said handing me the phone.

'It's like him but the mouth isn't quite right, he's always smiling, you've got him looking very gloomy,' she said.

'You did recognise it as the man you knew?' I asked.

'Oh yes! That's him alright, in a gloomy mood.'

'Do you think that anyone who knew him would recognise him?'

'Oh yes, sure to. It's him but gloomy, like I

53

said.'

'Thank you Miss, er, Garner,' I said, looking back in my notebook. 'If we need to ask you anything else I'll be in touch,' I said and rang off.

'She reckons the picture is a good likeness but a bit "gloomy",' I chuckled.

'He's a right to be a bit "gloomy", the poor buggers dead!' the DI chuckled.

There were another couple of phone calls before I left, saying that they recognised the man as a cinemagoer or getting into or out of a taxi on the market place. Nothing new was added to what we already knew, except of course, it re-enforced the fact that the picture was recognisable. DS Whittington agreed to look after the phones until eight o'clock and we left him to it at five-thirty.

The boys had spent the afternoon playing in the garden with Dick and Nelly Williams's girls, and were still there when I arrived home. Dad had found an old broken deckchair at their local church jumble sale, repaired it and given it to Alice so she could sit in the garden on afternoons like this and keep an eye on the children. She had gathered them inside and was in the process of washing hands and faces when Nelly came down the side of the house to collect the girls, and tapped on the back door.

'Hello! Only me!' she said opening the door. 'Dick would like a word with you, Will. He'd have come himself but his shoulder is giving him gyp this afternoon.'

'Okay, I'll pop down now before I take my boots off,' I nodded.

'Don't be long! Don't forget Henry is picking us

up at half past six!' Alice reminded me. 'It's their wedding anniversary,' she added for Nelly's benefit.'

'Yes, I know, two minutes,' I nodded.

I knocked on the door knowing that I was about to hear just how bad his shoulder was, and Dick shouted to come in.

'Hey-up Dick, Nelly says yer shoulder's playing you up,' I said; best get it over with, I thought.

'Not half, stabbing like a knife jabbing between me ribs; takes me breath away,' he said. 'Takes ages before I…'

'Nelly said you wanted to see me,' I said cutting him short.

'Yes, the drawing in the paper, I've seen him!' Dick winked.

'That's great! What's his name?' I asked eagerly.

'I didn't say I knew him, I said I'd seen him!'

'Can you remember where and when you saw him?'

'Oh, that's easy, at the hospital the day I got knocked off me bike. He was the first person I saw as I woke up. I was still a bit hazy as you can imagine, but it was him, definitely.'

'Mm, not the same chap, Dick,' I said, shaking my head.

'You don't know that,' he snapped.

'I'm reasonably sure, yer see the chap we are trying to find out about had been dead for a week by then.'

'Dead… Oh! It was his double then, or his twin brother, although I admit I wouldn't have put him at twenty-six stone. I suppose it must have been someone else.'

'Thanks anyway, we really are clutching at straws with this one.'

'You've no idea who he is?' Dick asked.

'We think his name is Bloor, but there's some doubt about it. I really can't tell you anything else, not because it's police business and all that, we just don't know anything else,' I said, as Nelly came back with the girls.

'Sorry, Will. I felt sure it was him,' he said.

'Thanks anyway,' I nodded as I left.

Henry's car pulled up outside just as I was combing my hair and slipping on the jacket of my best suit; my only suit, the one I wore to marry Alice.

The boys jumped out of the car the moment we arrived and raced to the front door. Mam was there to greet us and we all piled through to the best room, where meal placings had been laid.

'I suggest we eat now, I'm having a job to keep it all hot,' Flossie suggested. We all voiced our agreement. I for one was ravenous.

With the meal over, Dad stood up, 'I want to say a few words,' he said very solemnly.

'I bet Mam put him up to it,' Flossie laughed.

'Forced me, yer mean, no, I took no forcing. So shut up all of yer and listen,' he chuckled.

'I'm a very proud man, a very lucky man. I've a very happy marriage, or at least so my wife tells me,' he stopped for the ensuing laughter and Mam said something to him that I missed, though it made him laugh.

'I have, we have, three children with happy marriages, and four grandchildren, admittedly two of 'em live half a world away but we keep in touch by post and the photos we all saw last night. Henry and me have spent the afternoon putting them in a lovely leather album, we're not finished yet but it's looking really good so far,' he said and looked at Henry, who nodded his agreement.

'It doesn't seem like five years since I stood up like this, wishing the happy couple all the luck in the world and proposing a toast to my second daughter. There was one person missing then as there is now.'

'One family missing,' Mam corrected.

'Yer right, one family missing, though this afternoon, Edith rang from Canada, to wish Flossie and Henry a happy day. The line was a bit crackly but you could hear every word, Flossie held the thing so that we could all hear. My only regret was that we had just three minutes to say a million things. I think we all know that they are thinking about us, as we are about them!' he said and we all nodded.

'Henry assures me that what we have in our glasses is a drop of his fine old port, so without further ado, will you please raise your glasses to Flossie and Henry, many more happy years of marriage,' he said and took a gulp. 'By gum, that's a drop o' good stuff!' he coughed.

'I think my husband should reply to that,' Flossie said. Henry nodded and stood up.

'Where have five years gone? When I married my Flossie there was no doubt in my mind that I had made the right choice. I knew her for three years before we married, and met you all from time to time. The welcome you gave me was, I can't think of a single word that covers it, but I seemed to be part of the family right from the start. Even then, there was just a small shadow of doubt; how would it all pan out? Would we still be as happy spending every hour of the day with each other? Could I make a go of running my own practice? If you are a lucky man Mr Dexter, your daughter has made me a very lucky and happy man. Mr and Mrs Dexter, Mam and Dad, and Flossie I thank you for my happiness,' he said and raised his glass again.

The boys had snuggled down on a sofa in the corner and we all cleared the table. Alice and I washed and dried the pots; only fair since Mam and Flossie had prepared and cooked the meal. As we eventually sat down Alice asked Mam a question.

'Will and I met at Lomax's factory, but I know nothing about him as a boy. What was he like as a young lad, Mam?'

'I'd had two girls of course, they used to fight like cat and dog, no, not fight exactly. Argue! None-stop, whatever one said the other would say the opposite. They'd fall out two or three times a day. Then I found out after a few years I was going to have another child. I have to admit I was worried about it being another girl to add to the tribe. Then along comes Will, he stopped them in their tracks, falling over themselves to help, mothering him. Oh dear, will he turn out to be a spoilt brat I worried.'

'And did he?' Alice grinned and squeezed my hand.

'No, Dad saw to that. He was always able to find little jobs for Will to help him with, like when they made a vegetable garden out of our tiny bit of land at the back, and built a chicken house for our neighbour Mrs Lewis,' Mam said.

'I didn't know about that!' Alice said, and Mam went through it for her, adding things even I didn't remember.

'Oh, I am disappointed. I hoped Will would be more of a real little boy than that!' Alice smiled.

'I've not told the half of it. He used to catch spiders and put them in the girl's beds. I lost count of the number of times Edith near screamed the house down when she found one. You'd have thought murder was being committed!' Mam tittered.

'He put a frog in my bed once!' Flossie shuddered. 'A horrible slimy thing I had to change my bedding, so don't think he was a little goody-goody, far from it!' she added faking annoyance at the memory.

'Not to mention being caught scrumping by Bobby Barnes our local copper. Thinks, we didn't know about that,' Mam grinned.

'What is scrumping?' Alice asked.

'Jumping over someone's fence and pinching their apples!' Dad chuckled.

'How did you find out about that?' I asked.

'Never you mind; Mam's and Dad's always find out, as you'll learn with that pair!' Mam said nodding at the boys on the sofa. 'All in all, I don't suppose he's turned out too bad,' Mam smiled.

'Only one thing wrong with him,' Dad laughed, 'he had a perfectly good job, electrician he was, but no, he had to be a flippin' copper!' he shrugged, and we all laughed, me the hardest.

'It was Bobby Barnes that made me want to be a policeman,' I said. He made me take the apples back and apologise to the man. I thought that was very fair.'

'We know!' Mam and Dad said together and

59

everyone laughed.

First thing next morning DS Whittington ran through his notes on the calls he had taken the evening before.

'Five calls, all claiming to either know or have seen our Mr Bloor, I think we should call him Mr Bloor until that is actually proved to be wrong!' DS Whittington suggested.

'Agreed, the chap deserves a proper identity,' the DI nodded.

'The first call was from a woman at number six Courtney Street, claiming he was her window cleaner. I pointed out that the person we are looking for weighed twenty-six stone and she replied that I was wrong. "He's only thirteen or fourteen stone, but it's definitely him." I thanked her and said we'd be in touch if we needed to ask any further questions.' DS Whittington grinned.

'An attention seeker?' the DI asked.

'I don't think so, she seemed very convinced.'

'Keep it on file, who knows it could be a lead. What's next?'

'A chap who works as a shift foreman at Rolls Royce aero-engine division in Derby, lives in Crammingdon, reckons he used to have our chap on his shift, until three or four years ago. He couldn't remember his name, I mentioned that we thought it might be Bloor, but he didn't think so.'

'That sound like a possible lead, how did you suggest we'd follow it up?' the DI asked.

'He's going to take the newspaper to work with him to ask the people on his shift to see if anyone remembers him. I suggested that he asked the personnel department to try to chase it up for us. He agreed to try, and ring us at lunchtime today, sir.'

'That could be a possible; would you say he was convinced it was the same chap?'

'Yes, but then so did the next one,' Whittington grinned.

'Okay, let's have it.

'That was a lady from Edale Street, an elderly lady from the sound of her voice, a bit shaky it was, anyway she said she had seen him at the cinema.'

'Now that seems interesting,' the DI nodded. 'What did she say?'

'I pricked my ears up as well when she said that,' the DS grinned.

'Go on, what's so funny?'

'She said he was a big fat man in a black bowler hat. I was still wriggling on the hook at that, as you can imagine. Then she said he was with a little thin chap, always fooling about!' Whittington chuckled.

'A thin chap, always fooling about?'

'Yes, sir!' Whittington said, and burst out laughing. 'She said his name was definitely Hardy, sir,' he continued wiping his eyes.

'What's the joke... Oh, bloody hell; she was talking about the film. She was talking about, Laurel and bloody Hardy!'

'Quite convinced though, sir. I thanked her and said we'd be in touch if we needed any more information,' Whittington grinned.

'That's three, what was number four?'

'Now that was interesting, that was from a woman in Cavendish Road, saying he looked just like her sister's…'

'Window cleaner!' I jumped in.

'Right in one,' the DS nodded.

'Really?' I said.

'Her words were, "He looks just like my sister's window cleaner, but he's much smaller than you say in the paper, I bet he's a relation, the likeness is uncanny!" That's what she said.'

'The window cleaner could well be a lead,' the DI nodded. 'Number five?'

'This was a woman from Matlock, her husband works in Crammingdon and takes the *Argus* home with him. She claimed to know the man from working with him in the past; thought his name was Boon. I told her that someone else had suggested his name was Bloor, but she was adamant that it was Boon. I thanked her and said if we had any other questions we'd be in touch,' DS Whittington shrugged.

'All in all, we're not any further forward,' the DI said, as the phone on his desk rang. He picked it up and did his usual introduction. We couldn't hear the person at the other end but the DI's answer suggested that the call was of little use.

'Thank you sir, but I know for a fact, that the gentleman we are looking for couldn't possibly have been in Liverpool yesterday, sir,' the DI said. 'No that's perfectly alright sir, we rely on the goodwill of the public to assist us, thank you for taking the time,' he continued then replaced the phone with a shake of his head.

Throughout the morning, there were several other calls all adding little or nothing to our knowledge. The only interesting factor was that by then five callers all claimed that the man was their window cleaner.

'We need to find this window cleaner and ask if he recognises the picture and is there any relationship. It's probably a pretty long shot but it could hold the key,'

'It seems strange that so many people think he's their window cleaner but no one has a name or address for him,' I pointed out.

'Well now, Dexter, do you know the name and address of your window cleaner?' the DI grinned.

'Er... No, sir.'

'I know mine,' Whittington grinned. 'It's me!'

'Got the ladder and all the gear?' the DI asked.

'Yes, sir.'

'Then you can do mine once a fortnight,' the DI laughed.

True to his word, the foreman at Rolls Royce rang at just after one o'clock. The DI answered the phone, but passed it to me, as he was nipping out with DS Whittington to an urgent appointment with a pint of best bitter, and Tom Greatorix in the Kings Head.

'Hello, I'm DC Dexter, DS Whittington is not in the office at the moment but he told me you'd be ring-ing, sir.'

'I've asked around the lads on my shift and with the personnel department and I've too much to tell you over the phone. I should be in Crammingdon about half past five, is it okay if I drop in?' he asked.

'Yes, sir; that would be very kind of you, I'll let the front desk know to expect you and no doubt they will bring you straight up to our office!' I agreed. 'I've not got your name to hand at the moment, remind me what it is!'

'Barton, I'm Charles Barton.'

'Okay, thank you Mr Barton, I'll see you then,' I said and we closed the call.

4

DS Whittington and the DI had called in and gone again by the time Mr Barton arrived in the office.

'Please sit down Mr Barton.'

'Thanks.'

'I think you said you've some information for me?' I asked.

'You were right about his name, I said I didn't think it was Bloor, I always knew him as Dick; anyway, the personnel department assured me his name is Richard Sidney Bloor. This is his address,' he said passing me an official Rolls Royce headed slip. 'I've had to get all of what I'm going to tell you approved by my head of department.'

'That's most helpful thank you,' I nodded.

'He worked on my team, in Department 12, the research and special development department. We are working on a new aero-engine, hush-hush, so I can't tell you anything other than that.'

'I understand,' I nodded, wondering why he had even mentioned it.

'About five years ago my head of department told me that Dick Bloor was passing information to a third party; enough to get him dismissed but it wasn't that simple!'

'The company didn't prosecute him?' I asked,

surprised that it hadn't come to light.

'That would mean admitting we were working on a secret mission,' he grinned.

'Yes, I see that. So what happened to him?'

'The stuff he passed on was from very early in the project, things that later proved to be a bit of a dead-end. It seems it was decided not to make a big fuss about anything and to let our competitors continue working along the lines we had already discounted,' he grinned. 'The decision was taken to keep Bloor working on the defunct part of the project, with an assistant we could trust!'

'Crafty!' I nodded, 'letting him continue to pass on useless information.'

'Everything I'm telling you must be treated in the strictest secrecy, my department head realised that there was every possibility that your investigations would uncover this matter and decided to let you into as much information as he feels you need to know, rather than risk the possibility of the press getting involved.'

'I think I can guarantee that,' I said, hoping I could.

'My boss is very much in charge of the project, answering only to the board of directors. When he learned of Bloor's activities, he informed me but we were at a loss to know how to proceed! Then Bloor himself came up with the answer. Leaving the factory one night at the end of his shift he collapsed. He was still in my department and I had him moved into my office, no mean feat as you can imagine, awaiting the ambulance. In his pocket I found the latest bit of information he was about to pass on. It was of no consequence so I took it on my own back to replace it as though it hadn't been found!' he grinned.

'Yes, I'm with you so far!'

'It was then they found out that he was a diabetic; you do know that I suppose?'

'Yes,' I nodded.

'That gave the excuse for forcing him into early retirement on a full pension.'

'And he was none the wiser to the fact that he had been found out?'

'Neither, of course was the third party,' he smirked.

'Even craftier!' I said.

'We like to think so. As I said I am telling you all of this in the hope that my department can rely on your total discretion,' he said getting up to leave.

'I understand, I'll have to report what you've said to my inspector, but I see no problems,' I said.

'If anything else occurs to me I'll let you know, but I think that's the lot,' he nodded. 'Ah, yes there was something else that helped to dismiss him. He had become very clumsy, fumble-fingered, not good where intricate machinery is concerned.'

'Thank you Mr Barton, that's been a great help,' I said and took him back down the stairs.

At last, we had a firm lead on Mr Richard Sydney Bloor. We could now put a definite name to the man. I filed the information in my drawer and headed home.

The boys were in bed and Alice and I had just settled down for the evening, in front of the kitchen range. I was mulling over the local paper and Alice was knitting some winter pullovers for the boys. The phone rang and we looked at each other.

'I'd better answer it,' I shrugged.

'Mm; I'll get your coat!' she nodded.

'Dexter, It's DI Brierly, get yer skates on we've a missing lad. Tommy Grant, six years old last seen on Parson's Rec. playing with his mates, didn't arrive home at seven o'clock for his tea. His mam and dad have looked for him but there's no sign. Parson's Rec. as soon as yer can, bring yer whistle.'

'Right sir, I'm on my way!' I said, grabbing my flash light and whistle.

Parson's Recreation Ground, known locally as, the Rec. is a hefty piece of land about a mile by a half-mile, roughly oblong. There's a small kiddies play area, with slides and swings, a paddling pool and a sand pit. Alderman Herbert Parson bequeathed the ground, for the enjoyment of the people of Crammingdon, in his will, sometime around the turn of the century. Used enthusiastically since then for everything from visiting fairs and circuses to the local carnival and, with a chunk roped off for the local cricket club; it was loved by all.

DI Brierly was waiting for me at the main entrance.

'Evening Dexter. Sergeant Bell alerted me just before I rang you. He has eight of his chaps starting at the far end, four each side of the brook. The rest of his chaps are searching the streets around the area,' he said as DS Whittington joined us.

'Sorry I'm late sir, I was having a bath.'

'So your wife informed me. We've a missing six year old. Tommy Grant, last seen by his mates about half past six; they thought he'd gone home!'

'What's the plan, sir?' I asked.

'I'm going to stay here and coordinate the search. Whittington, you go over the bridge and search that side. Dexter this side and let's get the lad found before it gets properly dark.'

The sky was cloudless and at barely eight thirty, there was probably a little over an hour before it would be too dark to search.

In the distance, I could hear the uniformed chaps every so often, calling Tommy's name. I called myself of course and since the ground was flat, I covered a fair area quite quickly. I met the uniformed searchers coming towards me, about a quarter of an hour later, when I was about a third of the way down the Rec. Like me, they had found no sign of the boy.

Sergeant Bell's lads continued to search the area I had already done, just to double check.

'No sign of the little chap, sir,' Sergeant Bell said as he joined the DI and me.

'We'll just have to hope that your lads covering the streets have better luck.

'I doubt it, it's a still and quiet tonight; we'd have heard a whistle a mile off!' Bell said, and the DI nodded. By then the night was closing in.

'It's much too dark now to do anything more. I think we'll have to call it off until morning, what do you think Sergeant?' the DI asked.

'I hate to admit it, but I think you're right. At least it's a warm night; the lad should be warm enough,' Bell nodded.

'It should be light at five, start again then?'

'I agree,' Bell said.

Reluctantly, we three set off for home. Sergeant Bell left one of his men on the rec. in case little Tommy turned up, and had the rest of his shift combing the streets. Alice had waited up for me and within minutes of arriving home, I sat in front of the kitchen range with a bowl of homemade soup and a chunk of freshly baked bread.

I was up, dressed and breakfasted by four-thirty and on my way to Parson's Rec. The DI and DS Whittington were already there, as was Sergeant Bell and his men, including the nine officers that had patrolled the streets.

'Sergeant Bell, can I suggest that your men start a search of the outhouses locally?' The DI said.

'I was about to suggest that sir. How about leaving four or five of my chaps here to continue the search now we can see what we are doing?'

'If you can spare them, yes please. I want to make a detailed search of the brook; it was difficult to see it very well last night,' the DI nodded.

'You know that there's an old sheep-dip, don't you, sir?' Bell asked.

'No! Where is that?'

'Down the far end of the rec. by the Derby Road Bridge, It's not been used for years, I only just remembered it myself, sir,' Bell said with grimace.

'Is it still full of water?' the DI asked, scratching his chin.

'I would think so sir, it's just a widened and deepened part of the brook.'

'Still deep enough to dip sheep?'

'Definitely, sir!'

'Your boys started at that end, they'd have searched there sergeant, surely?'

'I only just remembered it myself, sir. You lot come here,' he shouted beckoning the uniformed group. 'Did anyone think to search the old sheep dip, last night?' His answer came with a dozen or so shaken heads and one officer stated that he was unaware of a sheep dip.

To be fair, the dip was, as the sergeant had said, an expansion of the brook beyond the bridge that marks the end of Parson's Rec. The brook flows under the bridge and into the deepened and widened stretch, where the washing took place. The un-washed sheep were gathered in a pen on the west side of the brook, un-ceremoniously thrown into the water and left to swim across and gathered into a pen on the east side. Original-ly, a boom across the brook ensured that the sheep had to swim across and not end up down-stream. Scant evi-dence remained of the boom, and the pens and surround-ing banks were overgrown!

Sergeant Bell, together with the men of his night shift was still on duty, refusing to go home until they had searched and eliminated all possible areas. One of his officers had located a pair of long rubber waders, "rub-ber trousers with boots on the end that tied around his waist", and been assigned the task of searching under the bridge. The bridge was a single arch, but the road over it wide and modern, with a pavement either side. The arch was low enough for the constable to need to stoop. He emerged from the bridge, five minutes or so later, on the sheep dip side of the road, shouted up that there was nothing under the bridge, and immediately stepped into the deepened section, disappearing up to his armpits, much the appreciation of those on the bank.

'Might as well stay in and search, now you're

wet, Constable Evans!' Sergeant Bell shouted, amid re-newed laughter.

'Thank you, Sarge,' he said gingerly stepping forward.

Bell detailed some of his men to walk back into the Rec. and search the brook now it was daylight. He assigned two more to search the brook downstream beyond the sheep dip. DI Brierly, DS Whittington and I searched the overgrown pens on either side.

PC Evans waded carefully from side to side slowly progressing towards the site of the boom, where the brook again took on its normal proportions. About halfway, he stopped and shouted!

'Something on the bottom, Sarge,' he yelled, throwing his helmet, the only dry part of him, to one of the coppers on the bank. Taking a massive gulp of air, he ducked below the murky surface, emerging a few seconds later.

'Can't see a bloody thing, but something is caught in the weeds at the bottom,' he said, gulping and ducking again. When he arose next time, the look on his face instantly stopped the grins and jolly banter on the bank, stone dead!

'It's him Sarge. Chuck us your penknife.'

'What's the problem, Evans?' Bell said, moving to the edge of the pen and tossing the knife to Evans.

'His ankles and one arm are tangled in the weeds. I'll have to cut him free,' he replied, opening the knife and ducking below the surface again. Four or five plunges later the top of a little head rose to the surface, it's hair gently billowing in the disturbed water.

'Just his ankles to free now, Sarge,' he gasped and Bell nodded.

Police Constable Eric Evans, gently gathered up the body of little Tommy Grant and carried it to the open end of the pen where the sheep had once been thrown in, and passed it to Sergeant Bell.

'Thank you Evans. Off home, and get yourself dry.'

'Right, Sarge. I'm glad we've found him, I just wish he'd still been…'

'I know. Off yer go,' Bell said, carrying the little lad's body to the pathway and carefully laying it down. One of the coppers covered it with his tunic.

'Sergeant Bell, thank you and your men, get them off home. We'll handle it now,' the DI said.

'Thank you sir, I'll arrange for a doctor and the pathologist, sir,' Bell said, turning to dismiss his men.

'Thank you, sergeant.'

'Whittington, you and Dexter go and see the lad's family, I'll stay with him.'

'Right sir,' we both agreed, though I'm sure neither of us was looking forward to the task.

The Grants lived within easy walking distance of the Rec. and I wheeled my cycle as we walked there, both deep in thought. I couldn't get the vision out of my mind of little Tommy's flesh, swollen and wrinkled by being immersed overnight in the near stagnant water of the sheep dip.

The small, well-maintained house was the left hand half of a pair of turn of the century semi-detached houses. The doors and window frames were mid green and had a freshly painted look about them, the windows sparkled, proof of regular cleaning. A neat little garden, glowing with early autumn colour, led to the front door and it swung open as we entered the front gate.

'Mr Grant?' DI Whittington asked. The man nodded.

'Have you found him?' he asked, though the look on his face betrayed the fact he had already guessed the answer.

'I'm Detective Sergeant Whittington and this is Detective Constable Dexter, can we come in please, sir?' Whittington asked.

'Aye; yes er… Yes, come in,' he said standing aside. His ruddy, outdoor complexion drained to grey in a couple of seconds.

'Is your wife in Mr Grant?'

'The doctor has given her something to make her sleep, she's been prancing around with worry all night! She's up in the bedroom; she's just settled I don't really want to disturb her,' Grant said.

'I understand, I think you'd better sit down, sir!' Whittington nodded.

'It's bad news, the boy's dead, aint he?'

'I'm sorry Mr Grant. We found him this morn-ing at first light,' DS Whittington nodded.

'What happened?'

'We don't know as yet. We need to talk to the kiddies he was playing with yesterday.'

'Where was he found?'

'He was discovered in the old sheep dip beyond Parson's Rec. Could Thomas swim Mr Grant?'

'Not really, two or three yards maybe. You're saying he was drowned?'

'I'm sorry…'

'Who is it Harry? Have they found our Tom-my?' We guessed the voice was Mrs Grant since it came from the top of the stairs.

'I'd better go up and tell her, better coming from me,' Mr Grant said and hurried up the stairs.

We could hear a few mumbled words as he quietly told his wife the bad news.

'No! No! No! Not my little Tommy! This is all your fault; I knew we shouldn't have let him out with that bunch of little bastards!' she screamed.

'They're not a bad bunch, we couldn't stop the lad, and he so wanted to go and…'

'Yes and now look what you've done… Now look what *you've* done Harry Grant. I hope you're bloody well pleased with yourself,' she said, and there was a heavy bump as Mrs Grant collapsed at the top of the stairs.

'Come and help me get her back in bed, please,' Mr Grant requested.

'Right, sir,' we both said, and climbed the stairs, though it wasn't a job we felt happy about.

Mrs Grant hadn't fainted, merely slumped against the wall between what turned out to be two bedroom doors.

'Come on Ida; let's get you back to bed,' Mr Grant said.

'Don't bloody touch me; murderer!' she yelled.

'Come on love don't be silly, I feel just as upset as you m' lo…'

'Upset, you feel upset. I don't feel upset, I want to die!' she said and kicked out at him from her position on the floor, hitting him just below the knee. Mr Grant staggered backwards and if DS Whittington hadn't grabbed him a bit swiftly, he'd have taken a tumble down the stairs. Mrs Grant slumped onto her side and tears flooded across her face, pooling on the polished lino of the landing. She wailed and kicked her arms and legs about in a child-like tantrum.

Harry Grant was also on the floor, with his trouser-leg pulled up, the ugly bulge at his knee suggested that the blow had displaced his kneecap. Gritting his teeth, he grabbed the bulge and snapped it back into place.

'It's an old footballing injury, it's made it weak, easy to pop out again, happens every couple of years, bloody painful, I'll strap it up once we get Ida in bed!'

Her sobbing and kicking about meant that for three or four minutes, we had no alternative but to leave her lying on the landing as her tears created a pool on the lino. Eventually the tears became deep sobs, as she cried herself out. Carefully the two of us lifted her and with Mr Grant's help with the covers, we got her into bed. She looked at him in a way that no wife should ever look at her husband; a way that suggested their marriage was broken in all but the formalities. She gave a last massive sob, closed her eyes and within a couple of seconds was fast asleep. The doctors' sedative kicking in, I suppose.

'It is, yer know, it's my fault!' he said as we helped him down the stairs and into the kitchen.

'Put the kettle on, would yer.' he asked me.

I nodded, filled it and lit the gas, as he opened a cupboard and from the assortment of raincoats, boots and shoes, he selected two pieces of wood about a foot long. Leather lined and shaped perfectly to his straightened leg, he slipped them over his knee and using the four leather straps and buckles pulled on a perfectly engineered splint.

'That's very clever Mr Grant,' I said as the kettle came to the boil.

'I do a bit of wood carving, or used to do any-way, the first time this happened on the football field at Castle Donnington they took me to hospital and popped it back into place and put it in plaster, cost the team five pounds and put an end to football for me. Six weeks it was on and when they cut it off I asked them to split it down each side,' he smiled.

'And you used it as a pattern for those,' I nod-ded, as I filled the teapot and gave it a stir. He nodded and grinned, a grin that quickly faded as he remembered why we were there.

'You said earlier, that you thought this was your fault, Mr Grant,' DS Whittington enquired, as I found three mugs.

'Tommy asked to go out with his mates, they all live in the street, and they're not bad kids! Full of devil-ment of course, knocking on yer door and running away, the usual kid's stuff; what my mates and me did at that age. Tommy's the youngest of the bunch and there on sufferance, I suppose. I'd asked where they were going and Tommy said to play on the Rec. I couldn't see any problem with that and said he could go but be back for six o'clock. We expected him back more or less on time, but, yer know what kids are like, we said six, knowing he'd be half an hour late just to push a bit and see how far he could stretch us. We've all done it; I know I did.'

'But your wife objected?' I suggested.

'Aye, made a real scene out of it *"Just letting him run riot!"* Not true, I just couldn't see the harm in it. Well she really let fly at me when I suggested that she couldn't keep the lad tied to her apron strings forever. We argued for a while until we realised the lad had

77

nipped off. She demanded that I go and fetch him back, I refused and she started to go herself. I grabbed her arm and stopped her, bloody hell he'd still be alive if I hadn't stopped her! *"If anything happens to him, it'll be your fault Harry Grant!"* she said and shoved me out of the back door. So, off went our Tommy on the scooter I'd made him,' Grant said.

'Tommy had a scooter?' Whittington asked.

'I made him one last Christmas; he never let it out of his sight. I think he'd have taken it to bed with him if we'd let him!'

'You say you made it, would you recognise it?' I asked.

'You're saying you've not found it?'

'We had no idea he had a scooter. It hadn't been found when we left the Rec, but then as I say we weren't looking for one.'

'You'll know it when you see it, I found an old broken table, a nice bit of beech; I made it out of that. It was a bit too big for him at Christmas; he could just about see over the handlebars. He's growing into it now, it's about... was, about right for him,' Grant said and burst into a flood of tears that spilt hot tea on his legs. We quietly sipped our tea whilst Mr Grant cried himself out.

'Mr Grant, I hate having to say this, but you or your wife will have to make a formal identification,' Whittington said.

'That'd better be me. I'll get the wife's sister to come and help out; can't stand the bloody woman but she'll help comfort Ida,' he nodded.

'It will probably be around midday tomorrow, there will have to be a post mortem,' Whittington said.

'Aye… aye; let me know when.'

'We'll send a car for you Mr Grant.'

'Aye, right.'

'Is there anything we can do for you, anyone we can call, before we go?' I asked.

'No, I'll sort it out thanks; it'll give me something to do! I know what I need to do, I'll get on with it as soon as you've gone,' he said, with a faraway look in his eyes

'Good day then Mr Grant.'

'Aye, *good day*… some bloody hopes!' he said and closed the front door behind us.

'What price that marriage, ah, Will?' DS Whittington asked as we closed the garden gate.

'If they stay together it'll be an armed standoff, each blaming the other!' I nodded.

'Not really, he's accepted it's his fault and she'll make sure he never forgets it! No matter what we find; whatever happened, the lad's still dead and Harry Grant will carry the can,' Whittington said and shook his head. We walked off in silence, the only sound the click-click as I wheeled my bike.

About half way to the end of the road, returning to DI Brierly at the Rec, the sound of a gunshot stopped us in our tracks, shortly followed by a second. We looked at each other each knowing what we were about to be confronted with once we had gained access to the Grant home.

Harry must have left the door unlocked, a simple turn of the handle and we were in. Guessing that the action had taken place upstairs, we raced to the bedroom. Mrs Grant was still in bed; her head showed a small bullet hole surrounded by powder burns just above her nose.

Her pillow, crimson and wet, had held most of the mass of blood and brains together. Harry, still twitching, lay on his back on the bed, across her legs; the Webley & Scott service revolver dangled momentarily from his right hand, then fell to the floor with a metallic thud that made us both jump. The contents of Harry's head splattered every wall. Frozen to the spot by what I was looking at, the sound of DS Whittington emptying his stomach in the lavatory bowl, awakened a similar need.

'Well that solves their problem!' Whittington said, rinsing his mouth in the wash-hand basin.

'And ours are just beginning!' I nodded.

There was a knock at the door, a neighbour shouted up the stairs.

'Is everything okay, Mrs Grant?'

'Come in but don't come up the stairs!' shouted Whittington and descended to the tiny hallway.

'What's happened?' the woman asked.

'Can I ask who you are?' said the DS.

'I'm Tessa Millington. I live two doors down on this side of the road. What happened?'

'It seems that Mr Grant killed his wife then shot himself, Mrs Millington; it is Missus?' Whittington said.

'Yes it is missus! Who are you two? Coppers, from the look of yer!'

'I'm DS Whittington and this is DC Dexter. We came to inform Mr and Mrs Grant that we had discovered the body of their son, Tommy.'

'You told them their son was dead? No wonder they shot themselves! Ida, that's Mrs Grant, thought that little devil was all sweetness and light, he could do no wrong in her eyes!'

'You're saying that their son was unruly?' the

DS asked.

'Phew, not half! A real little sod when he was out of their sight, not that Ida would hear a word against the little bugger!' she said shaking her head.

'Mr Grant suggested that it was just boyish devilment,' I pointed out.

'Aye, if you call throwing mud all over my clean washing, boyish devilment!'

'Are you sure it was him?' Whittington asked.

'Saw him do it through the bedroom window, I did. I banged on the window but by the time I got downstairs, he was gone. I went to see Ida, she called the boy in and asked him. Saintly? You should have seen it, talk about butter wouldn't melt; "No mam, I didn't do that!" he said cool as yer like. He's dead yer say?'

'Drowned in the old sheep dip, sometime last night.'

'He wanted a bloody good hiding, but not that!' she said, sadly shaking her head.

'Mr Grant told us that he had made the lad a wooden scooter, did you ever see it Mrs Millington?'

'Harry is good – was good with his hands, Tommy was so proud of that scooter, it was homemade, obviously but, don't go thinking it was a makeshift job. Well no doubt you've seen it.'

'We didn't know Tommy had a scooter until Mr Grant told us a few minutes ago,' I said.

'Oh. Well, it was a lovely wooden thing, all polished oak I think it was, with a lion's head carved on the front. It was the lad's pride and joy. He used to scoot to school and his mam would wheel it back.'

'So, we are going to be looking for a wooden scooter with a lion's head carved on the front?' The DI

81

said.

'I'm surprised you found Tommy without his scooter!'

'Mrs Millington, we understand that Mrs Grant had a sister, do you know where we can find her?'

'News to me, we weren't in each other's pockets if yer know what I mean, but I never saw anyone at the house. Sorry, I can't help yer there.'

'Thank you Mrs Millington, we'll have to leave it at that for now, we need to ring this in,' the DS said.

'You can use my phone,' she said.

'You are on the phone?'

'My Bill was one o' them breakdown truck drivers; often used to get called out in the middle of the night to a crashed car, to help clear the road.'

DS Whittington went with Mrs Millington to call the details in, whilst I stood guard at the Grants' front door. Thankfully, the front door was on the shaded side of the house, though the sun was slowly working its way towards me. I got to thinking about six year old Tommy Grant. I wondered if the mud on the washing, that Mrs Millington had told us about was the only incident in his young life. We needed to ask around the neighbours and to find the other kids that Tommy had gone off with yesterday. As I was mulling this over in my mind, DS Whittington returned.

'The DI's on his way, and an undertaker and the police surgeon,' he said, offering me a cigarette.

'I'm still on the pipe, Sarge but not at work,' I said shaking my head.

'If you've got it with you, light up, I think we deserve it,' he nodded.

'I don't bring it Sarge, then I'm not tempted!'

The police surgeon, Archibald Daniels, turned up about nine o'clock.

'What have we got, DS Whittington?' he asked as he locked his elderly but immaculate blue Humber.

'Mr and Mrs Grant. We are assuming Mr Grant shot and killed his wife, then turned to gun on himself.'

'Grant? The parents of the lad in the sheep dip?'

'Yes, we'd just informed them, and were on our way back to DI Brierly when we heard the shots.'

'That suggests you need to revise your technique for informing parents of bad news!' he laughed and headed up the stairs. 'Unusual décor!' he yelled from the top of the stairs. 'Red and grey randomly on white distemper!' he added, and burst out laughing.

'Is he always like that?' I asked.

'His way of dealing with this sort of thing! Look Will, learn to pass it off, make a joke of it if it helps but don't let it get to you,' Wittington said.

'Aye, I think I was coming to that conclusion!'

'Okay, put me in the picture; what exactly happened?' asked DI Brierly, stepping from one of the police cars. DS Whittington quickly ran through the sequence of events leading to us finding the bodies of the Grants.

'If the gun was in his hand, he must have shot her then done himself in,' the DI nodded, 'but why?'

'We asked ourselves that,' I admitted. 'Mrs Grant blamed her husband; he even started to blame himself. We think he saw a lifetime of regret and recrimination ahead and took the easy way out,' I added, Whittington nodded his agreement.

'What a bloody mess!' the DI said leaning against the front door frame.

'I couldn't agree more!' Archibald Daniels said with a broad grin on his face as he jogged back down the stairs. 'Quite simple, murder followed by the perpetrator's suicide. Life extinct at er, nine-o-nine,' he said looking at his pocket watch. 'I'll have them moved to the morgue and then it's Bob Armstrong's pigeon! Good day gentlemen.'

'Well, that was short and sweet!' The DI said.

'Although we weren't there when it happened, it's hard to see it any other way,' I suggested, and DS Whittington nodded his agreement. A uniformed officer arrived and stood guard at the door.

The DI and DS Whittington returned to Whitecross Yard in the police car. I of course, had to ride my bike.

As I rounded the street corner into Cavendish Road, I noticed a group of youngsters, about nine or ten years old. As I approached them they scattered, one running past me and into the front gate of a house on the corner. I followed him up the side of the house and around to the back door, in time to hear it slam.

I knocked on the door, and after a second knock, it was opened by a timid looking woman with her hair in curlers.

'Who are you? What do you want?' she asked, surprisingly fierce from the first impression she had given.

'I'm DC Dexter and I'd like a word with the young lad who just came in here,' I replied.

'Why, what's he supposed to have done?'

'I just wondered if he could tell me if he played on the Rec yesterday with little Tommy Grant?'

'He didn't have nothin' to do with that!'

'He was with a group of lads and girls just now, who scattered when they saw me. I need a word with him to see if he can tell me what happened that made Tommy fall into the old sheep dip.'

'Sorry, he can't help you!'

'I'm trying to determine what happened, to see if it was just an accident, before my inspector decides to call it murder,' I added.

'Murder... Just a minute,' she said and disappeared from the door, leaving it open.

'Edward Pollock, you come down here this minute,' she shouted up the stairs. 'You'd better come in.'

'Thank you, er, Mrs Pollock?' I queried.

'That's right,' she said holding the lad by the scuff of the neck and plonking him on a kitchen chair.

'Edward, early this morning we found little Tommy Grant at the bottom of the old sheep dip by Parsons Rec. He had drowned. Were you with the group that were playing with him yesterday afternoon?' I asked, and after looking at his mother, who was stern faced, he nodded.

'Can you tell me what happened?'

'We weren't playing with him, he's a nipper and he tags along wherever we go,' the lad said.

'He's younger than the rest of you?'

'He's only six, always annoyin' us. He always wants to be as good as us, better. Jack gets real mad with him sometimes, clouts him and sends him home but he never goes, just hangs around watching us.'

'So, what happened yesterday afternoon?' Mrs Pollock asked the lad, beating me to the question.

'Jack went up to him before he could turn and run and grabbed his scooter and rode round and round on

85

it, with Tommy trying to catch him.'

'Then what happened?' I asked.

'Tommy shouted, "Give me my scooter. I'll tell my Dad!" but Jack just laughed and chucked it in the brook! "There it is go and fetch it and then bugger off home".

'Edward! That's enough, of that sort of language!' Mrs Pollock snapped.

'That's what he said, Mam – honest.'

'Then what happened?' I asked.

'Tommy slipped down the bank and we all ran off laughing.'

'Jack didn't push him or throw him in?'

'Nobody touched him, he just went after his flippin' scooter!' the lad said with a look that suggested he was telling the truth.

'If that's what happened, then it was just a very sad accident. I need to talk to this boy Jack, what's his other name and where does he live? I asked.

'Don't know,' the lad said, looking away.

'Edward Pollock, you tell the officer this minute,' his mam said, grabbing the scruff of his neck.

'Jack Pine and he lives at number fifteen.' Clearly, Edward's mam stands no nonsense.

'Thank you Edward. We'll need to take your statement down at the police station later today, once I've had a word with your friend Jack,' I said. 'We have to get everything straight, of course,' I pointed out to Mrs Pollock who looked aghast at being so involved with the police; a look I'd often seen in similar circumstances.

I went to the front door of number fifteen and rattled the knocker.

'What?' asked a muscular man in shirtsleeves and braces.

'I'm DC Dexter, I need to have a word with your son, Jack.'

'And if he don't want to talk to you?'

'I can have a quiet word with him here, or send a couple of Bobbies' to take him down to Whitecross Yard,' I bluffed.

'I think you'll find it'll take more than a couple,' the man said.

'Mr Pine, something very tragic happened last night on Parsons Rec. My inspector is looking to treat it as murder, *I* think it was just a tragic accident, a word with Jack could clear it all up, without any unpleasantness,' I said trying to calm the situation.

'What 'appened then?'

I quickly told him that we had found the body of six-year old Tommy Grant, and needed to know what had happened to him.

'What does it matter? The Grants have topped themselves; I heard the gunshots! So, who gives a damn? I'm sure I bloody don't! And, if you want a word with our Jack, send yer bloody Bobbies,' he said and slammed the door.

'He slammed the door in your face?' the DI asked.

'He did and although I knocked a couple of times more he refused to answer,' I nodded.

'Time for a word with Sergeant Burdette, leave it to me!' he said and raced down the stairs to the front office.

'What did Edward Pollock tell you?' DS Whittington asked. I told him the gist of the matter.

'Sounds like a pretty realistic account of a kids tiff!'

'I think it is more or less what happened, just one of life's sad incidents,' I nodded.

'What's this chap Pine's problem, then?'

'Just doesn't like the police I suppose.' I grinned.

'Not on his own with that!' the DS nodded.

'I think we can leave that in the hands of our colleagues in uniform, they'll no doubt go round there mob-handed to arrest a nine year old boy. The newspapers will shout about it but it's not our problem,' he smiled. 'You reckon this lad Pollock is telling the truth?'

'Yes sir! His mother is only a slip of a woman but he does as she says, and I think he told it as it was.'

'Apart from needing to give evidence at the inquest I think we've wrapped it up. So let's get back to Mr Bloor.'

5

Because the disappearance of Tommy Grant and his subsequent discovery in the old sheep dip, then the deaths of his parents in quick succession had taken our full attention, I had been unable to tell the DI of my talk with Mr Barton my contact at Rolls Royce. I quickly ran through what I had learned.

'Then our man is definitely Bloor,' the DI nodded.

'Rolls Royce employment records say he is Richard Sidney Bloor,' I said.

'They reckon he's been passing information to a business rival but do they know who it is?'

'I'm not sure they'd tell us if they do, sir.'

'If Bloor has been unwittingly passing duff information to them, would they take revenge to the point of killing him?' the DI asked.

'Who knows; if they have spent loads of cash trying to make something work that Rolls Royce has already proved doesn't, perhaps they might be a bit put out!' I grinned. 'I think it's remote but perhaps we should bear it in mind as another possibility, sir, especially if they are forking out a hefty sum every time he hands it over. I'm assuming he was still doing it but that must have stopped when he retired.'

'Mm… Point taken. They gave you an address

for him, you say?'

'Yes, sir,' I said feeling in my desk drawer and handing him the company-headed slip.

'This address is Codnor, that's roughly between Eastwood and Ripley. Codnor is Derbyshire, I think, so let's get a car organised and have a word with Mrs Bloor, if there is one,' the DI nodded.

'It explains why Bloor was picked up by taxi in those two places,' DS Whittington suggested.

'Okay, agreed, but why not from home?' the DI pointed out.

'That's something we could ask his wife,' Whittington said.

'Dexter, whilst Whittington and I go to interview Mrs Bloor, look into who might want to have access to Rolls Royce research,' the DI suggested.

'Okay, but how do I do that, sir?'

'It's called detection, Dexter!' he grinned.

With the DI and DS Whittington off to Codnor, I set about finding the information the DI had suggested. I didn't want to upset Mr Barton, my contact at the factory, but I could see no alternative. I rang the number that I knew would contact him.

'Mr Barton, this is DC Dexter again, I don't want to say over the phone what I'm wanting to ask you. I wonder if you could call in to Whitecross Yard again for another chat?'

'I can't think what I can possibly add to what I've already told you,' he said impatiently.

'It may be nothing, but my inspector thought it worth getting your thoughts to try to eliminate his worries.'

'Can you give me a rough idea what his worries

are?'

'He wonders if the party that we spoke about, was killed by the…'

'Okay, don't say any more, I know what you're thinking, I'll have a word with my head of department and I'll ring you back. I can't promise that he'll allow me to say more than I already have.'

'Thank you sir, you have my word that it will go no further.' I said and he put the phone down.

That was the point at which the duty sergeant tapped on the door and poked his head into the room.

'There's a Mr Lennox asking to see you, is it okay for me to bring him up?'

'Ah! Mr Lennox the taxi driver?' I asked.

'That's right, says it's important.'

'Bring him up, please sergeant.' I said and a few moments later the man came in.

'Mr Lennox, what can I do for you?' I asked.

'Mr Dexter, I'm so sorry,' he said handing me a little leather case, about the size of a small book. I un-zipped the thing and looked inside.

'I'm sorry, I didn't know my son had found it in the cab; I caught him messing about with it this morning!'

'This is the kit you saw Mr Bloor using in your cab?' I asked, though there could be no other explanation.

'I wanted to be really angry with him; he knows that anything found in the cab has to be handed in, but knowing Edgar, that's my eldest lad, if I was angry he'd just clam-up. I realised that it was probably important to you so I took a different line with him. I said, "Oh, you've found it, my boss has been looking everywhere

91

for that. Where did you find it?" like I was relieved,' he shrugged.

'It is most important, thank you Mr Lennox. Where was it by the way?'

'It was down the back of the seat, I'd have found it when I cleaned the car the morning before I started work again after the holiday, but my lad had already found it of course. The kids each have a little bag of their own when we go in holiday. Ginny, Virginia, that's my wife, thinks it's important for them to be responsible for their own bits and bobs. It seems that on the way to Ginny's sister, Edgar was fiddling with his holiday pocket money, dropped it and it fell down the back of the seat. Looking for it he found this and put it in his bag.'

'Did he find his pocket money?' I grinned.

'He did, and I've come straight round with this, Mr Dexter,' he said nodding at the little pouch open on the desk.

'I might need to take his fingerprints, to eliminate them, but a child's prints should be pretty obvious I should think. Yours too as you've handled it.'

'That's no problem. Look, I've got to be on my way, I'm a bit late signing in already,' he said.

'I'll be in touch if we need to do that, and thank you Mr Lennox, I'm sure this is most important,' I said and showed him down the stairs.

I decided to get the pouch to Dr Armstrong, the pathologist, who also carries out some of our forensic work, but before I had looked up his number, the phone rang. It was Mr Barton from Rolls Royce.

'Is that DC Dexter?'

'It is. What can I do for you Mr Barton?'

'My boss has agreed to me giving you certain

information on the understanding that he will be informed if you intend to use it in a way that might be detrimental to the company,' he said.

'If we use it in a way that causes the company embarrassment; is that what you mean?' I asked.

'Rolls Royce has many customers around the world, we hold lots of confidential information about them. If it became known that that information was being divulged they might well consider cancelling their contracts.'

'I see. Perhaps it would be best if you told your information to my inspector.'

'I finish at four o'clock this afternoon. I could be with you about half-past, if that's okay?'

'He's out at the moment, but he should be back by then,' I said.

'Right; I'll see you then,' and we closed the call.

Things seemed to be on the move at last. I put the kettle on and rinsed the mugs, then looked for the number for Dr Armstrong in the DI's phone pad. His assistant answered on the third ring.

'Dr Armstrong is about to scrub-up, I'll see if he will talk to you,' he said when I told him who I was.

'DC Dexter, how can I help you?'

'I've just come into possession of Mr Bloor's injection kit,' I said.

'That will be interesting! You have it there you say?'

'I have but there's a slight problem, it was found in the taxi Mr Bloor had used. It's a longish story but the taxi driver's kids have been messing with it.'

'Oh well, after all this time, I suppose it was inevitable that someone would have handled it. Can you get it across to me or had I better send a hospital messenger?'

'I'll get one of the cars to bring it to you, as soon as possible,' I said.

'I'll be interested to see it. It could answer quite a few questions.'

The kettle came to the boil and I poured water into the teapot, and unwrapped my sandwiches. I suddenly realised I hadn't eaten since a hurried breakfast that morning, before heading to Parson's Rec.

Charles Barton, my contact at Rolls Royce arrived shortly after four-thirty as he had promised and the duty sergeant showed him to the office.

'Sit down Mr Barton, Detective Inspector Brierly, isn't back yet but I expect him any minute; can I offer you a cup of tea?' I asked.

'Thanks but no, I won't if it's all the same to you?' he said with a shake of his head.

'I've not been able to contact DI Brierly, so he doesn't know you're here. I suggest you wait until he arrives otherwise I'm afraid you'll have to repeat the whole thing when he does get here.

'That's fine. I need to be certain that he understands the delicate nature of what I am going to tell you.'

Luckily, the DI arrived within a couple of minutes of Mr Barton sitting down.

'Mr Barton has agreed to give us certain information, but I'll let him explain,' I said.

'As I'm sure DC Dexter has made you aware, my department is extremely hush-hush. We are constantly refining existing aero engines and developing new ones. Only those within the firm, with the need to know,

94

are aware of my department and most of them are top management. The person, whose death you are looking into was passing information about our work on a very special engine, to an interested party. DC Dexter contacted me early this afternoon, hinting that he would like to know the identity of that party. I was unable, perhaps unwilling, to divulge that information until I had cleared it with my head of department,' he said.

'I understand your reluctance to part with sensitive information, but I feel Mr Bloor's death may be attributable to your "industrial spies", is that the correct term?' the DI asked.

'I suppose it is,' Barton said.

'Tell me as much as you are allowed then please Mr Barton.'

'As I told DC Dexter last evening, we are developing a new aero-engine. What I didn't tell him was that we are working very closely with the Royal Air Force. They are expecting to put out specifications for a new all metal fighter-plane, capable of three-hundred-plus miles per hour.'

'Three-hundred, miles per hour,' the DI whistled.

'Nowhere near as tall an order as it might seem, no doubt you will remember the Schneider Trophy Race last year. The Supermarine aircraft exceeded four-hundred miles per hour with our R type engine.'

'But surely that was a racing aircraft, like racing cars, built for that one specific race, not intended to run for ever in normal conditions,' the DI suggested.

'A valid point, but the engine we are developing will be capable of propelling a fighter aircraft, a much heavier prospect than the race plane, to meet the proposed specification. As I told you, that specification does not exist yet, but it seems more than likely. We are working as though it is a forgone conclusion. That makes it very sensitive, both militarily and commercially,' he said and looked around the three of us. We nodded our understanding.

'Do you mean that even if the RAF don't want it, it could find a market with the commercial airlines?' DS Whittington asked.

'In a modified form, without doubt. I think I can say without seeming immodest, that Rolls Royce has a reputation for excellence second to none. That makes anything in the way of inside information very desirable and thus quite valuable to a competitor,' again he looked around for our agreement.

'That being the case, you must have a pretty good idea who those interested parties would be,' I suggested.

'A German Aircraft manufacturer, B&F, have shown a mild interest in purchasing our R type engines for a light trainer plane. Given the way the German political situation is progressing, no doubt they would make any specifications we divulged available to their engine manufacturing industry,' he shrugged.

'What's to stop them getting one of your existing engines and using that as a basis for their own?' the DI asked.

'Nothing, of course. But why copy an engine that was designed five or six years ago, when your rivals are already working on next year's engine,' he grinned.

'That is who you suspect Bloor was providing with information?' DS Whittington asked.

'It may not be that simple. We have a rival in

America; they make mostly rotary and radial engines, very good engines they are too, but they are running into problems with their development of more conventional engine types. That makes them equally, if not more interested in obtaining an insight into how we are thinking.'

'Two rivals! Could Bloor be dealing with them both?' the DI asked.

'We hadn't thought of that. That would be a very dangerous game, it could get…'

'You killed?' the DI suggested.

'It's a very good way to upset some serious players, especially once they found that what they were being given was very expensive, useless information,' he nodded.

'No doubt, both of these companies have representatives in this country. Can you give me any idea who they are?' the DI asked.

'B&F have an office in Swindon, very low-key. They use private companies to carry out any servicing requirements they may have! Peters & Walker, our American rivals, have a service area at Croydon Airport and another near Edinburgh. That is all I'm authorised to tell you gentlemen,' Mr Barton said and rose to leave.

'Thank you Mr Barton, I hope that Bloor's activities have nothing to do with his death, or it could provoke an international incident,' the DI said as we all shook his hand. 'I'll show you out.'

Just as we were about to leave for the night, a uniformed constable met us at the bottom of the stairs.

'What do you want me to do with this?' he asked, holding up a little wooden scooter with a lion's head carved above the front wheel.

'Where did you find it?' the DI asked.

'Lodged in the weeds about a hundred yards before the Derby Road Bridge. Almost underwater, I just noticed the rear wheel sticking out!'

'Take it down to archives, I'll decide what to do with it in the morning,' the DI said, with a shake of his head.

The boys were busy drawing and crayoning when I arrived home.

'You must be worn out my sweet,' Alice said as I walked through the door, and the boys stopped and ran to meet me.

'Did you find the missing child?' she asked.

'I'll tell you later,' I said, giving her a look that said "not in front of the boys", and she nodded her understanding.

'Have you only had your sandwiches to eat?'

'Yes, I'm absolutely starving,' I admitted.

'I've made a pie with some steak and kidney the butcher had, it was expensive, but it should last over the weekend. It's about done. Just time for you to get a wash, and have a shave if you're going to come anywhere near me,' she laughed.

I played with the boys until it was their bedtime, then took them to bed and read them a story. Once they had nodded off, I told Alice the sad tale of little Tommy Grant, including the discovery of his scooter.

'I could tell from the look on the DI's face that he was at a loss as to how to deal with the thing,' I said.

'No one will want it if they know where it came from,' she said. 'I think you should suggest it is given to the local orphanage,'

'We will need to make sure that there are no relatives who might have a claim, but I think that's a good idea, I'll tell DI Brierly what you think,' I nodded.

As I lay in bed, I realised that with Mr Barton's appearance in the office, I hadn't found out about the call that DI Brierly and DS Whittington had made on Mrs Bloor. Life as a detective was going to be much more complicated than that of a mere bobby, and it could wait until the morning. I put my arm around Alice and dismissed it until then.

Saturday morning started as they so often do in Late August, with a slight mistiness that suggests once the sun burns the mist away, it will turn hot and sultry. Even at seven-thirty it was a warm bike-ride to White-cross Yard.

DI Brierly was already in the office, he had made a cup of tea, so had clearly been there some time. A slight hint of whisky was in the air; I guessed he had added a little nip to his brew.

'Morning Dexter. Pour yourself a cuppa, it has only just brewed.

'Morning, sir,' I replied and poured the steaming brew.

'I've put a little of the hard stuff in mine because I remembered that little scooter and it knocked the stuffing out of me for some reason,' he said with a weak smile. 'I went down to archives and brought it up here, I've not a bloody clue why.'

'It does look sad, leaning against the wall waiting for an owner that will never come,' I nodded.

'I can't help thinking that less than thirty-six hours ago, a family of three were living a fairly normal life; okay with their fair share of problems, but what family hasn't? Then a child accidentally dies because of a childish act and almost in the blink of an eye, the whole family is wiped of the face of the earth. Makes you realise just how delicate human life really is!' he said with a shrug.

'It is a very sad story, sir! I suppose you will be required at the inquest?' I suggested.

'Yes, ten-thirty this morning I've got to be there and DS Whittington has been called to give evidence of the two shootings. I think the coroner will look upon the three deaths almost as one event.'

'Now might not be the time to sir, but Alice suggested that assuming there is no family claim on it, the scooter is donated to St Joseph's!'

'To the orphanage. Yes… yes, that's a nice idea,' he nodded.

'Changing the subject, sir. How did your interview with Mrs Bloor go?'

'What a strange person she turned out to be! I told her the bad news about her husband and she just shrugged, said she'd seen his picture in the paper. I asked her why she hadn't come forward with information; and she said she knew he'd kill himself one day with his stupid way of going on,' he said shaking his head.

'Sounds like she didn't care if he lived or died, sir.'

'That's the way I saw it, not only that, she didn't care who knew how she felt.'

'That must make her a definite suspect, once we can be absolutely certain he was murdered,' I said.

'Hard to see it any other way. She is, after all a

very presentable woman; smart attractive, almost sure to have admirers,' he nodded. 'Okay, she's in her fifties, but well preserved, looks a good few years younger than that.'

'You think that could be another angle, sir?'

'It wouldn't be the first time that one side of a love-triangle gets eliminated,' he grinned. 'It can be a very strong motive!'

'You think we need to look into it?' I asked.

'Already in hand, Dexter. I've got the local boys looking into Mrs Bloor's background and poking around to see if she has any, er… Paramours!'

'That's a very old fashioned term sir,' I chuck-led.

'It's a very old situation, Dexter, it probably goes back to when we lived in caves, perhaps even before that. One of the strongest motives for many things,' he nodded. 'It must have been very frustrating for a per-sonable woman like that to be married to our massively overweight Mr Bloor.'

'Mm,' I agreed.

By twelve-thirty, the DI and DS Whittington were back from the inquest.

'Following our evidence the coroner has ad-journed the inquest pending further enquiries by the uni-form lads. He asked us to oversee their operation and inform him of any new information. I'm going to put you in charge of coordinating that,' he said nodding at DS Whittington.

'Is there likely to be any new information, sir?' I asked.

'Young Jack Pine admitted grabbing Tommy's scooter and chucking it in the brook and he saw Tommy go down the bank after it and they all ran off. The coroner returned a "Death by misadventure" verdict on little Tommy, but he has left the deaths of the lad's parents open. As I said, that is how it stands.'

A few moments later, the DI made the decision that we leave it all until Monday morning.

It was nice to have a day and a half, being a family. We spent the Sunday on a bus ride to the delightful little town of Wirksworth. The steeply sloping streets and market place were alive with folk enjoying the fine weather and a church fete was in full swing. The boys shared the pushchair, alternately riding, walking or being carried on my shoulders, using my hair to steer me to their next point of interest. All part of being a dad I suppose!

One of the stalls had a selection of good second hand toys; George fell in love with a pull-along wooden duck that flapped its wings as it moved, and Will couldn't take his eyes off a pressed metal toy police car.

'The siren should work as you push it along, but it's broken, I'm afaid,' the stallholder winked.

'A bit noisy was it?' Alice asked.

'Not so much noisy as annoying, it was my lad's and after a couple of days the siren stopped working!' he said tongue in cheek. 'But it could easily be repaired.'

'I don't think I'll bother.' I grinned.

'Very wise,' he nodded.

The boys were ready for bed by the time we got home and were soon fast asleep.

Monday the 23rd of August, the three of us sat over what the DI called "the thinking cup"; the first mug of tea of the day, discussing the death of Mr Bloor and its different aspects.

'It seems to me that there are three possible suspects,' the DI said. 'Mrs Bloor; her lover, assuming there is one, and the company or companies he was passing information to.'

'That's four, sir!' DS Whittington pointed out.

'You know what I mean! My money is on the lover,' the DI said raising a questioning eyebrow.

'I think one of the two companies felt annoyed at being given bad information,' I offered.

'No, it will turn out to be the wife, but I can't see how,' Whittington nodded.

'The local lads in Codnor are looking into the possibility that Mrs Bloor has a lover, I'm going to pull a few strings to get a look at Mrs Bloor's background, You Dexter, find out what you can about the two business rivals,' the DI said.

'I'll go and see what the uniform lads have found out about the Grants,' DS Whittington nodded. 'I want to get that sorted as soon as possible and get the case closed,' he said, and the DI nodded his agreement as Whittington went down the stairs.

The DI had gone out and I sat mulling over Bloor's contact with the other companies. I couldn't see where to start. The death of Bloor broke the chain with the interested companies. No, that isn't true! Bloor becoming ill and being pensioned off over four years ago broke the chain. Why kill Bloor four or five years later? Perhaps the company or companies had only just found out that he had given false information. Then another possibility clicked a light on in my brain. What if, Bloor

103

didn't admit to them that he no longer worked at Rolls Royce, and continued to pass on seemingly feasible information? That's a completely different kettle of fish. That would really make them angry enough to kill. Removed from the day-to-day working of a research department, could he really be knowledgeable enough to come up with information to fool Rolls Royce's business rivals? I rang Mr Barton, my contact at Rolls Royce.

'Mr Barton, this is DC Dexter, I wonder if we could have another little chat?'

'I've given you all the information I've been authorised to give you. I'm sorry I have nothing to add to what you already know,' he said.

'I understand that this is a delicate situation, but I'm part of a team investigating a murder. I'm not entirely happy that you have been totally honest with me.'

'I have given you everything that I know, and also some extra information the head of my department added. If there is anything being withheld it is not being withheld by me,' he snapped.

'I apologise, that didn't come out as I intended, I'm not accusing you personally. I think that we are both being kept away from vital information.'

'I couldn't possibly comment on that, however I will see my head of department and suggest that you are unhappy with the explanation they have given,' he said. 'I will ring you back as soon as possible.'

The DI was back just after midday.

'Well, I have been a busy little bee!' he said as he dropped into his chair and nodded towards the kettle.

'Got some good leads then, sir?' I asked, getting the tea on the go.

'I've been having a word with Inspector Fellows

at Codnor to see if I could get their lot moving a bit. One of his lads had searched the parish records. Mr & Mrs Bloor were married in January 1922. He is on record as a research worker at Rolls Royce. She is down as a secretary at the same place. Presumably, she gave up her job on marriage, I need to check that out of course, but it is normal. Her maiden name was Annette Smith. Her mother was one of the witnesses. His brother Thomas James Bloor was the other. Guess what occupation he is recorded as having?' The DI grinned.

'No idea, sir. Oh! Could it be window cleaner, sir?'

'You clever little bugger, yes, window cleaner.'

'Have you traced him, sir?'

'No. That's a nice little job for you, Dexter.'

'Thank you, sir.'

'How far have you got, tracing leads on the spy companies?'

'I wondered if Bloor was continuing to pass on duff information even after he had been pensioned off, sir,' I said.

'Now that really would be dangerous!' the DI said sucking his breath through his teeth,

'There seemed to be a problem. Would he be able to provide information of a high enough calibre to fool a major company?'

'We already know that his information was sending them down the wrong track, and that Rolls Royce provided that information. I think I know where you're going with this, Dexter,' the DI grinned.

'I'm expecting a call before too long that should take us a little way forwards, sir,' I nodded.

The call came just before two o'clock.

'Crammingdon CID, Detective Inspector Brierly speaking.'

There was an unheard reply. Then the DI said.

'I see, sir. Thank you sir, I appreciate that,' and then replaced the receiver.

'Dexter organise a car for us, we're going to Derby,' he said. 'Come on, get yer backside into gear, we have to be there for three o'clock!'

'Right, sir.'

Sergeant Mellors was at the front desk and switched on the police-box lights. Since their installation two years ago, the system had reduced the incident response time considerably. The set-up consisted of twenty odd police-boxes, arranged around the town all containing a phone and a small fold down writing surface. A telephone connected them to Whitecross Yard. A switch on the duty sergeant's desk could instantly put on a blue flashing light on top of each box. This alerted passing patrols, on foot or in car to an urgent situation. He flicked the switch just as DI Brierly entered the front office.

'Ah, glad I've caught yer Tom. You know John Bell is retiring at the end of the week?'

'Sergeant Bell, yes,' the DI agreed.

'Done his thirty years, virtually without a blemish, the uniform lads are putting on a surprise party for the old bugger. We want CID to be there, what do you say?' he asked as his phone rang, and whoever was at the other end introduced themselves.

'Back here quick as yer can,' he said and put the phone down.

'Car on its way, he's at the corner of Whitaker

Lane, less than two minutes at a guess. Anyway what do you say about John's surprise do?'

'I say count us in,' the DI said looking at me and I nodded my agreement. 'I think I can speak for DS Whittington and DC Harrington, stick them on the list.'

'I'm glad you said that because... Okay it'll do when you get back!'

The screech of brakes outside the main entrance had interrupted him as our transport arrived.

We already had the okay to work in the Derby force area, provided we kept them informed that we were on their patch and the DI had done so.

As we walked into the reception area, a well-dressed young woman met us.

'Good afternoon. Welcome to Rolls Royce Limited, I'm Janice Durham, I assume you are the gentlemen from Crammingdon!' she said, glancing through the huge glass doors at our police car standing outside on the parking area.

'That's correct, a bit of a give-away,' he grinned nodding at it.

'My superior has asked me to dismiss your car, as he is going to arrange your transport back to Crammingdon, sir.'

'That's very good of him, Dexter, dismiss the car!'

With the car on its way back home, I joined Miss Durham and the DI. I'm not sure what I was expecting in the way of grandeur, this being the headquarters of a world famous company, whatever it was I was not disappointed. I suppose the building and its interior is best described as Art Deco, yet unmistakably functional. Miss Durham led us down a short corridor and to a beautiful oak door, where she tapped politely.

'Come!' shouted a deep voice.

'Your guests from Crammingdon, sir.'

'Show them in Miss Durham,' she stepped out of the way and waved us in.

'DI Tom Brierly and this is DC William Dexter. Pleased to meet you, sir,' the DI said holding out his hand as we advanced to the tall, thin man who had stepped from the biggest desk I had ever seen.

He introduced himself, but asked us not to write down his name, for reasons of secrecy 'I'm the director of the project, perhaps if you recorded me as "Mr Hooper",' he suggested.

'Please take a seat, gentlemen. This is our Mr Barton, though I think you are already acquainted.' We thanked him and sank into sumptuous leather armchairs.

'I think Mr Barton has told you as much as we are prepared to admit, so perhaps if you are willing to put your own cards on the table we might more easily come to a mutual exchange of information,' *Mr Hooper* said, with raised eyebrows.

'As I'm sure you are aware we are investigating the murder of one of your past employees, Richard Sidney Bloor,' The DI stated.

'I have his file here,' he said.

'DC Dexter found the body of Mr Bloor in a cinema on Crammingdon marketplace. It was clear from wrappers that he had consumed at least two large bars of chocolate covered confectionary. Mr Bloor was massively overweight and it was initially assumed that his death was through natural causes, probably a heart attack,' the DI said.

'You now consider that he was murdered; are

108

you at liberty to give further details?'

'Since we are being frank with each other I see no reason to withhold the state of our investigations so far. Though like you I must ask that what I am about to tell you stays in this room.'

'Understood,' Mr Hooper, said and Barton nodded.

'Once we realised that Mr Bloor had not died of natural causes, we placed his picture in the local press, and Mr Barton was one of the people who responded to our request for a name, as at the time we had no idea who he was.'

'Mr Barton came to me, asking how and if he should contact you. I worried that your investigations might well uncover certain information that I needed to keep confidential, and because of that, I decided to allow him to give you enough to set you on the right tracks with a name. Hoping that would be all you needed.'

'Mr Barton informed us that Bloor was passing information to a third party; information that would lead them down a blind alley. Is that correct sir?' the DI asked.

'I saw it as a useful delaying tactic.'

'Initially Mr Barton was loath to suggest who the third party might be. I am following several lines of enquiry, and at my request, DC Dexter again contacted Mr Barton for further information. Information I understand he first cleared with you.'

'You are thinking Bloor was killed by one of our competitors once they found out his information was useless, is that it? Hooper asked.

'Mr Barton admitted that Bloor had been fed with useless information up to the point when he collapsed in the factory and was subsequently diagnosed with diabetes, roughly five years ago.'

'That gave me what I was looking for: an excuse to end his employment without actually being seen to dismiss him,' he nodded.

'That is more or less what you told DC Dexter, is it not, Mr Barton?' the DI asked.

'It is!' Barton said turning to his boss, 'with your approval, sir?'

'Agreed.'

'Now that leaves me with a couple of problems. Why would it take nearly five years for your competitors to find out that it was duff information they had received, and would it make them sufficiently aggrieved to kill him? That set us on another tack: was Bloor continuing to give information to your competitors, and had they only recently found out that it was, er... of little use. That continuing information would need to be sufficiently accurate to keep them interested. If that was indeed the case, where was the new information being obtained?' the DI enquired, with raised eyebrows.

'I can see that you're a man not easily thrown off the scent, Detective Inspector. I summoned Mr Bloor to my office, once he was back at work after his illness and he admitted that he was suffering from diabetes. I confronted him with the fact that I had long been aware that he was passing information to a third party. I pointed out that we were perfectly within our rights to sack and begin prosecutions against him there and then. However, we were prepared to retire him on a full pension on the grounds of ill health, on the understanding that he agreed to pass on information that would continue to delay them. Information I would ensure that they would find interesting,' he grinned.

'Information that could get him killed!'

'Being a double agent, which he undoubtedly was, is a dangerous game, Detective Inspector.'

'I assume Bloor agreed to your suggestion.'

'He had little choice, Inspector. Consider it; a life of ease on a full and very fair pension plus whatever he was being paid by our competitors, or dismissal on the spot, arrest and legal action. Not a hard choice, I suspect.'

'Was Mr Bloor still passing on your information at the time of his death, sir?' the DI asked.

'I can confirm that the last information I allowed him to pass on was to the effect that there had been a change of specification from the design department, following continued problems with the existing design development.'

'He was to admit that his information was of no use?'

'No indeed, he was merely passing on information as to the latest development in his department. In research and development circles, it is not uncommon for a close to be called on a particular avenue, once it becomes clear that it has become a blind alley. Having said that, the data from the project is always stored for possible use in the future.'

'How happy was he with the fact that he was to pass on that information? In effect he was to tell them the design had been scrapped,' the DI asked.

'He was not exactly over the moon, but even he admitted that we had run with the situation to the point; that our competitors must have begun to find it incredible that we were continuing to try to make a leading aero engine from such a problematic design. He was told to tell them that in due course, once the new design was in development he would continue to provide the latest information.'

'Not a situation I would have enjoyed,' the DI nodded.

'My last contact with him was on the day before he died. He had passed on the information and his paymasters had accepted it in the normal way,' he said. 'That is as far as I am able to tell you; even Mr Barton, here was not aware that we had continued to feed Bloor with dis-information,' he grinned.

'I did wonder, sir,' Barton nodded.

'So there it is, Inspector. Cards on the table, as I promised!'

'Thank you for your frankness, sir.'

'I find it difficult to believe that our competitors would kill Bloor, with the possibility of new information in the pipeline,' Mr Hooper said. 'Might I ask how you came to the conclusion that he had been murdered? Cards on the table as you suggested, Inspector.'

'We happen to know that Bloor was injecting himself with huge doses of insulin before devouring extra sugary items, whilst at the cinema. We know that on the day he died, he had injected, but the post-mortem showed no sign of insulin, save a small trace that would be left from the previous injection,' the DI said.

'How strange!'

'That is how the investigation stands, sir. I am sure you have an idea which of your two business rivals was paying Mr Bloor. Is that something you are prepared to divulge?'

'Ah yes, it was our German competitors B&F!'

'Thank you, sir. I think that is all I need to know.'

'Total discretion, Inspector.'

'From both sides, sir.'

'Agreed,' he said as we shook hands. He pressed a bell and Miss Durham arrived to conduct us out. 'Your transport awaits, gentlemen,' she smiled.

A shiny black Rolls Royce limousine, stood outside the main entrance. We sank into the cream leather seats and moved, no, floated over the ground back to Whitecross Yard.

'You were very quiet in the car, Dexter,' the DI commented, as we climbed the stairs to the CID office, 'I expected you to have something to add to the proceedings.'

'I have sir, but I suspected that despite the glass screen, the chauffeur might be able to hear what was said, so I limited my comments to the quality of the car. I suspect that is why you did the same, sir,' I grinned.

'I admit I had the same thoughts. Go on then what did you think to Mr Hooper?'

'I think he's a very shrewd man using an ex-employee to delay or outwit a competitor. But I see a problem in what he is thinking, sir.'

'Go on, Dexter.'

'It seems to me that a major competitor would quickly smell a rat; recognise that the information that they were being given was near worthless, sir,' I suggested.

'Mm… possibly. Where are you going with this, Dexter?'

'Purely for the sake of argument, let's say Bloor was passing information once, or maybe twice a month.

113

That would give a lot of time for B&F to recognise that they were being hoodwinked; even enough time for them to start looking for their own solutions.'

'Once they recognised that, surely they would tell Bloor to stop messing them about.'

'Come up with real information or forget our association, and please can we have our money back,' I grinned.

'Only, perhaps not quite that politely,' the DI nodded.

'So, Bloor contacts one of his old mates in the development department, and starts passing the genuine information to his paymasters.'

'You're thinking Bloor brings in an accomplice, for a share of the pay-out,' the DI suggested.

'Probably, sir.'

'If he can't come up with the real stuff, and can't come up with the money to pay them back, they wouldn't be best pleased. That's a pretty good motive for putting an end to Bloor,' the DI nodded.

'Two other possibilities exist, though sir,' I pointed out.

'Go on.'

'What if Bloor *was* able to access the genuine information via this possible associate, and Hooper found out!'

'*He* wouldn't be a happy chappy,' the DI nodded. 'I doubt he'd go to the extent of bumping Bloor off though Dexter!'

'Agreed, sir.'

'But you said two possibilities, Dexter.'

'This is a real long shot. Again, it's only a "what if", sir. What if, for some reason, Hooper was actually giving real information to Bloor for him to pass on?'

'Why would he do that?' the DI asked.

'I can't see any possible reason why he would, sir. It just occurred to me a few moments ago.'

'I think we'll put that down as a *very* long shot!'

'I agree, sir,' I nodded with grin.

There was a knock at the door and Sergeant Mellors entered.

'If you remember, I wanted to ask a favour before you went out, sir,' he said.

'Ask away, Sergeant.'

'The lads think it would be nice if you were to say a few words at John's party, sir,' he grinned.

'Why me?' the DI asked.

'Come on, sir, you've always been good friends.'

'True, we've worked well together over the years. But, I hate standing up and...'

'It would mean a lot to him, if it came from you, sir,' Mellors pleaded.

'Oh, bloody hell! Okay, when is the party?'

'Tomorrow night. In the Town End Tavern, sir.'

'Tomorrow night!'

'Yes, sir!'

'Why tomorrow night when he doesn't retire until Friday?' the DI asked.

'He's there every Tuesday night if he's not working. We intend it to be a real surprise for him, sir.'

'A bit of a bloody surprise to me as well!'

'But, you will do it, sir?'

'Yes. Yes... though what I'm going to say I've no bloody idea,' the DI said, shaking his head.

'Thank you, sir; I'd better get back to the desk,'

he nodded and left.

'What the bloody hell are you grinning at, Dexter?'

'*Am* I grinning, sir?' I asked in fake innocence.

'Yes you are, but I've just thought of a way to wipe the smile off you face, Dexter.'

'Oh?'

'As you know, Dexter, I'm a very busy man, so you can write my little speech for me,' he grinned.

'Ah! What do I... er...?'

'Exactly,' he grinned. 'Not smiling now, Dexter.'

'No, sir.'

I'd done most of my training under Sergeant Bell; a strict but fair man, I'd always thought. A man who liked a pint in his off duty hours, but wise enough not to lose the respect of his men by overdoing it, a man who had completed his thirty year, virtually without a blemish. Those had been Sergeant Mellors words as we left for our appointment at Rolls Royce. *Virtually,* without a blemish! I needed a word with Sergeant Mellors.

He was just leaving at the end of his shift as I trotted down the stairs from the office.

'Sergeant, could I have a quick word?' I asked.

'It'll cost you a pint in The Greyhound,' he nodded.

'Fair enough,' I said, and we strolled across to the old Georgian pub.

The Greyhound was surprisingly busy for the early evening, probably due to the warmth of the day and so, with a pint of their best bitter it our hands, we found a table outside at the back of the pub in an area they called the beer garden, though most people would have called it, a little back yard.

'I think I know what you want to talk about,' he smiled. 'Tom Brierly has passed the buck. He wants you to write his little speech for him.'

'That's it,' I agreed. 'And I haven't a clue where to start.'

'Crafty old bugger! Go on then, ask away.'

'You said that Sergeant Bell had done thirty years without a blemish!'

'No, I said, virtually without a blemish. Thirty years and never a foot wrong. Come on son, what are the chances of that?'

'Pretty slim,' I agreed, 'so what did he do?'

'It happened about five years before I joined. I found it out by accident, so you didn't get this from me,' he said, raising one eyebrow!

'Agreed.'

'Well it was like this…'

6

'What are you writing?' Alice asked as she came down from tucking the boys into bed.

'A retirement speech for DI Brierly.'

'I didn't know he was retiring.'

'He's not, Sergeant Bell is. DI Brierly has been asked to give a speech and he's given me the job of writing it for him.'

'How did that come about?'

'I grinned at the wrong time… It's a long story.'

'What, have you got so far?' she asked and I passed it to her.

I couldn't take my notes down to the woman who does our typing, because Sergeant Bell was on duty, and likely to pop into her tiny office at any moment. Neither could I hand them to DI Brierly with all the changes and crossings-out. The only answer was to be in the office early, and I was just putting the finishing touches to the rewritten manuscript when the DI came in.

'In bright and early this morning, Dexter?'

'Yes, sir. Just putting the final polish on your speech, sir.

'Show me,' he said and I handed it over.

'Mm, not bad, not bad,' he said then his eyes lit

up. 'I didn't know that! How the bloody hell did you find that out?'

'It's called detective work, sir,' I grinned.

'Bugger off, someone has told you that.'

'I couldn't possibly say, sir.'

'Mm! That'll make the old bugger squirm a bit,' he chuckled. 'Er… It's not very long.'

'I thought there might be comments you would want to make, there must be some things you remember, having worked with him for twenty-odd years,' I replied.

'Well yes, there was the time… No I'll save that until tonight,' he chuckled.

The phone rang and the DI answered it in his usual way. The voice at the other end was merely a mumble.

'Thank you Doctor, that is more or less what we expected,' he said and replaced the phone.

'That was Doctor Armstrong. Bloor's little medicine pouch, you sent him, has shown some interesting results. Firstly, he admitted to being surprised how small and neat it is. He traced it to a high quality German manufacturer. He reckons that it is less than half the size we are using in this country. It seems it is not currently available here and he can't explain how Bloor came to have it. I think we can have a pretty good guess, don't you Dexter?'

'His German contact, sir?'

'Oh yes. Secondly, the little file of insulin is not actually insulin, he thinks it's water!' the DI said. 'He's sent it off to some lab or other to confirm his findings.'

'That's why there was no insulin in his body, even though the taxi driver saw him inject.'

'Whatever it turns out to be, it's hard to see this

119

as anything other than murder now,' he DI nodded.

'It doesn't tell us who did it though, sir.'

'Someone, with access to the pouch.'

'Mrs Bloor; who else could it be?' I asked.

'What about Thomas James Bloor, brother and window cleaner?'

'I suppose so. Does this mean we are discounting the commercial involvement in Bloor's death?' I asked.

'Not entirely, but this finding seems to make it a lot less likely,' the DI said.

'Do you have an address for the window cleaner?'

'Yes, just around the corner from Bloor in Codnor.'

'I thought you had asked Codnor police to try to find out if Mrs Bloor had any romantic entanglements, sir.'

'Come on Dexter, it's hardly top priority for them, and people are reluctant to answer that sort of question unless they have a personal axe to grind,' he replied.

True sir, but it is a worthwhile line of enquiry.'

'I'll give them a ring to see how they are getting on, once I've got this little speech in my head. I hate to see people reading a speech, so I'm damned if I'm going to.'

The DI grabbed my little manuscript and headed to the stairs. I guessed he was looking for somewhere quiet to do his practicing. DS Whittington came in and with a nodded good morning went straight out again having picked up his handcuffs and a fresh notebook.

I sat reading and rereading the reports and statements, looking for something that might get my mind working in a new direction. The cardboard box, about the size of a shoebox, containing the personal effects of Richard Sidney Bloor, I picked it up and placed it on the desk. I lifted the lid and gazed down on the meagre contents. There was nothing there, that I didn't already know about and a reminder of just how little we actually knew about the man. I lifted the items out individually and placed them beside the box.

Something was wrong but I couldn't put my finger on it. I handled each one for a moment or two to see if it would jog my memory of the afternoon I discovered Bloor's body. I could clearly remember finding each item on his person, but when nothing fresh seemed to appear, I replaced them one by one back in the box. The freshly laundered handkerchief, still smelling slightly of lavender; the bunch of keys that we had tried in the stolen Bentley, belonging to the bookmaker; Bloor's wallet still containing the banknotes; the garage business card; and the little silver hip flask. My hand lingered on the hip flask – something about the hip flask. I guessed it was important, but I just couldn't place my finger on what it was. I mentally prodded myself, *"Come on Dexter, think,"* What was it? *I* hadn't found the flask. I was kneeling in the central aisle, talking to Phyllis, the box office girl. The doctor, the police surgeon, had rolled Bloor over in his seat and found it in his back pocket. I could remember turning to look at him when he shouted. In my mind's eye I could see him holding the flask aloft, something was nagging at me, some detail I was failing to remember. That little piece of mental film, played over-and-over in my mind, but the end was missing, what was the ending?

"If somethin's stumpin' yer, do somethin' else. Give yer mind time to sort it out, without any pressure, it'll come, you see if it don't!" Dad had said those words to me a dozen times over the years, and I'd lost count of the number of times this had come true.

I decided on the time honoured English tradition, of make a cup of tea. I rinsed out yesterday's milk bottle and jogged down the stairs to exchange it for one from the morning delivery.

'Ah, Acting DC Dexter, what's going on?' asked Sergeant Bell.

'Sorry Sarge, I'm not with you,' I blustered.

'Mm, I see, you as well, eh?'

'Sorry Sarge, I don't understand.'

'DI Brierly is pacing up and down in the back yard, reading something, over and over I'd guess since he's still at it. That's strange enough but when I poked my head out of the door, a few minutes ago, to ask him if he wanted a cuppa, he shoved the bit of paper in his pocket like greased lightning! I may be getting old and past it but I'm not that senile that I can't see that somethin's up,' he said scratching his chin.

'I'm sorry, I couldn't say Sarge.'

'Couldn't or won't? Don't worry, I'll find out. I'll lay odds that before I start my shift tomorrow morning I'll have found out,' he nodded and turned back to his desk.

As I climbed the stairs back to the CID office, I had to grin to myself. If all runs to plan, he will have found out before he goes to bed.

Alice was, of course aware that I would be attending Sergeant Bell's party and had made the usual lunchtime sandwiches and was not expecting me home in time for the evening meal. Unfortunately I had come out in such a rush I had left them on the kitchen table. When I realised that, I went across the road to the little greengrocer's shop and asked the chap's wife to rustle something up for me.

'Forgotten you're pack-up Mr Dexter?'

'Yes, out in a bit of a rush this morning,' I nodded.

'Leave us yer ten pence and I'll get young Bob to drop 'em cross the road to you. By the way what happened about that chap in the cinema?'

'Still working on it Joe.'

'Did you ever find out what is name was?' he asked. I couldn't see any reason for withholding it now we knew.

'A chap named Bloor, that's about all we know,' I shrugged.

'Can't have been natural causes if you're still looking into it,' the said, closing one eye.

'Sorry Joe, I can't tell you anything else, mainly because we don't know anything else,' I grinned. As I left, he gave me a look that suggested he could tell I was being a bit cagey with what I was prepared to tell.

As I reached the pavement the newsagent's daughter caught my eye; she was in their shop window setting up a display of diaries for the coming year. Not yet September and there she was arranging 1933 diaries and calendars. Knowing our local newsagent, he would have bought a large quantity of them at a special price, hoping to make a good profit by cornering the market early. I strolled over and tapped on the window to attract her attention. 'Bit early for that lot, isn't it?' I said, raising my voice enough to be heard through the glass.

'We've sold three already! I suggest you get yours now before they're all gone,' she grinned, holding up a little dark brown, leather bound diary.

'What is it?' she asked. 'Close your mouth I can see what you had for breakfast.'

I realised I was standing looking at her open mouthed. Light had dawned. I was looking at the answer to the problem I had left in the office. 'You've just solved a problem for me. If you weren't behind glass, I'd give you a big kiss.' I grinned.

'Thank heavens for a sheet of glass.' she said sticking her tongue out at me and turning her nose up in haughty fun.

The doctor had held up the hip flask and a little diary, just as Winifred, the newsagent's daughter had done. The missing item was Mr Bloor's diary, although, one problem remained, where was it now? It should have been with the hip flask and the rest of Bloor's things in that cardboard box. I increased my step and headed up the stairs. The DI was sitting at his desk, grinning from ear to ear.

'I guess you've learned your lines, sir,' I said as I entered the office.

'Indeed I have. I've made a few minor altera-tions to what you have written, adding my own bits like you suggested, but all in all, I think you've done a good job. I intend to make the old bugger squirm a bit, espe-cially since he's unlikely to get the chance to return the compliment when I retire in eight years time!' he chuck-led.

'Nothing hurtful I hope sir. I did my training under Sergeant Bell, and always found him firm but fair.

He's always been good to me, sir.'

'No, no; no one has greater respect for John Bell than me. But I can still pull his leg, and give him a red face, without threatening our friendship,' he chuckled.

'Right, sir.'

'You were going to ring Codnor police to see if they'd made any progress on Mrs Bloor's … er.'

'Romantic entanglements?' the DI suggested.

'Yes, sir.'

'Mm, I'll do it now, Dexter'

'Before you do sir, I've been looking through all the evidence in the case, the statements and other bits of information, but nothing came to light. Then I looked in the box with Mr Bloor's effects in and noticed something is missing,' I said, lifting the box onto his desk.

'That's all we've ever had,' the DI replied having a quick sort through.

'Where is Bloor's diary, sir?'

'I've never seen a diary. Are you sure there was one?'

'Yes, sir. I distinctly remember Dr Daniels holding up the hip flask, then a moment or two later he held up Bloor's diary. It was poorly lit in the cinema, so I can't be sure of the colour but probably dark blue, brown or black.'

'From memory of that day, DS Whittington and I were in court giving evidence in the Singleton trial, so it must have been DC Harrington who met you at the cinema,' the DI said, scratching the back of his neck.

'That's right,' I agreed.

'I'll give him a ring. Put the kettle on Dexter.'

'Right, sir.' I realised I'd forgotten to collect a replacement bottle of milk from the front office, having been tackled and questioned by Sergeant Bell, and went down to get a bottle. The sergeant was standing in the little typist's office talking to Mrs Burton our typist, proving the wisdom of me hand writing the DI's edited script.

'Forgot the milk, Sarge!' I said holding the bottle up for him to see and heading for the stairs in double quick time to prevent a further quizzing.

'He's gone bloody fishing. If he's well enough to go fishing, he's well enough to come back to work!' the DI snapped, as I re-entered the office.

Not wishing ill on DC Harrington, I hoped he wouldn't return to work before I'd seen the end of the strange case of our Mr Bloor.

'Perhaps, he's just gently exercising his arm and shoulder, sir,' I suggested.

'You're right, he's off on the sick, so it's up to him how he uses his time I suppose,' the DI nodded. 'I've asked his wife to get him to ring as soon as he gets home.'

'It would be nice to find Bloor's diary, sir,' I said, returning to the subject that was still whizzing around my brain.

'And to find it contained all the names, addresses and telephone numbers of everyone he's ever met, together with the name of his murderer double underlined in red ink! Come on Dexter, it's a diary but I suppose it might have a couple of interesting facts, if we can work out what they are,'

'I suppose so. I wonder if Dr Daniels can remember what happened to it.'

'Give him a ring then Dexter, if it will make you happy,' he shrugged.

'Right, sir.'

I rang his surgery to find that Dr Daniels was away for a few days, taking the kids to the seaside and that the practice was being looked after by a locum, Dr Smithers who, of course, knew nothing of the episode with Bloor.

'He's given me a number to ring him every night after surgery, just to keep him in the picture. I could ask him to ring you tomorrow morning if it is important,' Smithers suggested.

'If you'd do that please Dr Smithers,' I said.

'I've made a note on my pad, will do,' he agreed and we ended the call.

'I'd better ring Inspector Fellows at Condor whilst I'm thinking about it. Oh, and Dexter.'

'Sir?'

'You were making a cup of tea, look slippy about it. I'm spitting bloody feathers here!'

The tea was starting to cool in the mugs as the DI replaced the phone.

'It seems that the only possibly romantic connection the Codnor boys can come up with is a frequent male visitor to the Bloor house; nearly every Thursday, at half past two! According to a nosey neighbour, a Mrs Rogers, he goes in and stays about forty minutes to an hour,' he grinned.

'Thursday afternoon, is that whilst Bloor is at the cinema, sir?'

'Whilst he's out, yes.'

'Naughty, naughty,' I said, shaking my head.

'Extra marital-thingy isn't against the law, Dexter.'

'No sir, but plotting a murder is, surely?'

'Yes, but how the hell do we prove that?'

'Do they know who the man is, sir?'

'Well not as yet, but according to the neighbour, the man quite openly parks his car on the road outside the Bloor residence. She's promised to ring them next time it's there. It seems that once they came across Mrs Rogers, they stopped doing door to door so as not to alert Mrs Bloor to our interest, or, possibly because that was as far as they are prepared to go in helping us. So it's up to her now.'

'That's another thing we need to wait for,' I shrugged.

'That's detective work, Dexter. We'll get there in the end,' he nodded.

The phone rang just before four o'clock. The DI had been summoned across to "Heaven", our pet name for the plush offices above the old stables; the official residence of the Chief Constable and his assistant, so it was up to me to answer it. I started the usual introduction.

'Afternoon Will. It's me, George,' Harrington said, stopping me half way.

'Afternoon, how did the fishing go?' I asked.

'What do you think?' he laughed.

'No fish?'

'Plenty of fish, but they were all just out of range having a good giggle no doubt at my attempts to get 'em to bite. But it was nice just lazing in the sun, and watching the world, well the river, go by anyway!'

'How's the arm?'

'The doctor had a look at it this morning; there was a little bit of infection in one of the stitches but he bled it and put a pad of cotton wool with that iodine stuff

128

on it, hurt more than the bloody knife wound, but other than that he seemed happy with it. I go back to see him again next week.'

'That's good news.' *For both of us, I thought. The longer he's away the longer I'm in CID* 'The DI is across the yard, don't ask why, the phone rang and he upped and went, a bit grim faced. He asked you to call to clear up a bit of a problem. Do you know what happened to Mr Bloor's diary?'

'The chap in the cinema?'

'That's right, do you know what happened to his diary?'

'I don't remember a diary, er... A wallet with one and a half quid in it, a bunch of keys, and a hip flask, I think that was it,' he said straining to remember.

'We have all of that, plus a hanky,' I agreed, 'but no diary.'

'That's right, I'd forgotten the hanky! As I re-call, when I got there, the doctor was just finishing up, shutting his bag. The keys, and wallet and stuff were on the seat at the side of the chap you called Bloor, but I don't remember a diary. No I'm sure there was no dia-ry,' he said, adamantly.

'Thanks, George! Glad you're on the mend.'

'If I think of anything, I'll pop in or give you a ring,' he said as we put the phone down.

The Town End Tavern had put on a nice spread in the room above the bar. One of the uniformed lads had made sure that Sergeant Bell was leaning in his usu-al place at the public bar. The rest of the party, consist-ing of most of the shift that had just finished with him and the four of us from CID, were concealed in various locations, in and around the pub awaiting the entry signal. Just as we got the troop-in signal, a car pulled up at the front door of the pub and out got none other than the Chief Constable and his assistant, effectively subduing the merriment in an instant.

'Good evening, gentlemen. Well, come on what are we waiting for?' he asked, as he and the Assistant Chief Constable threw their uniform caps in the rear of the car.

The spread had more or less been consumed by something like forty hungry coppers of various ranks, plus a few old timers. Some I remembered and some I didn't. The makeshift bar had sent down for additional stock when Sergeant Mellors brought the gathering to order by banging the handle of a knife on the bar.

'Order!' he shouted.

'Mine's another pint of mild,' yelled one of the old timers that I didn't recognise, amid laughter.

'Clap that man in irons!' yelled the Chief Constable, adding to the laughter.

'Come on you bloody lot, put a sock in it, beggin' yer pardon, sir, DI Brierly would like to say a few words,' Mellors yelled.

'Before that, by your leave Detective Inspector, I've a few words of my own I'd like to say.' the C.C. stated. The DI nodded his approval.

'When I arrived in Crammingdon, nearly two years ago now, I wondered quite what I had let myself in for. Crammingdon force was still coming to terms, with the sudden retirement on health grounds of my predecessor, Sir Montague Kenning and the Assistant Chief Constable, due to retire anyway. The policing of a town environment was new to me, from being a chief inspector in a rural part of Cambridgeshire, and I might easily have struggled with a number of things, not least the local accent,' he said, amid renewed laughter. 'I was however, aware of one thing, always keep in good books with your men on the ground. They always have their finger on the pulse of what's happening out there, none better that the man we are here toasting tonight. From day one of my service on this force, Sergeant Johnathan Fotheringhay B...' The group erupted in laughter and catcalls, and the chief raised a hand for silence. 'Sergeant Johnathon Fotheringhay Bell was my...' *"Spy in the camp,"* suggested another old timer, amid more laughter.

'I was going to say my prompt on local etiquette. For which I am eternally grateful. Thank you gentlemen,' the C.C. said and the group nodded and applauded. 'Over to you, Detective Inspector!'

'Just a moment please, sir. I'd like to reply to that,' Bell said, and the chief nodded.

'It's been a pleasurable experience working for you sir, until tonight that is. I have, over the years, managed to keep my second Christian name a deep dark secret. However, that is no longer the case.' More laughter. 'I look forward to a happy retirement in the happy knowledge that I no longer need to keep it hidden. I'm not ashamed of the name. It just seems a bit too highbrow for a plain police sergeant. Thank you for your kind comments, sir,' he said and raised his glass to the Chief Constable.

'Detective Inspector Brierly,' Mellors said, again calling for order, and the DI advanced to the front of the group amid an assortment of cheers and catcalls.

Eventually silence was restored and the DI was able to speak.

'Good evening everyone, I do not propose to make a lengthy speech...' Shouts of hooray, and sit down then amid more laughter and merriment.

'Shut up you lot, let the DI speak,' shouted Mellors.

'First of all I'd like to thank the Chief Constable for stealing my *Fotheringhay* punch line,' More laughter and the C.C. grinned.

'I've known and worked with John "F" Bell...', more laughter, '...on and off for the best part of twenty years. In that time he has had a stain free record. Well, *almost* stain free, isn't that right John?' the DI grinned and John Bell looked a bit bewildered and the gathering was hushed. 'Most recently, there was the case of a short-lived Assistant Chief Constable, who happened by sheer chance to get himself locked in one of the cells overnight. Was there not, John?' Bell grinned and scratched his chin, the Chief Constable looked interested, and the crowd were lapping it up. 'I won't name the man but I happen to know he came from the London area; he was a stickler for correct procedures. Whenever, during his short reign of terror, he happened to be over in the business side of the station and saw an empty cell, he would enter and make a list of any irregularities that needed attention. On one particular occasion, an especially busy Saturday night, he went into a cell, no doubt with his notebook at the ready, when the door swung shut. I'm told he claimed to have shouted for help, but amid the cries of drunks and pickpockets, he was warned like all others to be quiet, or else! Sergeant Bell was one of two sergeants on duty, it being as I said a Saturday night, and he returned to the streets immediately following the dirty deed. The duty sergeant was deep in arrest paperwork and ignored the shouts. The man was found the next morning, somewhat dishevelled, isn't that right, John?' the DI grinned and Bell shrugged, amid more laughter.

'I remember the incident well!' said the chief. 'I found the man, my new assistant chief, a real pain in the... most difficult to work with!' More cheers and laughter. 'If John's actions, always assuming it was him, was the reason for the man's instant resignation, then I have even more to thank him for than I thought.' More merriment.

'Own up time John, did you or did you not, accidentally close the cell door on the then Assistant Chief Constable?' the DI asked.

'The man seemed to have it in for me. Three times in the week before the incident in question he had reprimanded me for petty things, in front of my men. My pocket watch, when checked with his, was one minute slow! Two days later, he noticed that my tunic was stained and not fit for duty; I pointed out that a drunk had been sick on it that morning, and he told me that back-chatting him constituted defying a senior officer. The following day, he noticed that my boots and trouser bottoms were muddy. I didn't bother explaining that I had chased and arrested a burglar, escaping across a muddy field. So, yes I shut the man in cell six and it was no bloody accident.' Yells and screams of laughter.

'Now we come to the incident of the Market Inn, after closing time, John!' the DI pointed out, once Mellors had again brought silence with great difficulty.

'It seems that PC Bell, as he was then, and his

133

companion officer had an arrangement allowing them to call into the back of the pub, around midnight to allow for the consuming of a swift pint of suitable refreshment, provided they turned a blind eye to the late drinking in the bar on occasions, these no doubt being claimed as closed-door parties. I have no doubt that these arrangements also included other members of the force, depending on the shift patterns. On the particular occasion in question, John and his mate were caught at the bar at midnight, closing time being ten o'clock of course, by their duty sergeant who had received a phone call to the effect that this practice was in progress. By the time the landlord had answered the hammering on the door, the pair had attempted to scarper out of the back door and were detained by the sergeant who had nipped around the back suspecting that such might well be the case. Two glasses on the bar contained nothing more incriminating than lemonade. How was that John?' the DI asked.

'It was ginger beer actually and they were always on the bar for such an occasion, so that the beer glasses could be emptied into the sink and ginger beer seemed to have been the tipple. I always wondered who made the complaint. We were quiet as mice, ten minutes maximum and always went in by the back door,' Bell grinned.

'I have that information also. The landlord's wife was fed up with the late nights and phoned in a complaint that Sergeant Watson had to pursue. In effect she shopped her old man.' More laughter.

'Sergeant Bell, consider yourself suspended until further notice, as from Monday morning,' the Chief Constable smiled. 'Gentlemen, we'll leave you to your party, no drinking after time mind. I'm sure I speak for everyone here in wishing you a long, healthy and happy retirement. Good night everyone,' he nodded and the senior officers left.

Several more stories were told as you might expect, some by Sergeant Bell himself. The most memorable being a tale that involved him as a young copper just before the Great War. It involved a meeting of the Suffragette Movement that he was helping to police, ensuring that it went off peacefully. I'll try to use his own words as far as I can remember them.

"Although Mortonby village is in the county area, fearing trouble and intent on keeping control of the situation, their Chief Constable asked for a couple of extra men from the Crammingdon force and myself and a PC Jefferson went along to assist. The village hall, a goodly size for a small village was crammed full with the local women folk not to mention twenty police officers. It was clear that the women folk saw the presence of so many coppers as provocative, and the crowd looked like turning riotous even before the meeting started. The sergeant in charge of the affair had the good sense to arrange with the organiser to go up on the little stage and address the meeting. He pointed out that although we were there to ensure the meeting passed off peacefully, as the law required, many of his men agreed with the sentiments of the gathering, and would not be happy having to make arrests; and requested that the meeting be calm and dignified. Two local speakers took the stage first, both of them saying more or less the same thing. It was clear that by the end of the second speaker, the gathering was starting to lose interest and feel that they had heard nothing new and began chatting among themselves. The third speaker was a lady from the local suf-frage headquarters in Nottingham. A very small woman, she could hardly see over the tall lectern and before she went on stage, one of the local women placed an up-turned beer crate and then for some obscure reason put a tin tray borrowed from the local pub, on top. With due introduction, she marched on stage, to muted applause. As she trod on to the makeshift step, the tin tray slid sideways and the poor woman went all her length across the stage spilling her handful of notes and losing her hat. The gathering forgot its little conversations and a gasp ran around the hall. Several people, myself included went to her aid and someone gathered her notes. After a couple of minutes it was clear the woman had suffered no damage other than to her dignity and she again stepped up, this time minus the tray. Her opening remark broke the ice brilliantly and the meeting ended with us coppers being offered tea and homemade cakes!"

'So what did she say Sarge?' a young copper asked.

"She said, *"Now that I have your attention!"* It brought the house down!' he grinned.

It turned out that Sergeant Bell had three days of unclaimed holiday entitlement, meaning that was the last time we would see him in his official capacity. The party broke up at ten o'clock and although I hadn't consumed a huge amount of drink, I thought it wise to push my bicycle back home.

7

I arrived at Whitecross yard next morning to find a new murder on the books.

Over a number of years, it had become the regular duty of police officers to move tramps and beggars from under the railway bridges on South Street and Magdalen Row. Most officers on night duty in the area turned a blind eye when finding them sleeping in the shelter of the bridge overnight, making sure that they were moved on before signing off duty at eight in the morning.

On making the wake-up call at the South Street bridge, that morning, PC Arthur Watts found the body of a vagrant, an occasional sleeper there known to him as Norwich Jimmy, in a dirty and blood soaked blanket.

Unless Jimmy had managed to cut his own throat to the extent of nearly decapitating himself, it was a clear case of murder. A second man, known simply as Doug, was asleep in an equally dirty but blood free blanket some feet away. When woken by PC Watts the man admitted to arguing with Jimmy during the night, about the favours of a female vagrant, Golden Lily. According to Doug, Golden Lily had made to doss down with the pair under the bridge and both Jimmy and Doug had suggested that she might like to "grace their blanket" in exchange for a share of the chosen ones' bottle of scotch whisky.

Again, according to Doug, Golden Lily, had told them both to go away, in rather more florid terms than that and had wandered off to find another place to sleep. On finding Norwich Jimmy lying dead, PC Watts had blown his whistle and was soon joined by a young police officer PC Newland. Newland went off to phone the station leaving Watts to stand guard on Jimmy's body.

The call came through to CID and was answered by DI Brierly, just as I entered the office.

'Grab a car Dexter, before they all go off in patrol!'

'Right, sir,' I said, and trotted down the stairs to detain one of them before they left.

'Looks like Mr Bloor is going to take a back seat again; we've a murdered vagrant on our hands!' the DI said as we seated ourselves in the back of PV3.

PC Watts gave us the events as he knew them and PC Newland had gone off to try to find the whereabouts of Golden Lily. He returned a few moments later with a human specimen, presumably female, though that seemed open to debate. Newland had clearly arrested her since she was in handcuffs.

''Ere, this copper 'as arrested me, just because I got a knife,' she screamed.

'No, I arrested you because you threatened me with it,' Newland said.

'Well he as good as accused me of murder.'

'I asked you if you knew anything about the suspicious death under the railway bridge and you threatened me with your knife. I relieved you of the weapon and arrested you,' Newland explained.

'Who's dead anyway?' she said and stepped forward to see. 'Oh my gawd; it's Jimmy!' she said and

138

went white as a sheet, even under several months, if not years of facial grime. 'Oh, shitting bugger! I killed him!' she said, and slumped against the wall.

'You admit killing this man?' the DI asked once Lily had again become coherent.

'I thought I'd dreamt it, not this. Say I never killed him,' she said, staring the DI in the face.

'You did have a knife,' the DI replied. 'Where is it now constable?'

'I knocked it out of her hand and it went into the bushes, sir,' Newland said.

'Right, she's going nowhere, go and find it, Dexter, go with him.'

'Right, sir,' we said together and set off to where Golden Lily had been arrested.

'I found her asleep in there,' Newland said, pointing to an old open-fronted hut, like a bus-shelter. 'She was fast asleep and when I shook her awake she went for me with the knife, I knocked it out of her hand, and it went over there,' he said and nodded at a clump of hawthorn bushes.

Newland located it after a short prickly search, and lifted it out holding it by the handle.

'There's no blood on it,' he said.

'So it's unlikely to be the murder weapon. Just as well since you've just destroyed Lily's fingerprints, idiot.'

'Oh, bugger! Why did I do that?'

'Because you are young, in-experienced and a bloody idiot,' I said, and the poor chap could only nod. 'Come on, no point hanging around here.'

In the absence of the police surgeon, Mr Armstrong the hospital pathologist had come to the scene to certify "life extinct." He was unpacking his bag as we arrived at the bridge.

'I think I can pronounce life extinct, at er… nine forty-seven,' Armstrong said, as a black van turned up, and he indicated to the two occupants to load the body. 'I was about to start a post mortem when you rang, I'll be on to this one as soon as possible, probably this afternoon. I'll take the blanket as well, though I don't suppose it will tell me anything I can't already tell from that knife wound.'

'This lady is Golden Lily. She seems to think she has killed the victim, with this,' I ventured holding up the knife we had found in the undergrowth.

'I doubt it. The blade it nowhere near clean, but I see no signs of blood on it. I'll take it and give it the once over but I'd say it's not the weapon that killed this poor chap,' Armstrong said slipped it in his bag.

The two police officers, the DI and I made a thorough search of the area, including the vagrant we had woken, finding nothing new.

'Whoever did the dreadful deed must have taken the murder weapon with him or her.'

'Would a woman be capable of that degree of injury?' I asked.

'Unlikely I agree, but nothing ceases to amaze me, Dexter!' he said shaking his head. 'Come, things to do,' he said and headed towards the waiting patrol car.

As we entered the CID office, DS Whittington was just pouring boiling water into the teapot.

'Morning sir,' he said. 'Thought you'd both be ready for a cuppa; saw your car pull into the yard!'

'You see, Dexter. That is what makes the difference between a copper and a detective; the ability to read the mind of your senior officer even through a dirty window,' the DI grinned.

True to his word Dr Smithers, Dr Daniels locum had asked Daniels to ring us. We were out of course, but he had left a number where we could reach him.

'Dexter, give Dr Daniels a ring, I want to hear what DS Whittington had found out about little Tommy Grant's parents.'

'Right, sir,' I said, and looked at the number on the pad. Guessing that I would need our switchboard operator to get the number for me I picked up the phone and gave the number. The operator told me that it might take a minute or two and promised to ring me as soon as she had made the connection.

DS Whittington had poured the tea and settled himself at our desk ready to give the DI the information he had obtained.

'When acting DC Dexter and I went to inform the lad's parents of the sad outcome to our search, they gave the impression of being a far from happy couple. For reasons, I'll go into in a moment, Mrs Ida Grant, was very antagonistic towards her husband. According to the neighbour, Mrs Millington, who came to the door just after we found the bodies of Mr and Mrs Grant, Ida Grant suspected her husband was having an affair with another woman. Harry Grant had confided to Mrs Millington's husband one Sunday lunch time in the local pub saying, he was very busy at work and was putting in all the hours he could to get a bit of money put aside for a rainy day and that he had shown his pay packet with the overtime payments to his wife but she was still convinced that he was having an affair,'

'Even though he can prove he's at work, his

missus won't be persuaded?' the DI asked.

'So Mrs Millington gave me to believe.'

'So the poor devil was on a hiding to nothing.'

'Hard to see it any other way, sir. Ida Grant had already convinced her husband that little Tommy's death was his fault. It seems to me very much along the lines that Dexter and I decided at the time. Harry Grant couldn't convince his wife he wasn't having an affair, she was giving him hell for no reason; I guess he could see no possibility of them ever coming to terms with Tommy's death. It could take years to learn to live with, even if you weren't firing guilt at each other. No doubt with his mind in a whirl of emotions, he remembered his old service revolver and created an end to it, for them both,' DS Whittington said, shaking his head.

'No-one has suggested anything else?' the DI asked.

'Being a work day when it happened, few people were at home, house to house, even in the street that backs on to the Grant's house could add nothing to Mrs Millington's account, sir!'

'Case closed, then, DS Whittington.'

'I think so, sir,' he agreed.

'Okay! Come with me, we'll put that to the Assistant Chief and get his approval to set it before the coroner,' the DI said and they left me to wait for Dr Daniel's call to come through.

I began to think about Norwich Jimmy, wondering about the motive behind his murder. It couldn't be for his possessions, I reasoned, but possessions of course are relative. What I, as a reasonably well paid police officer, might not see as an item worth killing for, could be completely beyond reach at that end of human existence;

half a bottle of whisky at Jimmy's social standing might well be enough. Done in a drunken stupor, only half remembered, one thing seemed certain, whoever had killed Norwich Jimmy, would have been covered in blood.

The phone rang, putting a stop to my thoughts. The operator confirmed that this was my call to Dr Daniels.

'Dr Daniels, this is DC Dexter, I'm sorry I wasn't able to take your call this morning, I was attending another murder.'

'So I was told. What can I do for you, make it snappy please, my few days off are ticking away rapidly,' he replied.

'Just one thing sir. The afternoon you attended the death of the man in the cinema, I believe you found a hip flask and a small diary?' I said jogging his memory.

'That is so. However I don't think it was a diary, more a notebook.'

'I assumed it was a diary, but I didn't actually handle it,' I admitted.

'I suppose it was a diary of sorts, not printed with the days of the month like a real diary but I did flick through it quickly and noticed that the entries were headed with a date.'

'It seems to have gone missing. Can you remember where you last saw it, sir?'

'Do you mean, what did I do with it, Detective Constable?'

'I suppose I do, sir,' I agreed.

'I put it with the rest of the things you found, on the seat beside, him! I understand you now have a name for the chap?'

'Yes sir, he is a Mr Bloor.'

'Means nothing to me I'm afraid. Wait a minute, I remember now. I didn't put the notebook, diary or whatever it was on the seat. I initially placed it with the other things, then realised that in that bloody awful light it was hard to see, it was practically the same colour as the seat. I slipped it in the chap's inside jacket pocket,' he yelled. 'I meant to tell you as I left but it must have slipped my mind,' he said.

'I handed over to DS Whittington on his arrival, telling him that everything I'd found was on the seat beside the victim,' I said.

'My apologies DC Dexter, remiss of me, you should find it in Mr Bloor's inside pocket. Now I must be going I've two children desperate the re-organise Blackpool beach,' he said, suggesting that that didn't rate all that highly on his own list of pastimes.'

Bloor's clothes, of course, were in a brown paper parcel under our sink. The DI and DS Whittington re-entered the office as I placed the parcel on our shared desk.

'Bloor's clothes; thinking of chucking 'em out, Dexter?' the DI challenged.

'No sir, Dr Daniels claims to have replaced the diary in Bloor's inside pocket, sir. I was about to take a look.'

'Mm! Rather you than me, Dexter. Carry on.'

'Right, sir,' I said and began to undo the string, marvelling at the fact that we obviously hadn't needed to go under the sink in over a fortnight.

Mr Bloor's inside pocket was empty. All of his pockets were empty. I sorted through the whole parcel; shirt; trousers; and under clothes, finding no sign of the elusive diary, whilst the DI and DS Whittington stood

144

back as though they were afraid something would leap out and attack them.

'Nothing, sir,' I said shaking my head, and the DI grinned.

'I'll get this typed up and across to the Assistant Chief, No doubt he'll inform the coroner, sir,' DS Whittington said, waving a couple of hand written sheets of notes.

'Okay,' the DI nodded.

'What's the next move now, sir?' I asked, a bit disappointed at being thwarted by the diary once again.

'Was Dr Daniels certain that he'd put the diary in Bloor's pocket?'

'I reckon so, sir.'

'I suppose it might just have the killer's name underlined in red ink,' he chuckled.

'I think it could be important, sir.'

'Of course, it *could be,* that's your task for the day, find it Dexter.'

'Thank you, sir.'

'It'll keep you out of mischief,' he laughed. 'But, before you do…'

'Put the kettle on, sir?'

'You are getting good at this, aren't you Dexter?' he nodded.

'Yes, sir,' I chuckled.

'I think I'm going to take another look at the place where the tramp was killed. I can't help thinking that we've overlooked something,' the DI said once the tea ceremony was completed.

'Do you need me, sir?'

'No, DS Whittington is just on his way back

from Heaven, I'll take him.' the DI said turning from the window overlooking the back yard.

'Am I still to track down Bloor's diary, sir?'

'Yes, as I said it will keep you out of mischief,' he smiled and headed down to the front office, no doubt to gather DS Whittington.

As I've already said, my early training as a PC was done under the very close scrutiny of the now re-tired Sergeant Bell. One thing he had impressed on me was to recognise how fleeting, thoughts and ideas can be. *"Get it down on paper, lad."* With that in mind, I grabbed a scrap of paper and jotted my thoughts as to how the notebook/diary could have gone missing.

Doctor Daniels had found the book. I could re-member him holding it in the air, so the thing actually existed. He had originally thought that he had placed it on the seat beside Bloor, but then remembered placing it in Bloor's inside pocket, considering at the time that in the dim auditorium lights it might well have been missed. I actually thought that unlikely but could see his reasoning.

By the time Bloor's body was autopsied, the book had gone missing. I assumed a search of the vic-tims clothing would form part of the examination and since the book had not been commented on by Dr Arm-strong, the pathologist, then he had not found it. I rang him, and he confirmed that a search of clothing is always carried out no matter what the circumstances and that, since he actually carried the search out himself, he could confirm no notebook was found on the man's person.

Therefore, somewhere between Dr Daniels plac-ing the thing in Bloor's pocket and him arriving on the Autopsy table the notebook had disappeared.

146

I tried to piece together my memories of the afternoon Bloor was discovered. As you might imagine, I had been over the actual discovery, several times in my mind and was sure that I had it straight, certainly up until the doctor arrived and I started to interview Phyllis the box office girl. The doctor had pronounced life extinct at five-o-seven; had discovered the hip flask and notebook and was leaving just as DC Harrington arrived, Daniels quickly informed him of his findings. DC Harrington did another search of the surrounding area, approved the removal of Bloor's body and rang the undertakers. The removal of such a large man had proved problematic. The plain wooden coffin was only just big enough to hold him and once the poor chap's body was enclosed four wooden handles were attached and DC Harrington and I assisted the two undertakers' men to carry it down the central aisle toward the screen then out through the emergency exist at the rear of the cinema.

I rang the undertaker's to ascertain if Bloor's body had been taken directly to the hospital pathology department. The person at the other end remembered the incident, mainly because of the weight involved. According to him, the department was closed for the night and the body was taken to their premises. Normally it would have been taken into their "chapel of rest", but because of the enormity of the task, a decision was made to leave it in the van overnight.

'Mr Bloor had a notebook in his pocket, it has gone missing, is there any chance you have it?' I asked.

'I'm not quite sure what you are insinuating, DC Dexter, but I can assure you that the deceased remains arrived at the hospital, exactly as they were collected from the cinema!' he snapped.

'I was not suggesting that anyone had taken it, simply that you might have found a small notebook and be unsure to whom it belonged,' I said hoping to calm the man down.

'I see, although that was not the way your question appeared. However, I can confirm, that no such book has been found, and as you might imagine, the contents of our transport casket are examined after each use. Sorry DC Dexter I cannot help you.'

Perhaps I could have handled that better.

Okay I thought, take the situation one-step back. Dr Daniels put the notebook in Bloor's pocket, and I have no doubt that he did, yet by the time it got to the autopsy it was not there. It had not been lost in the transit coffin or casket as the undertaker seemed to prefer to call it; it could not have been lost in the undertaker's premises since the coffin had remained in their van overnight; the only conclusion left was that it was lost at the cinema. I rang the Magnificent Cinema and the manager answered the call.

'Mr Worthy?'

'It is. Who's calling, please?'

'This is DC Dexter. I was the officer you called to the cinema a couple of weeks ago.'

'Oh! To the stout gentleman?'

'That's correct. We have established that the man's name is actually Bloor. Dr Daniels found a hip flask and a small notebook in his search of Mr Bloor's clothing. We have the hip flask but not the notebook. Is there any chance it has been found in the cinema, sir?' I asked.

'I remember him finding the hip flask and putting it on the seat beside the poor chap. At that point, I remembered there had been a problem with the sound on the second film and went to the projection box to speak to the projectionist. If Dr Daniels found a notebook, I certainly didn't see one,' he said.

'Is it possible that one has been handed in?'

'We have a lost property box, also a book recording anything we find. A notebook you say, well that shouldn't take much finding among mostly gloves and scarves; I could kit out a bus queue with assorted gloves, provided they didn't need them to match,' he chuckled. 'A notebook right, I'll pop through to the box office, we keep everything there; it's where people ask about lost items, I won't be a moment,'

I heard the sound of the phone being placed on his desk, the creak of his chair and the opening of a door, then silence for a minute or so. The door opened, the chair creaked and the phone was picked up again.

'You're in luck, I have a small brown leather notebook. According to the lost property book it was found and handed in at the end of the evening performance that night. Whoever handed it in stated that it had been found in the middle of row nine on the left hand side of the aisle. Well away from Mr Bloor, I can only imagine it must have been accidentally kicked there,' Worthy said.

'It must have slipped out of his pocket in the struggle to fit the chap into the transit coffin,' I suggested.

'Wherever it was we failed to connect it with the poor chap. I've some shopping to do first thing in the morning, I can drop it at Whitecross Yard then if that will be soon enough?' he asked.

'That will be fine Mr Worthy,' I agreed, and we

finished the call. I couldn't see that a few more hours without the thing would make all that much difference after all there was no guarantee the information it held would add anything to the case. At least we now knew where it was, Always assuming it actually belonged to Mr Bloor. My mind began to wonder to our other murder case.

The coverage in the local press of the murder of Norwich Jimmy was scant to say the least. The man was a tramp; seen by society as a worthless individual, and many people would have muttered "good riddance" to the poor chap. All of these people, down on their luck have a story to tell. Although I had only been in the police force for a little over two years and was still a very junior officer, I had seen several so-called tramps arrested for drunkenness. Occasionally a story stood out, like that of William Everidge. I had first met him only a couple of months into my police career. Although the locals had come to call him "Billy", William Everidge had once been a highly respected schoolmaster. When his sons were killed early on in the Great War, he lost interest in life, and only a freak event brought him back to being a respected member of Crammingdon society. Sadly, William was no longer with us, but Crammingdon had a special reason to remember him and his part in solving another murder.

I determined to try to find out the history behind Norwich Jimmy.

True to his word, just after eight-thirty, Mr Worthy delivered the notebook I hoped belonged to Mr Bloor, and Sergeant Mellors brought it up to the office.

Is that the infamous notebook, Dexter?' the DI asked a few moments later when he arrived in the office.

'It is sir!' I shrugged, and handed it to him.

'Oh, dear. No killer underlined in red ink,' he grinned. 'Just a collection of letters and numbers, some sort of code you reckon?'

'Is it worth trying to crack it, or should we put it to a specialist, sir?' I asked.

'I'll give you a morning to crack it then we'll seek someone to cast an eye over it. I'll leave you to it, I'm meeting DS Whittington on Parson's Rec.'

'Have you found some more information on Billy Grant, sir?'

'No, some kids found a knife in the undergrowth. Whittington believes it could be Norwich Jimmy's murder weapon.'

'Do we know anything more about the chap, sir?'

'Quite a bit actually; I'll tell all when I get back,' he nodded and trotted back down the stairs, leaving me with the notebook.

Once I realised that Mr Bloor was dead, I had done a check of his pockets, to try to establish the chap's name. His hip flask and notebook only came to light when the doctor turned the body over, for whatever reason, meaning they must have been in a back pocket. I would have thought that a hipflask particularly, would have been uncomfortable in a back pocket, but that was certainly where they were. The unremarkable brown leather notebook had a piece of elastic attached to the rear cover, forming a loop used to separate the pages and keep his place. In this case, it seemed to mark a point between the used and unused pages. I started at the front looking at the jumble of numbers. There was a date as the heading to each jumble, meaning that, although the notebook was not a diary in the true sense of the word the entries were placed in chronological order. The first entry dated 24th of June 1927 with the letter "S" then below it about forty numbers, in double figures, some of them preceded by a minus sign. The first few groups:

-06 -14 01   -18 -15 -07 -14 -01   -18 01

I could make nothing of them, unless the groupings represented words.

I grabbed a scrap of paper and began to make a few attempts at decoding the first message. After about ten minutes and half a sheet of crossings out, I had a brain wave. I remembered being told at school that "E" is the most common letter in the English language. I counted the total of each of the individual numbers in the message. Assuming that each group was in fact a word the most common number in the message was minus fourteen, no less that nine of them in nine words, the next most common being zero one. I was stumped, deciding to fall back on the English belief; if all else fails, make a cup of tea.

George Harrington poked his head through the door just as I was stirring the pot.

'How's that for timing?' he smiled.

'I wondered who the smell of tea would summon,' I replied.

'What's this?' he asked looking at my decoding attempts.

'This is the notebook of the chap...' I explained giving him the full story.

'Let's have a look. The secret is to determine

which number represents "E", it's the most…'

'Common letter in the English language, I know. I reckon it's minus fourteen, see?' I nodded.

'Okay. Agreed, that's "E", I make it nine of 'em! Does that work in the next entry?'

'Right, it's dated, 20th July 1927 01,' I said passing it to him.

'Not enough minus fourteens! Minus fifteen is the most common in this entry,' he pointed out.

'We'll have to get someone who understands these things to look at it,' I shrugged.

'Can't give up yet, Will. Pour that tea and let's talk about something else, and let our brains stew on the problem for a bit,' he grinned.

'Mm, okay, how's the arm now?' I asked noting he was not wearing the sling.

'The doctor reckons the bugger damaged the muscle, I'm doing exercises to help build it up again. I've got limited movement and power in it now; I'd probably fail the force's fitness test,' he said shaking his head.

'That's bad news. Are the exercises' working?'

'It's getting stronger slowly, but I might never get back to fully fit. I was hoping to take my sergeant's exam in the New Year. Just got to wait and see I suppose.'

We chatted for a while about personal matters and decided on another cup of tea, before looking again at the coded notebook.

The phone rang and I answered it.

'Armstrong, here. I've got the results of the tests done on Mr Bloor's insulin phial.'

'The DI is out at the moment, sir. This is DC

Dexter but you can give me the results if you wish,' I said.

'I'll be sending them in a report later today but I thought you should know as soon as possible. Mr Bloor's insulin has been replaced, at some point by water. Plain common tap water, as I suspected. Not only that but they can even tell what area the water comes from.'

'Really?'

'They can't say which tap it came out of, but they do state that it comes from the Ripley, Eastwood, and Heanor area.'

'How would they know that?' I asked.

'It'll all be in the report, but they analysed minerals etcetera dissolved in the water, it differs slightly from area to area!'

'I see. Thank you Doctor, that's most helpful,' I said, and put the phone down. Bloor lived in Codnor, slap bang in the middle of the supply area.

'Do you reckon we can accept these dates as being correct?' George asked, tapping his index finger on the notebook.

'I think it's about the time that Bloor started passing information to the German company, which means the book could be a diary of his dealings.'

'Would he keep a thing as damning as that?'

'It is in code, so he wanted it to be secure,' I suggested.

'Okay, let's assume that the book is, as you say, a log of where and when, presumably kept as a means of covering this back if things became awkward. If that is the case, unless the man is a cypher wizard it has to be pretty simple to decode; something he could keep in his

154

head!' he suggested.

'Agreed.'

'If we as two intelligent police officers can't crack it we need our backsides kicking.'

'Not so sure about that,' I smiled.

'You don't think we'd need our backsides kicking?' he queried.

'No! Not that, I'm questioning the two intelligent police officers,' I grinned.

'Okay, one intelligent police officer and you. Come on let's give it a go, what have we got to lose?'

I moved my chair around to the same side of the desk as Harrington so that we could both see the book without constantly passing it between us.

'Okay, we are pretty sure that minus fourteen is the letter "E". I wonder what the next most common letter is, they didn't tell me that at school, but there must be one,' I shrugged.

'Mm, probably another vowel, say "I" or "O", at a guess! Is there an old newspaper up here?'

'Last night's *Argus* is in my bag, I didn't get time to read it so I brought it in,' I nodded.

'Right, give me a couple of pages. If we each choose a piece of text, about a hundred words and count those two vowels, that should give us an idea what the next letter could be,' he suggested.

'I can't think of anything better,' I admitted.

We set about doing our individual counts, jotting the totals at the side of the page, and a couple of minutes later we compared notes.

'I make it, twenty-one "I's" and twenty-eight "O's",' Harrington grinned, 'a clear winner.'

'Twenty-six "I's" and twenty-two "O's",' I

155

grinned.

'Bugger!'

'I did another count, I also counted "T's", in my bit there was thirty-one of them.'

'Oh well, the idea was good!'

As we sat wondering what, if anything could be the next move, rapid footsteps resounded on the stairs and the door burst open.

'Hi, Dad!' a bright eyed, tousle haired lad of about nine rushed into the room.

'This is my lad Alfie, Alfie has been annoying Sergeant Mellors; has he had enough of you?' Harrington grinned.

'He showed me the cells and the policeman with the funny way of talking let me sit in his police car. I'm hungry.'

'What a surprise! We're going to meet Mam and Artie at twelve o'clock.'

'Ah!'

'Twelve o'clock!' he said then turning to me, 'The missus is taking Arthur my youngest to the dentist. He's really choked, he hoped it could be when he'd gone back to school, and have some time off,' George smirked.

'What yer doing Dad?' the lad asked leaning over the desk.

'Trying to break a code, now sit quietly and read your comic.'

'I didn't know you had to do alpha-numeric codes in the police.'

'What?' we said together.

'Dr Crippen gives them to us some times, if he has to leave the room to see the headmaster or anything.'

'I assume you mean Mr Crippen your teacher?'

'Yes, but we all call him that, or Mr Actually-Virtually,' the boy said, suddenly becoming solemn.

'I can see why you call him Dr Crippen, but where does actually virtually come from?' George asked.

'He ends every sentence with actually or virtually! We *used* to call him Mr Actually-Virtually.'

'Not to his face though, I'll bet,'

'We don't call him that anymore, Dad. Not since we learned about what happened to him in the war.'

'Go on son.'

'He was an intelligence officer, captured by the Germans in the Battle of the Somme, tortured with electric shocks. The headmaster caught us laughing about him one day after his lesson and we thought he'd be mad at us. Instead, he took us all into his study and told us Mr Crippen's story. He said that teaching is a great ..er…'

'Ordeal?' I suggested.

'That's it; teaching is a great ordeal for him and that we should be grown up men and understand how he had suffered; that made us all cry,' young Alfie said and we both nodded.

'Now he's just plain Dr Crippen?'

'Mm.'

'So, are you any good at these, alpha-whatever's?'

'Yes, but you need a key letter!'

'Oh well, that's it then,' George shrugged.

'Let's have a look,' the lad said and I passed it across to him.

'To start with, you write all the letters of the alphabet out in a long line across the page,' he said doing just that. 'If you don't know the key letter you have to find out the most common set of numbers in the message, Dr Crippen says the most common…'

'Is the letter "E",' we said together and the lad nodded a bit crestfallen.

'We think that minus fourteen is "E",' I said.

'Looks like it. The key letter is always zero. Then you count off the letters to the left of zero as minus numbers, and those to the right as just numbers,' the lad grinned and began to write minus fourteen under his letter "E" on his alphabet.

'You're saying "E" if that's what it is, is fourteen letters to the left of the key letter?' I suggested. The boy nodded and continued to write the numbers on his bit of paper.

'Looks like "S", is the key letter,' he said

'There's an "S" at the end of the date heading,' I pointed out, as the lad completed his chart to the left and right of his key letter.

'Easy,' he said and began to jot the letters below his chart to form the message, "Met Adler at Stone Haven Cottage first delivery completed, 200"

'I think that deserves an ice cream,' I said.

'Three at least,' the boy grinned.

'It's a deal, your dad will pay,' I nodded.

'Only, if he can tell us where Stone Haven Cottage is,' George laughed.

'Daaaad!'

'I think I can guess roughly where it is, I'll get in touch with the post office in the area, they're sure to know.' I said, feeling in my pocket and giving the lad a shilling.

'Wow, thanks,' he said showing it to his dad.

'I think you've earned it son,' Harrington said.

'For being smarter than two policemen?' the boy said with a cheeky grin.

'Don't push yer luck, son.'

'Sorry, Dad.'

'Come on time to go and meet yer Mam,' Harrington said looking at his watch.

'Alfie,' I said.

'Yes.'

'Thanks,' I said, adding, 'this is top secret,' and tapped the side of my nose. His face lit up and he tapped the side of his nose. We had a secret pact. I couldn't stop myself from shaking my head in wonder at the ease that the lad had solved our problem. A bob's worth of ice cream was very small beer.

'The date on the next message was "20th July 1927 01" meaning, according to the lad, that the new key letter was 01 on our list. I rewrote the list using "T" as the key letter and hey-presto "E" became minus fifteen, just as we had suspected. I phoned the GPO offices in Eastwood, Heanor and Ripley, asking if they knew of a Stone Haven Cottage. They each promised to phone me back as soon as possible. In the meantime, I set about deciphering the rest of Bloor's notebook.

By the time the DI arrived in the office, I had all but finished the list of entries, made simple by the fact that the large majority were much along the same lines as the first; the fact of a meeting, followed by 200. I assumed, that indicated that Bloor had been paid £200. Presumably, by the mysterious Mr or Mrs Adler; I wondered if that was also a code name.

'I'm impressed, Dexter. I never thought you'd get further than a pile of waste paper.' the DI said.

'DC Harrington popped in and…'

'Harrington gave you a hand?'

'No, sir. Alfie, his nine year old showed us the way, sir. It seems he sometimes gets given these codes to crack at school.'

'A nine year old showed you the way. I wonder what is the earliest age we can recruit to CID,' he said shaking his head. 'You'd better try to trace this cottage.'

'Already in hand, sir,' I nodded.

'How many entries still to do, Dexter?'

'Five, that brings me up to date with the day Bloor died, sir.'

'Time for a decision of management,' the DI said.

'You mean, put the kettle on, sir?'

'Got it in one, Dexter,' he grinned.

'You said you had new information about the murder of Norwich Jimmy,' I reminded him as I did the honours.

'DS Whittington's enquiries came up with a string of burglaries and thefts, mostly from people who offered to help Jimmy. It seems he would go from house to house giving the hard luck story and begging for help. If he found a person willing to give him a helping hand he'd hang around for a few days gradually becoming more civilised making them think he was a reformed character. Then when they least expected it, wham, savings and jewellery and anything he could carry disappeared with Norwich Jimmy,' the DI said, shaking his head. 'He only returned to our patch a couple of weeks ago, looking for his next victim no doubt. He normally carries an old leather shoulder bag. DS Whittington found one a few yards from the bridge. It had a razor, soap, flannel and a key from the left luggage office at Nottingham station.

'He's a real wrong 'un,' I said.

'They don't come much worse,' the DI said, then continued, 'DS Whittington has taken the knife the boys' found on the Rec to Dr Armstrong to see if it fits the bill. Then he's off to Nottingham to try the key. Why would a tramp need the key to a left luggage box unless he has something to hide?'

'Ah yes, Dr Armstrong phoned this morning to say that Bloor's insulin had been swapped for water, he could even tell which water company the water came from. Codnor, Bloor's home is right in the middle of the area they cover!'

'Is it now? That's very interesting!'

We sat with our tea and I explained the entries in Bloor's notebook. DI Brierly agreed that the figures at the end of each message must relate to the amount the German company had paid for the information.

'I wonder if the date of that trade delegation is about the time of the first entry!' the DI suggested.

'Mr Hooper, could probably say, sir!'

'Mm, give him a ring!' the DI said passing me the phone.

He was not in his office according to Janice Durham, the young lady who had met us on our visit to the RR headquarters.

'I don't think my boss would mind you being given the information you are requesting, but I daren't let you have it without his actual agreement. I will tell him you rang and what you'd like to know and ring you back in the morning,' she said, and I relayed her answer

161

to the DI.

'I don't think we really need to know that, do we Dexter?'

'It would just be nice to tie the first entry in the book to around the time of the German trade delegation, sir!'

'True, one more bit of information, can never do any harm!'

At around four o'clock, the phone rang and DI Brierly lifted the receiver.

'Ah, that was DC Dexter, I'll put him on!' he said passing the phone over to me. 'Ripley, Post Office!'

'Hello, DC Dexter Speaking!'

'You were asking about a Stone Haven Cottage!'

'I was! Have you tracked it down?' I asked eagerly.

'Not exactly, all mail for Stone Haven Cottage is redirected to our sub-office in Long Thorley and picked up there every couple of days.'

'So you don't know where Stone Haven Cottage actually is?' I asked.

'All I can tell you is that we have a pigeon-hole at our sorting office for mail to Stone Haven Cottage, with a redirect to Long Thorley, for collection!'

'Is that normal?'

'It's a bit irregular, but the fee is paid every month to renew the arrangement. Four bob a month, everyone is entitled to have mail redirected provided that they pay the fee,' the chap said.

'Okay, I can see that but how does the mail get to you in the first place?' I asked.

'It arrives addressed to Stone Haven Cottage, c/o

Ripley Sorting Office Derbyshire. That gets it put in its pigeon-hole and sent to Long Thorley next delivery.'

'So you don't actually know where Stone Haven Cottage is?'

'Sorry, not a clue, it could be anywhere! Your only chance of finding it would be to trace the person who collects the stuff from Long Thorley. But you're in luck, there's a letter due for delivery to that office last delivery this afternoon.'

'Mm, okay, thank you for that, I'll make arrangements to sort that out.'

'Sorry I can't be of more help, good luck,' he said and we closed the call.

'You don't look very optimistic, Dexter,' the DI said.

'I'd like to follow it up, sir. I think...' I said and told him why I thought it important.

'Long Thorley? Where the hell's that?'

'I'm not sure, sir,' I admitted.

'Then you'd better look it up, Dexter.'

'Yes, sir,' I said and went down to the front desk to locate the Ordnance Survey maps.

'Looking for somewhere in particular?' Sergeant Mellors asked.

'Long Thorley, Sarge.'

'Never heard of it!' he admitted.

'I think I could be in the Ripley Codnor area, but that's only a guess.'

'You'll need this map then!' he said dragging out a well-thumbed Ordnance Survey map of the area. He spread it on the front desk.

'Well beggar me, just look at that, smack in the middle,' he said. It was true the tiny hamlet, was near

163

enough in the middle of the map.

'Not much of a place from the look of it; a couple of dozen houses, looks like they're mostly farm attached cottages; a public house; a post office and a disused windmill. Talk about the back of beyond,' he said shaking his head.

My eye had fallen on something completely different. About a mile to the west of the village was a disused quarry going by the name of Haven Quarry. The place was quite small, the sort of size created when extracting the stone for a single large building.

'I think that's what I'm looking for Sarge,' I said pointing at the quarry. 'What year is this map?'

'No doubt there is a newer version, but we haven't got it; outside our patch.'

'I'll nip over and see if the library has got one.'

'What are you thinking lad?'

'I'm looking for a place called Stone Haven Cottage, near Long Thorley. I'm wondering if a cottage has been built by the quarry, since this version of the map.'

'It's certainly a logical name for a cottage in that location.'

The library had a current version of the same map, and sure enough, by the time of the resurvey, a cottage had appeared, probably built using stone from the quarry, and the whole area was part of a small wood.

'You took your time, Dexter. I assume from that expression on your face you've struck lucky again,' the DI said as I entered the office.

'I think I've located it, sir.'

'Remind me what you were looking for. You've been so long I'd almost forgotten you worked here.'

'Stone Haven Cottage, sir.'

164

Ah yes, so it was; and…?'

'I know where it is, sir, or at least I'm pretty sure where it is,' I said, and explained my thinking to him.

'I can go with you on that, well done Dexter.'

'Thank you, sir.'

'About ten miles away, Dexter.'

'About that, yes.'

'Off yer go then lad. See if you're right,' he grinned. 'The ride will do you good.'

'Thank you, sir.'

The remote cottage stood about halfway between Ripley and Eastwood, half a mile or so northeast of a line drawn directly between the two, hidden in a small copse. The gateway was unmarked and a casual passer-by would dismiss the half-open five-bar gate as being the entrance to a little used pasture, with a small wood half a mile up the overgrown track. The casual passer-by would be wrong. Beneath the covering of weeds, the track was firm, well-compacted road stone. A close inspection showed that a car or possibly a small van had recently driven along it: whether in or out, I could not tell.

The track turned slightly as it entered the copse further obscuring the dwelling from idle inspection. The cottage once I had reached it was in a reasonable state of repair. A two-storey structure, probably built in the early 1920's, stone built with a slate roof. A large lean-to shelter at the side acted as a garage for the car or van and stood empty. I leaned by cycle against the front wall and pressed the bell push by the front door. I was surprised to hear a modern electric bell ringing somewhere in the interior. Not expecting the door to open, without having to ring a second time, perhaps not even then if the occupants were out as the lack of vehicle suggested. I had turned my back and was looking through the trees back towards the field gate, noting that from this point it was possible to see it in the distance, through the trees, even though the cottage was invisible from the road.

So intrigued was I by the fact that I was surprised when a polite female voice said-

'Can I help you, sir?'

In her mid-fifties, the woman had what must have been in youth, jet-black hair, still impressively black, but now with odd strands running to grey. Strangely, for that hair colouring, her round and pleasant face was awash with summer freckles.

'Mrs Adler?' I asked.

'No! I am Mrs Tooley, Mr and Mrs Adler's housekeeper. Can I ask who you are and what it is about?'

'I'm Detective Constable Dexter, I wonder if it would be possible to speak to Mr Adler, please?'

'Mr and Mrs Adler are out at the moment, not expected back until tomorrow. Is it about the picture in the paper?' she asked.

'Do you mean this picture?' I asked opening my notebook and unfolding my copy of the artists drawing.

'Yes! Oh, you had better come in. I can tell you about it. Would you like a cup of tea?' she asked.

'Never been known to refuse,' I grinned as she showed me through to the kitchen.

'I must admit, I wondered if Mr Adler had contacted the police. You see I saw the picture in an old copy of Crammingdon *Argos*; Mr and Mrs Adler don't have a newspaper. I go to see my sister Betty in Crammingdon once a fortnight on my day off and she saves me all of the back copies of the *Argos*. I can't say that I'm all that interested really. Stuck out here in the wilds, half the stuff in it is meaningless to me.'

'You say your sisters live in Crammingdon?' I asked, as she poured water into a little chromium plated teapot.

'Like I said, I go to her house once a fortnight to hear the family news. That's when I saw it, the picture, I was sure it was Mr Bloor.'

'You know him?'

'He comes... came here about every ten days or so. I brought that copy back with me and showed it to Mrs Adler; I don't have a lot to do with Mr Adler, he's an Austrian and a very quiet man. Milk and sugar?' she asked laying out pretty little cups and saucers.

'Yes, both please. What did Mrs Adler say to the picture?'

'Mrs Adler is German, though you'd never guess it she speaks English beautifully, she was surprised when I showed it to her. Shocked you might say, though she got over it very quickly. I thought at the time she was upset to see that he had died.'

'But now you're not so sure?'

'I'll let it stand for a couple of minutes.' she said, stirring the pot and putting a knitted tea cosy over it. 'Well, she said, "Thank you Mrs Tooley, I'll show this to my husband." And she took the paper from me.'

'Then what happened?' I asked.

'She took it through to Mr Adler as I said, but she didn't fully close the door, then they started speaking in German.'

'So you've no idea what was said?' I suggested,

167

but the grin on her face suggested otherwise.

'I went to a posh school in Nottingham. German was one of my subjects,' Mrs Tooley smiled.

'The Adler's *knew* you could speak German?'

'When Mrs Adler interviewed me for the job about six or seven years ago,' she said, pouring the tea and sliding a cup across the scrubbed top of the kitchen table and indicating the milk and sugar, 'I guessed from the way she asked if I spoke German, that it was important to her that I didn't.'

'You told her that you didn't?'

'Actually it's true. I understand it, but I never really learned the intricacies of the spoken grammar. It's a very complicated and precise language.'

'Really then you spoke the truth, you don't speak German. That's very naughty,' I smiled. 'What did they say about the picture?'

'I can't remember the exact words, but Mr Adler wasn't surprised. "He had it coming, the fat fool!" or something like that. Then Mrs Adler said, "What am I to tell her?" and he said. "Oh, tell her not to worry, that I will inform the police that we know the man and can give them a name." She came out and spoke to me in German; she often did that when they had been speaking together, pretending to forget I didn't understand. But really trying to catch me out, I think.'

'But you were ready to be tested?'

'Oh, yes,' she nodded.

'She told you that Mr Adler would get in touch with us?'

'Yes. Did he?' Mrs Tooley asked and I shook my head.

'No, I wonder why?' she said. I didn't answer

but posed another question.

'When Mr Bloor came, how did he arrive?'

'Mr Adler picked him up, from his home I suppose.'

'Mr Adler collected him in his car?'

'Yes, then they gave him a first class lunch, treated like royalty he was, then afterwards he and Mr Adler would shut themselves in the office for about twenty minutes.'

'They closed the door?'

'Yes, I couldn't hear. In any case, Mrs Adler was always hovering around finding things for me to do. Something's going on isn't it? Why didn't Mr Adler get in touch?'

'Mrs Tooley, please tell the Adler's that I called, and that I wouldn't say why, but that I have asked them to call me so that I can arrange an appointment.'

'Can I say that I think it's about him telling you about the picture?'

'Yes, but nothing about this little conversation.'

'Yes, okay,' she said and nodded.

'Is there anything else that seems strange, out of place or character?' I asked.

'Not really, except, if it was a Tuesday or a Thursday when he came, he always seemed to be in a hurry, as though he had something else he needed to do. Mr Adler always picked him up about an hour earlier than other days and they eat that much earlier. I always wondered why,' she shrugged.

'Perhaps he did just have another appointment on those days,' I nodded, remembering that the Magnificent Cinema had afternoon matinees on Tuesdays and Thursdays.

'I suppose that must be it,' she agreed. 'Then there's the fact that Mr Adler has two engineering magazines delivered by post. He cuts adverts and articles out of them, then burns them within a few days in the garden incinerator; I always wondered why,' she added.

'I have a background in engineering, and occasionally buy one of the magazines, if something catches my eye,' I admitted. 'My wife is always complaining that I never get rid of them; perhaps Mr Adler is a very tidy man,' I suggested.

'He is a very tidy man. I think perhaps that must be it.'

'Remember to say that I called and wouldn't say why.'

'Do you think Mr and Mrs Adler, killed Mr Bloor?' she asked, clearly the thought had just come to her.

'No! I shouldn't think so,' I chuckled. 'If their relationship with Mr Bloor was what I think, they had every reason to want him alive,' I added, though I was far from convinced.

'So, I'm not in any danger?'

'Good heavens no!' I said with a shake of my head, and I honestly didn't think she was.

8

'That's very interesting Dexter,' the DI agreed. 'I'd better accompany you once they tell you when. It rather looks, as we expected, that Mr Adler was Bloor's contact with the German engine company.'

'Hard to see it any other way, sir.'

'I wonder how they got in contact in the first place.'

'That might be worth looking into, sir. It might give us a lead into why he was killed,' I suggested.

'I wonder if Mr Hooper has any ideas.'

'Am I to ring him and tell him we now have a name that we think was Bloor's contact?'

'Mm… He might have heard of Adler. Yes Dexter, give him a ring.'

'I think I'll have to go through Mr Barton.'

'Okay, do it.'

Initially my talk with Mr Barton lasted only a few seconds, he agreed to approach Mr Hooper and ask if the name Adler meant anything to him. He phoned back within the hour to say his boss did indeed remember a Mr Adler, who was part of a trade delegation that he had shown around the factory eight or nine years ago. The name had stuck in his memory because it is the German name for a fish eagle, a bird that he found very interesting being a keen bird watcher.

'So, it seems sir, that Hooper's love of the sea eagle made the name stick in his mind,' I said, giving the DI the result of my calls.

'Meaning that if the chap's name had been, Schmitt or von Kloppenburg, he would have been instantly forgotten?' the DI grinned.

'Probably, sir,' I agreed.

'One thing you'll find the more you do this job, it's always the silly little things, the things that people are expected to overlook that are the real clues,' the DI said.

'It doesn't mean that the Adler's killed Bloor though, sir.'

'I know… I know.'

The phone rang and the DI answered.

'Ah, very good sir,' was all he said then replaced the receiver. 'I've been summoned over to Heaven; I wonder what the bloody hell I've done now?'

I was in the office about twenty minutes early next morning. It seemed to me that we were on the verge of solving the case. Although I was eager to get the culprit pinpointed, I was sad that it would probably mean an end to my secondment to DI Brierly's team.

When the DI came in, he instantly approached the Assistant Chief Constable for the use of a car for most of the day.

'We've got a bit of running around to do today. First off I want to go to see Mrs Bloor again to inform her that we are aware that her husband's insulin had, at some point been changed for water. It will be interesting to see her reactions,' he grinned.

DS Whittington came into the office a few seconds later.

'Morning sir, Will!'

'How did you get on yesterday?' the DI asked.

'I left the knife, the one we think killed Norfolk Jimmy, the one the lads found, on Parson's rec. with Dr Armstrong, with a promise to get the results to you by lunchtime, sir.'

'Did he think it seemed promising?'

'You know the good Doctor, sir! A very hard man to tie down. If I'm honest I don't hold out much hope; he seemed less than impressed!'

'It did seem to be a bit of a long shot, at least we'll know in a couple of hours. What about the key?'

'I found Norfolk Jimmy's locker in Nottingham Victoria railway station. The attendant looked up the number on the key and located the locker it. He wasn't too happy about me opening it, until I pointed out that the key holder had been murdered. Even so, he demanded to see my warrant card, and read every word, checked me against the photograph and stood over me whilst I opened it,'

'That's what comes of being such a shifty-looking character!' the DI laughed. 'Go on then, what was inside?' he asked.

'Before I actually opened it, I asked the attendant, a Mr Edmund Brewer, if he could describe the key holder. He looked at me as though I'd asked him the winner of the next Grand National, he said, "They come in, they show me their key, if the payment is up to date, they do what they came to do and they go out," then he said. "I don't ask to see a bloody birth certificate." Sarky beggar!'

'So he couldn't tell you what the chap looked like?'

'No, sir. To be fair he did point out that with over two hundred lockers, some of them rented for years on end and lots changing hands two or three times a day he couldn't remember many of the day to day clients. I pointed out that the man who had been murdered was a down and out, a tramp sir.'

'What did he say to that?'

'He said in that case he would have remembered, and looked again in his book. He turned the book around for me to see, whoever paid for the key was in a position to shell out five quid for a year's rental. "Not a lot of tramps would be able to do that," he said, and I had to agree,' the DS shrugged.

'We already know that he played a double life; presumably he loads and unloads the locker when he's taken advantage of a kindly house holder and gone through the miraculous change into a respectable human being,' the DI suggested.

'That's the way I'm thinking, sir.'

'So, when you opened the locker, what did you find?'

'A suitcase, sir.'

'Okay, where is it?'

'Still at the Railway station, it's too heavy to carry from there, so I left it there last night. I've arranged for it to be delivered, should be here any time, sir,' Whittington said and dropped the little key on the desk.

It was the first time I had seen it and I instantly realised its similarity to another small key, one we had thought to be a car ignition key, the key on the ring found in Bloor's pocket that day in the cinema.

'That looks like Bloor's key, sir,' I said.

'It could be a left luggage locker or a dozen other things!' the DI pointed out. 'But I agree it's not bound to be an ignition key!'

'Is it worth taking it with us this morning, to see if it fits anything at Bloor's home, sir?'

'That's the next logical step,' the DI agreed.
The phone rang and DI Brierly picked it up and introduced himself.

'Ah, yes, DS Whittington is carrying out that investigation, I'll put him on,' he said and passed to phone over.

'That's brilliant, I'm on my way,' he said after listening for a minute or so

'The Derby lads have apprehended a tramp with what looks like extensive blood stains to his shirt and trousers. He claims that he's never been anywhere near Crammigdon and has never heard of Norfolk Jimmy. It seems, when arrested he had a large sheath knife, also equally bloody,' the DS smiled.

'How does he account for the blood stains? The DI asked.

'It seems he claims to have cut himself shaving, sir!' the DS chuckled.

'Unlikely but not impossible,' I said. 'Depends how much blood we are talking about!'

'Agreed, except that according to the lad on the phone, the man has several months growth of beard!'

'Perhaps he was trying to shave Norfolk Jimmy but standing too close,' the DI laughed.

'If I get a move on I can catch the train to Derby and be there by ten o'clock, sir.'

'Yes, do that. It will be nice to get that one tied

up and out of our hair.' The DI nodded, and DS Whittington galloped down the stairs. Halfway down he turned and came back into the office. 'The suitcase has just come through the door, sir. Am I to get the chap to bring it up?'

'Yes, shove it under my desk, it'll have to wait until we get back. Come on Dexter, let's go and try that key.'

In the car, the DI told me the reason for his visit to the Assistant Chief Constable the previous day.

'I've got a little surprise for you Dexter.'

'Really, sir?'

'The chief thinks that our department should have its own transport.'

'Oh!' was all I could muster.

'You remember Mr Cox, Cox's Garage, the chap who taught you to drive?'

'Yes, sir. I'm unlikely ever to forget, I smashed up his little Riley Monaco with him in it!' I grinned.

'Oh, yes, well it seems that he has said he would be prepared to let my department have two second-hand cars and maintain them, provided the force pays for the fuel. The CC jumped at the idea and asked for my thoughts. I suggested that one should be mainly for my use, the other for DS Whittington's use. He agreed, but suggested that we should be able to drive ourselves rather than take a patrol driver out of circulation since that rather defeats the object.'

'That's true, sir!'

'It seems we will be getting delivery of the cars in a couple of days and since you can drive and I can't you can be my chauffeur!'

'Right, sir,' I nodded.

'However since your secondment to me is only temporary, you can also teach me to drive.'

'What?'

'Now then, Dexter. "What, sir" I think you mean,' he grinned.

'Yes, sir.'

It was the first time I had seen Mr Bloor's house; a pleasant medium sized detached house on a well-kept road. A large ornamental tree, a type of acer I think, grew in a raised, circular brick built area, surrounded by pinkish-red gravel The leaves of the tree were already beginning to turn colour and would probably, compliment the gravel in due course. A small Austin car stood in the driveway sporting a set of ladders overhanging its tiny length by a good few feet at either end. Wedged between the rungs of the ladder was a metal bucket.

'Looks like Bloor's window-cleaner brother is in attendance on the widowed Mrs Bloor,' the DI grinned as we stepped out of the squad car.

'Two birds with one stone, sir?' I asked.

'Be nice to see what they have to say for themselves,' the DI agreed.

'You again!' snapped the woman who opened the door.

'I said I'd probably need to have another word, Mrs Bloor, This is DC Dexter, can we come in?'

'I suppose so. Come through to the kitchen, my brother in law is here having a cup of tea before he does my windows,' she said opening the door.

The man nodded as we walked in. It was easy to see why so many people thought the picture in the paper was this window cleaner, the resemblance was uncanny. Facially he was a very good match but as the witnesses had pointed out the man was much smaller but size is relative of course; he was the same sort of height but this chap must still have topped the scales at eighteen stones. I pitied the set of ladders that had to take his weight on a regular basis.

'Good morning sir, I'm Detective Inspector Brierly and this is DC Dexter. Could I ask your name please, sir?'

'Thomas Bloor, you're here no doubt investigating the death of my brother.'

'We are indeed, sir. We now know that he injected himself with tap water rather than insulin. Our problem is, did he do that knowingly or had someone changed it?' the DI said.

'Me being the logical candidate, I suppose,' Mrs Bloor replied, placing her hands on her hips and scowling.

'We know from analysis of the water in his phial that it originated in this area. You live just around the corner I believe, sir?'

'Making me, another possible suspect I suppose?' The window cleaner snapped, and Mrs Bloor added, 'Well, I'm not guilty. It was only a matter of time before he killed himself, no self-control. You know he used to go to the pictures of an afternoon and scoff great dollops of chocolate covered fudge and things?'

'You did tell us that the last time we spoke, though we knew in any case; the pathologist gave us a pretty exhaustive list of his stomach contents. DC Dexter was first on the scene and found the wrappings of two large chocolate coated bars. So yes, we were aware that he, er… over-indulged!'

'Over-indulged! The man couldn't stop. He was bad enough when he was at work, but after they retired him because of his diabetes, he ate non-stop.' she snapped.

'I bet you don't know he was passing information to the Germans; information about some secret project he was working on before they retired him,' Bloor's brother said with a cocky wobble of his head.

'As a matter of fact we do know, sir, though might I ask how you happen to know?' the DI asked.

'I know my own brother, thinks he was so bloody clever. He actually admitted it to me one night in the Oak & Acorn, the pub at the end of the road. He swore me to secrecy of course. He reckoned he had their blessing to pass on the stuff!'

'You're saying his employers were allowing him to pass on their secret information?' the DI bluffed, pretending that this was news to us.

'I thought he was just bluffing, trying to look big, that was our Rick, always trying to be the important man. I told him I thought he was bluffing, and shook my head in disbelief at him,' the window cleaner said.

'He obviously convinced you,' the DI suggested.

'He even told me the chap's name that was his *paymaster* he called him… er… Antler, I think it was, something like that anyway!'

'He actually told you that he was passing information to a rival of his employer?' the DI asked, continuing the bluff, to see where it would lead I supposed.

'They'd retired him on health grounds by then, but someone at the factory was still feeding him information to pass on.'

179

'He was playing a very dangerous game, Mr Bloor,' I commented.

'A lot more dangerous than you think. He was passing on duff information. He told me that and giggled. They'll bloody kill you if they find out, I told him, but he shook his head and grinned at me; that was our Ricky for yer. Cocky as they come. Now look how clever he's been. They've done him in like I said.'

'That certainly looks like a possibility,' the DI nodded.

'Have a guess how much he reckoned they were paying him.'

'No idea,' the DI said, though I of course knew we had a pretty accurate idea.

'Two hundred quid... Two hundred quid for information! I don't end up with that for cleaning windows all bloody year!

'I does seem a bit far-fetched,' the DI nodded.

'He showed me his wallet; he'd got two o' them big white fivers and ten or twelve quid in pound notes. "Plenty more where that came from," he said and tapped the side of his nose.'

'He convinced you?' I asked.

'He said it was all safe and sound somewhere. Though he didn't say where.'

'I'm sorry to have to ask you this but we found a keyring on your husband's body Mrs Bloor, can you identify any of them?' I asked handing her the little bunch.

'That's his front door key; that one's for the back, that's his workshop key, but I don't recognise that one, something in his workshop probably,' she shrugged, handing them back.

'I'll have to look in there then, Mrs Bloor,' the DI pointed out.

'Will it make a difference if I refuse?'

'I'm afraid it won't. We are treating this as a murder enquiry.'

'You'd better go and have a look then,' she snapped, opening the back door and indicating a large, well-constructed wooden shed under the boughs of a massive oak.

'This would take some breaking into,' the DI said.

The door refused to open although the key had turned in it easily. I tried it a second time and with a well-oiled and satisfying click, the lock released. A turn of the handle and we were in. I found a light switch and clicked on three large overhead lights; the place was brighter that a summers day. The engineer in me quickly appreciated the well-equipped small workshop with old fashioned but good quality small machine tools placed along the walls, though it was obvious from the layers of dust on them that they had lain unused for several years at a guess. Some smaller individual lights could give extra illumination to certain of the machines, as needed. From the piles of parts and part-assembled projects it seemed that Bloor had repaired clocks, perhaps as a hobby or maybe as a spare time job; a big man doing very fiddly work.

My mind went instantly back to my time at Lomax's workshop; the top fitter there was "Charlie", a huge man, not by Bloor's standard of course but to a fifteen-year old apprentice, big and fat. Yet he could assemble the most intricate of machinery with the patience of a saint. He had the biggest workbench in the shop with a long shelf underneath between the legs. It had become common practice to pile any unwanted parts or scrapped projects under his bench when he wasn't looking, just for the fun of it. When eventually, he had to stoop to retrieve a fallen part. "Where the bloody hell has that lot come from?" he would yell, much to everyone's amusement.

'What's that smell, Dexter?' the DI asked, bringing me back to the present.

'Some sort of acid or chemicals at a guess, sir,' I said, noticing that a partition divided the place, and a second door closed it off. I tried the handle and it opened revealing something of a surprise.

'Ah, now we know what the chemicals are,' the DI grinned.

This part of the workshop had the layout of a small darkroom. In front of us a bench had developing dishes and tanks, a small sink with a tap placed under a heavily shuttered window and on the left hand wall an enlarger with a box of photo paper. On the other side, on a wide shelf, an electric print drier stood open awaiting its next task. Under the shelf was a metal cupboard, with a little keyhole. Our unknown key slipped in perfectly and with a smooth little turn, it opened.

The cupboard, almost a safe, seemed on first glance simply to be a store for boxes of unexposed photo paper. Four boxes sat there one on top of the other, the top one was obviously a fresh, unused box but the three below had their paper seals broken. I lifted them out and placed them on the workbench beside the sink. Moving the top one aside, I opened the lid of the first unsealed one.

'Well, well, well! That's interesting, Dexter.'

'Yes, sir.'

We were looking at a mass of ten by eight prints of the plans of intricate machinery, presumably the secret engine. Shuffling through the stack of prints in the first box it was clear that not only the complete drawings were shown but also small sections of what was obviously the same drawing showing more clearly fine detail of particular areas. The second box was more interesting still, it contained not only photographs of the plan drawings but also pictures of the actual components, some of them with their individual parts laid out as though ready to be assembled.

'What do you make of this, sir?' I asked.

'It seems to me that Mr Bloor was receiving his information from Hooper by 35mm negative cassettes, developing them and printing them off, keeping a set of the final prints for himself,' the DI suggested.

'That's the way I see it,' I agreed.

'They look pretty authentic to me, but what do I know?'

'At a guess, I'd say that these are actual photos of the real work in progress. Would anyone go to the trouble of making actual false parts so as to be able to photograph them and pass them off as real?' I said shaking my head.

'Are you suggesting that Mr Hooper is passing on the real stuff, rather than the duff information he claims?'

'I'd say someone is. That could probably be the reason Bloor was getting away with it for so long without the German company smelling a rat,' I added.

'Because there's no rat to smell!' he nodded, walking over to the little developing tank and inspecting the empty film cassettes lying at the side of it.

'My guess is he develops the negatives, prints off a set of prints for himself, for his own interest or possibly to sell on at some future date, then passes on the negatives to his contact, presumably Mr Adler, who sends them off by post to the interested party, sir.'

'I reckon that's about the size of it. We'll take these pictures with us, Dexter.'

'I think so, sir!' I said gathering them back into their boxes.

'I wonder what's in this box, Dexter.'

'More prints, I should think, sir,' I said as he raised the lid.

'Blimey! Just look at that bloody lot.'
The box contained a stack of five-pound notes. At a rough guess well in excess of five hundred pounds.

'We need to take this with us. We'd better take it back into the house, count it in front of Mrs Bloor and give her a receipt for it all,' the DI said.

'If this is the result of spying, do we need to explain why we are taking it?'

'It probably is as you point out, the result of dirty work at the mill, but I intend to keep this above board. I don't want some clever-dick lawyer trying to make out that we tried to pocket this little hoard,' the DI nodded.

We took the haul into the house and both Mrs Bloor and her window-cleaning brother-in-law sat wide eyed at the content of box three. DI Brierly signed a receipt for the three boxes and their contents and we said good day, leaving the pair somewhat shell-shocked.

'Time to pay our mysterious Director another visit, don't you think?' the DI grinned.

'Oh, yes, sir,' I nodded.

At just before midday we piled back into police vehicle one (PV1), normally driven by my old mate "Bong" the ex-New South Wales copper, but today his place was taken by PC Goldman, a chap new to the force, having transferred from Gloucester.

'I think we need to check with Mr Hooper to see if this is actually the stuff he gave to Bloor,' the DI said.

'I'll ring my contact Mr Barton as soon as we get back,' I nodded.

'Then we've time to drop in on Mr Cox to see what vehicles he's going to provide us with.'

'I suppose so, sir, it is more or less on our way,' I said, a bit tongue in cheek, since the place was in completely the other direction.

'Don't *you* want to have a little look?'

'Well, yes I suppose I do, sir,' I admitted.

'Cox's garage, please driver!'

'Right, sir.'

The man found us a place on the forecourt out of the way of the pumps and parked up to await our return. Mr Cox must have seen us arrive, and came out of the showroom doors to meet us.

'Good morning, what can I do for you gentlemen?' he asked holding out his hand.

'Good morning Mr Cox, you know acting DC Dexter, I think,' the DI said shaking his hand.

'Oh, yes! We know each other quite well, don't we?' he chuckled as we shook hands.

'What happened to that lovely little Riley?' I asked.

'It wasn't possible to do anything with it, much

185

too badly damaged. We've saved some of the parts, but it was insured, so I only lost a bit of profit. We lived to tell the tale and that's the main thing,' he grinned.

'We were just passing, and thought we'd drop in to have a look at the cars you've kindly offered us.' the DI said, looking at me in a way that said, "don't tell him we've actually come five miles out of our way."

'I hope you're not expecting sparkling limousines 'cause if you are you're in for a disappointment,' he grinned

'I'm sure we will be more than happy with whatever you can offer. As I'm sure you know, at the moment we have to rob the patrol lads of a car if we need to go further than a couple of miles.'

'So the Chief Constable was telling me the other day when we were playing a round of golf at our club. You don't play I assume, Inspector?'

'Rather too busy at the moment to have the time to play, sir.'

'Oh well, one day perhaps. These are the two cars I've earmarked for you,' he said pointing at a dark blue Singer saloon and a Ford saloon in mid grey, both of them the four door versions.

'They're a bit ordinary,' the DI said, 'Oh, sorry, that seems ungrateful.'

'Your chief suggested that they should be inconspicuous, "nondescript" was the word he used. I presume his thinking was along the lines that they shouldn't over advertise the fact that they belong to the force,' Cox said. 'They are both sound, safe motors but I just can't sell them. Mike's had a little play with them. I think you know what I mean?' he said with a wink at me.

'Oh, yes,' I nodded.

'Go on, let me into the secret,' the DI said, scratching his chin.

'Mike is my ace mechanic. No, that's not fair to the chap, he's a highly skilled engineer. These little motors look like ordinary run of the mill cars, but if you need to ask them to give chase they will hold their own with bigger motors in a cops-and-robbers situation,' Mr Cox grinned.

'What exactly does he do to them?'

'Now, you're asking. I just tell him to give it the works, and leave it to him. But I can tell you this, he's been on them for two days non-stop.'

'Look, I've some paperwork to complete, so have a look to your hearts content. They will be with you first thing in the morning,' he said, leaving us to inspect them, not that either of us had the first clue, what we were looking at.

'I fancy this one,' the DI said, sitting in the Singer. 'My wife's got one of their sewing machines,' he grinned and fiddled with the gear stick.

'I think it's a different company, sir,' I suggested.

'I know! I know!' he grinned.

'It is a nice looker, sir,' I admitted.

'Reckon you could teach me in this, Dexter?'

'I can try, sir,' I replied without any great enthusiasm. 'Perhaps, DS Whittington might make a better job of it, sir! He has driven a lot more than me, sir.'

'I want you to do it, that's an order.'

'Very good, sir,' I said.

'Don't look like that, Dexter,' he chuckled.

'Sorry, sir.'

'Come on let's go and ring Mr Barton, get these

photos cleared up.'

Mr Barton was in a meeting when I rang and the person I spoke to agreed to get him to ring me back as soon as he was available.

There was a message on my desk asking me to contact my old friend Marco Tizzoni. Marco has a stall on Crammingdon Market, selling his musical talents. More than a busker, he was once a famous musician but sadly blindness overtook him at the peak of his career. His place in Crammingdon society is well accepted. Crammingdon on market day without Marco's music doesn't bear thinking about. His message simply asked me to call and see him at the end of my shift. I rang Alice to tell her I would be a bit late and she asked me to give her good wishes to Marco.

Mr Barton rang about three o'clock and arranged for us to meet with Mr Hooper first thing next morning.

Marco has a room on the first floor of a house on the corner of the market place. The outer door is always open and I climbed the stairs to his room. Even before I reached the landing he shouted,

'Come in my friend the door is open.'

'How did you know it was me?' I asked.

'How did I know it was you, he asks. Phew, I hear your come a miles away. I hear you walk across marketplace. Once a copper, always a copper, you walk different to ordinary folk,' he laughed. 'You would like I should make you some coffee?'

'That would be very nice, yes please Mr Tizzoni.'

'Mr Tizzoni, Mr broody Tizzoni. I am Marco;

you are Will, we are friends is that not so?'

'It is Marco, it is. So, what can I do for you?' I asked.

'First the coffee, then I tell you my problem. Tell me how is your wife and your two little chaps?' he shouted from his little kitchen.

'They are fine growing fast, just starting to fall out once in a while.'

'Fall out of what? Are they hurt?'

'No, argue, disagree, fall out of friendship!' I laughed.

'Phew, don't to worry of that, is good they fall out. When I was boy in Italy I fight with my brother all of the time. We not hit each other only, the hurtful words you understand?'

'Yes, I think that's what my two are doing.'

'My Mama, she could have us laughing again in two minutes no matter how angry we become.'

'I think Alice would like to know that secret, she sends her love by the way.'

'And I send to her, she is lovely lady you lucky young bugger.'

'I know. But how did your mother get you laughing again?'

'She make us clean the windows.'

'My boys are only two Marco, a bit young to be cleaning windows,' I chuckled as he brought in the coffee.

'Okay, it won't work yet, but soon. It so easy and work every time. One clean inside, one clean outside of same window. Have to face each other, soon one cloth is following other cloth, or dodging about trying not to be followed, you understand?'

'I see soon the fun makes them laugh and be friends again,' I said.

'It is so, I could not tell you how many times my Mama made us clean the windows, even when we were nearly men. "You will clean the windows or you will get no food at my table," she would shout. We would laugh, shake the hands and not clean the windows but remember and it was enough,' he smiled and shook his head. 'Happy times, my friend.'

'I have only sisters, they would look after me all the time it was like having three mothers, I laughed, But you wanted to speak to me, something is bothering you?'

'Someone is coming into my room.'

'Things are missing?'

'No, not until yesterday. Everything is still here, but is moved. I know where everything is, I have to find without the eyes, you understand?'

'Yes, I have seen you do it, pick something up and put it back in exactly the same place,' I agreed.

'It is like someone is playing little tricks on me when I am out in the market.'

'You lock your door of course?'

'Will, I not a fool, I lock my door every time I go out and at night when I go to bed. Somebodys is getting in and playing the tricks. But yesterday, WORSE!'

'What happened yesterday?'

'Yesterday was the funeral of my old friend Saul Schulman, he sell me my furniture, you remember I tell you?'

'I remember.'

'While I am out some bugger get in, and take my money and my squeeze-box.'

'Someone broke in?'

'No they must have key, nothing is broken.'

'I'm sorry to hear that Marco, I'll have a word with my boss and get the fingerprint boys round in the morning,' I suggested.

'Will that get my accordion back again?'

'Probably not. In the meantime, I'll fit you a new lock sometime in the next few days. That should stop whoever it is getting in.'

'I am sorry to trouble you my friend!'

'Tell me about your accordion and I'll get the boys on the beat to look out in the pawn-brokers,' I said.

'It is old, not the best but worth ten, maybe fifteen pounds…'

He gave me a full description of the instrument including a maker's serial number. I assured him that I'd do my best, but he knew there was not a great chance of success.

'How much money was taken, Marco?' I asked.

'Twelve pounds and some silver I hadn't counted, probably about seven shillings, I think.'

'Is that all of your money? I'm not being nosey I just want to be sure you are not without money,' I said.

'I have some money in the bank, I am not without, but it is in a savings account, I need to give notice to make a er… what is the word?'

'Withdrawal?'

'Mm, withdrawal.'

'I can let you have ten shillings to tide you over, but I'll need it back as soon as you get your money.'

'That is kind Will, I'm not in need of money for a few days, but thank you my friend.'

'I'll set things in motion to get fingerprints done and look out for your accordion. I'd better be going to see my boys before they go to bed. Thanks for the coffee.'

As I walk down the stairs, Joe Watson the local ironmonger was coming in the door carrying a tool bag and when he saw me he stepped aside.

'Ah, just the chap, Marco has been burgled, can you have a look at his lock and put a suitable one aside for me? I've told him I'll replace it for him.'

'Just going to do it now, Mr Dexter. The lads on the market have paid for the lock, and I'm fitting it for them as my donation,' he grinned.

'Oh, dear! He won't like that, he'll be glad that he has friends that want to help him but he'll see it as charity and that won't go down too well,' I pointed out.

'We discussed that this afternoon, we have a little plan to outwit the silly old bugger. Like you said he will want to pay us back, fair enough, we'll let him pay then put the money back in his hat, bit by bit,' he chuckled.

'I bruddy heard that you buggers,' Marco shouted and we both burst out laughing.

I arrived home just as Alice was getting the boys ready for bed. They demanded that I read them a story, the one that had become their favourite in recent weeks. A story about a rabbit with ears that could do magic things. In the story they particularly liked he turned a nasty old farmer into a worm for the day. I'm not sure that that sort of story is good for them but Alice says it is okay, so I suppose it is. After all, it certainly didn't seem to frighten them or give them nightmares, they just laughed.

With the boys settled down and our evening

meals over, we sat by the fire and chatted about the day we had had.

'Dick is getting very restless, hobbling around on his crutch not able to do much. Nelly bought him a jigsaw puzzle of a sailing ship to try to distract him, he tried to do it for about an hour, got it all wrong, got mad and threw it in the fire. Nelly got angry with him and now they're not talking. She was round here all morning, complaining about his moods and thinking he must have had a knock to the head,' Alice said with a shake of her head.

'Ought I to go around and chat with him for a few minutes?'

'If you want, but sit and tell me about your day my sweet,' she said and rested her hand on mine.

I told her about Marco's problem, and about talking to Joe Watson at the bottom of Marco's stairs, heading to replace his lock.

'Marco heard you talking! What happened when Joe got up to Marco's room?'

'I don't know, I skipped off a bit smartish,' I grinned.

'You coward, William Dexter!' she laughed.

9

Our appointment with Mr Hooper, the director of the secret project, was set for nine-thirty and the DI and I were on our way in patrol car PV1 normally driven by my pal Bong, but today driven by PC Goldman.

'I've booked the car for the rest of the day, since I propose to go and see the Adler's after we've done at the factory.'

'Have they rung in and made an appointment, sir?' I asked.

'They have not. I think we'll go and give them a little surprise, don't you?' he asked.

'I think you're right, sir,' I admitted.

We were met at the reception desk by the same young woman that we had seen before, and shown through to his office.

'Please take a seat gentlemen, can I offer you coffee?' he asked, and we both accepted.

'Clearly you still have a problem, so how can I help?'

'When we last spoke, you told us that you had been using Mr Bloor to continue providing information, false information to his German contacts, is that correct, sir?' the DI asked.

'That is correct, and I asked you to be discreet in your use of that knowledge,' he admitted.

'I can assure you that we have treated it with the utmost discretion, sir. That is why we are here now to ask if some information we have found in Bloor's possession derived from you. DC Dexter here has an engineering background and he is unhappy about what we have found!'

'Unhappy! In what way, DC Dexter?'

'It seems to me that what we have found is genuine information. I'm no expert in aircraft engines, but this seems like proper working drawings,' I said.

'I had to make sure that what we supplied was at least feasible; the other side would soon realise that what they were being fed was pure bilge-water if it didn't at least look realistic. As you might imagine it has been something of a nightmare trying to run, in effect two projects, a real one and a believable fake. Are you at liberty to show me what you have found?' he asked, with a frown.

The DI opened his briefcase and spread the photographs we had found in Bloor's shed across his desk. Hooper picked up one of them, studied it for a few moments before opening a drawer and extracting a magnifying glass. Having examined it with great care, he put it down and picked up another, scrutinising it again with the glass. All the time his face was draining in colour and his eyes became wide and unblinking. Quickly he shuffled through the rest of the pile, stopping occasionally to give some feature special examination. He seemed particularly interested in the photographs that showed the actual parts in their dismantled form.

'You found these in Bloor's possession?' he asked.

'Mr Bloor is of course dead. However, they

195

were in his shed-cum-darkroom. You seem perturbed, sir.'

There was a knock on the door.

'Yes, what is it?' he shouted.

'Your coffee, sir.'

Quickly he gathered the photos into a pile and turned them face down, 'Come!' he shouted. The tray was placed on his desk and the girl poured three cups, he thanked her and she left.

'Please help yourselves to milk, sugar, biscuits,' he said, shuffling through the photos again and shaking his head.

'I hate to admit it, but these photographs are in fact what DC Dexter suspected. They are current working drawings, and pictures of the actual component parts. Bloor can only have got these from someone in the experimental development division, or perhaps from our precision casting section. This is most perturbing, it means our rivals are neck and neck with us in developing a high performance aero engine.'

'How far advanced is the engine, sir,' I asked.

'It was flown secretly last week at er... I'd better not tell you where, but it performed slightly below expectations, but not beyond a final twiddle and tweak. So, in answer to your question, the bloody thing's as good as finished.'

'And the Germans are a stone's throw behind!' the DI suggested.

'With these they can only be a very short throw, yes!' he said, placing his elbows on the desk and resting his head in his hands.

'This is definitely not the information you were authorising Bloor to pass on?'

'Most certainly not! How it came into his possession I hate to think,' he said and clicked a switch on what was clearly an internal intercom set. 'Janice, would you ask Mr Barton to come to my office, please?'

"Yes, sir," the electronic voice at the other end replied.

'I need to get to the bottom of this pretty damned quickly' he said, turning back to us. Before he could make any further comments, the intercom buzzed.

'Yes.'

"I'm sorry sir Mr Barton is not in today, sir. He rang in sick this morning. It seems he complained of some sort of tummy upset, sir."

'I see. Thank you Janice,' he said. 'In that case would you ask Mr Jackson to come here, please?'

"Certainly, sir."

'You heard that I suppose?' he asked and we both nodded.

'Mr Jackson is Mr Barton's assistant, hopefully he may be able the shed some light on what is going on.'

'I realise how distressing this must be for you, but our only interest is finding Mr Bloor's killer. We think that he was passing information to a Mr Adler, a German gentleman, I believe the name mean something to you, sir?' the DI asked.

'Mr Barton asked me that, as DC Dexter had suggested the name. I told him that I remembered a Mr Adler as part of a trade delegation about six years ago. Did he pass that on to you?' Hooper asked.

'Yes sir, he suggested that you especially remembered the name as it means sea eagle in German,' I nodded.

'That's not strictly true, Adler means eagle, and

197

is often used for any large bird of prey. However, I personally always think of it as referring to a fish eagle. It was what my grandfather called them, and the name stuck in my mind,' he nodded and told us a little about his grandfather's life as a committed angler.

The intercom buzzed, 'Yes, Janice?'

'Mr Jackson is here, sir.'

'Show him in please.'

There was a tap on the door and Mr Jackson entered the room.

'Take a seat Jeff,' Hooper nodded.

'Thank you, sir.'

'I understand Mr Barton has rung in sick.'

'So I believe, sir, he said he was feeling a bit off colour last night, as he left sir.'

'I see. What do you make of these?' Hooper asked pushing the photos across his desk towards Jackson.

'Could I borrow the glass a moment please, sir?' he asked and Hooper passed it to him.

'They seem to be photographs of the current drawings, sir,' he said.

'The current, working drawings?'

'I'd say so, yes sir.'

'Then have you any idea how these photographs happen to be in the possession of Richard Bloor?'

'Richard Bloor? Oh, Dick Bloor the chap that collapsed years ago, took early retirement?'

'That's the chap! How could he have these photos?' Mr Hooper asked and Jackson slowly shook his head, then after some thought he replied.

'There is one possibility, but I don't like to even mention it, sir!'

'This is important, sir. Whatever you know or even suspect, might have got Mr Bloor killed,' the DI pointed out.

'Yes, if you know anything, please tell us,' Hooper agreed.

'I think Mr Barton and Mr Bloor must have kept in touch after Dick retired. I recall two or three years ago, one night I was on my way home. I used to catch the trolley bus to the Spot in Derby, then walk up Babbington Lane to my home on Burton Road. Well, this particular night I got off the trolley, fancying a pint. It had been a really hot day, June or July I think it was, and I had a real good thirst on me. I crossed the spot and went into the Cheshire Cheese, but they were out of bitter ale, so I went to the Green Man, a bit expensive, but like I said I had a thirst on me.'

'I assume this is going somewhere, Jeff?' Mr Hooper asked.

'Yes sir, just setting the scene so to speak. Well whom do I see in there but Mr Barton and Dick, Dick Bloor. They were deep in conversation, sitting at one of the tables over by the window. Now to me it seemed odd, I often meet folk I remember from the past in pubs, we stand at the bar and chat of this and that, know what I mean. This pair were discussing something they obviously wanted to be on their own with. When they saw me, they had a quick word together, like they had been caught out in something they wanted kept secret. Anyway they called me over. I went and said hello, to be sociable like, then I made an excuse swallowed me pint and went. I admit, I did wonder what was going on, I suppose that's why I remember the incident.'

'You only saw them the once?' the DI asked.

'It was hot again the next day, but the Cheshire had its bitter on again so I didn't go in the Green Man again. Not been in since.'

'Jeff, are you suggesting that Mr Barton was passing this information to Mr Bloor?' Mr Hooper asked.

'Well sir, he's always the one who sees everyone else off the department each day, stays and locks up! Easy to take a few snaps before you go.'

'That's a very strong accusation, Jeff.'

'Can't think of anything else, sir.'

'Thank you, Jeff. For the moment, please keep what we have talked about under you hat, most important that it stays in this room.'

'Right, sir,' he said and went.

'When I first spoke to Mr Barton, he pretended not to know Mr Bloor, sir,' I said to Hooper.

'Why would he do that, I wonder!'

'Perhaps he was trying to reduce the possibility of becoming involved in whatever was going on,' the DI suggested.

'I can't believe that Mr Barton, a trusted employee, would betray the company like this. Though what other explanation can there be?' Hooper said, shaking his head.

'Sir, can I assure you that what we have learned here, today, will be treated with the utmost discretion and used solely in as much as it bears on the murder of Mr Bloor,' the DI said.

'Thank god for that! If this were to become common knowledge our customers would be most perturbed.'

'I assume you are thinking of your military customers?'

'Of course, engines out in the general commercial world are free and open to be inspected wherever they may happen to be. Those in military use are subject to the maximum of security.

There is a glimmer of hope in the situation, a colleague at one of the airframe companies has hinted that their latest design, still a deep-dark secret, will require an engine of a radical design. Although the original Air Ministry specification remains unchanged, it is a minimum specification. Anything that can exceed it will be looked at very favourably.'

'What you are saying is that a new aeroplane is being developed that means the engine you have just completed, is already out of date? In that case, it would mean, that your German competitors are already behind. Is that correct, sir?' I asked.

'You are very perceptive, DC Dexter. We are constantly looking to improve our existing engines, but also looking into the future to create ground breaking designs to keep us ahead of the opposition,' he grinned. 'Again, please treat my last remarks with the utmost secrecy, gentlemen,' he added and we both agreed.

'I wonder which is the more difficult, trying to unravel secrets, as we do, or trying to create them and run with them as Hooper has tried to do?' the DI said with a shake of his head as we settled back into the patrol car.

'I think trying to unravel them is a lot more fun, sir.'

'Interesting though that was, we are still no nearer deciding who killed cock robin.'

'Mr Barton has gone missing just as suspicion arises that someone in his department has been providing real information to Bloor. He has to be the prime suspect and I think Mr Hooper thought so too,' I suggested.

'That's how it came across to me as well, Dexter!'

'If Bloor was feeding genuine information to Adler, surely Bloor's death would deal a blow to Adler's plans, sir.'

'Making him a lot less likely to have killed Bloor, I agree, but we can't count him out, we still need a word. By the way, did you find out if Adler's cottage is on the same water supply as the Bloor house?' the DI asked.

'It didn't occur to me sir.'

'Tut-tut, Dexter.'

'Sorry, sir.'

'We'll attempt to get a sample of their water when we're there.'

'Mrs Tooley, the Adler's housekeeper, should be able to provide a small bottle for us, sir.'

'Or we could just ask the water company if they supply Stone Haven Cottage.'

'That might be easier, sir.'

'This Mrs Tooley, how did she come across to you?'

'I think she's a very shrewd woman, she suspects that something is going on, but wise enough to keep her own counsel. At the same time I think she would be keeping her eyes and ears open, gathering information,' I said.

'You don't see her as a gossip?'

'I think she would find it difficult to gossip, the

cottage is over a mile from the village, and I couldn't see another house anywhere near,' I grinned, just as a violent explosion, like rifle shot nearby, shook the car. The car continued to shake, zigzagging across the narrow country lane as the driver slowed the vehicle and eventually stopped it at the side of the road.

'I think we've got a puncture, sir,' PC Goldman said.

'We rather gathered that! Can you deal with it?' the DI asked, as we both got out.

'Yes sir, but it'll take a minute or two.'

'Leave you to it then. Come on Dexter, we might as well lean on this gate.'

Once again the weather was warm, comfortably warm, not the heavy and sultry stuff we'd been having of late but pleasant with a hint of a gentle breeze. In the field we were looking at, a small herd of cows were lying down chewing the cud. Lazily, I opened the conversation.

'We've already suggested that Bloor's death might be inconvenient for Adler, but that doesn't necessarily count him out. What if Bloor was becoming greedy, asking for more money, or perhaps threatening to expose Adler?'

'Good point, Dexter. On the other hand, what if Adler, recognising that the engine was as good as done, killed Bloor to cover his tracks,' the DI suggested.

'Killing Bloor would make sense in that case and meantime Mr Hooper thinks that all Adler knows is what he has fed to Bloor.'

'That puts Adler right back in the frame,' the DI nodded. 'How long for that wheel, Constable?'

'About ten minutes, sir,'

'Make it eight.'

Expecting to have to open the Adler's field gate wide enough to admit the car I was surprised to see it stood fully open. Arriving at the cottage, two cars were already there; a dark grey Daimler stood under the lean-to, presumably the Adler's vehicle; a large black Morris had pulled up in a careless way, blocking the drive, meaning we had to walk the last few yards to the front door. We left PC Goldman with the car in case it became necessary to move it. As we reached the door it opened silently even before we rang the bell, a tall woman with a thin slightly severe face stood looking at us. She attempted a welcoming smile but missed her desired effect by a mile.

'Mrs Tooley told me to expect you. We should have rung you to make an appointment but we have both been rather busy. Please come in,' she said, with a rather theatrical wave of her hand. Her mouth continued to smile a welcome, but her eyes did not.

'Thank you,' we both said, and she stood aside for us to enter.

'I'm Detective Constable Dexter, I called and spoke to Mrs Tooley yesterday and this is Detective Inspector Brierly.'

'I am Gertrude Adler. Mrs Tooley has asked for the day off, but she said that you wanted to speak to my husband, she assumed it was about that poor man Mr Bloor,' she said, closing the door.

'Just a few questions, Mrs Adler, nothing of great importance, just trying to fill in the man's background, you understand,' the DI nodded.

'You'd better come through to my husband's

office,' she said, turning to lead the way. She opened the office door, and again stood aside to allow us to enter, then followed us in.

Two men in identical suits, trilby hats plonked un-ceremoniously on their heads, presumably the occupants of the Morris, sat bound and gagged in chairs hidden to us until the door had closed. A third man, I guessed to be Mr Adler, stood over them with a handgun that I recognised as a German Luger pistol.

'Good afternoon, gentlemen. As you can see we were half expecting you!' the man said in a faintly German accent, turning the gun on us and smiling the smile of a person whose plan has come to fruition.

'Give me the pistol Erik, and tie them up,' the woman said and Adler passed it to her after moving us either side of the two other occupants.

'We only were expecting two visitors. I am sorry I am without more chairs, so I also regret you must stand,' he smiled, taking a length of rope from his desk, and began to tie the DI to the side of one of the chairs, whilst Mrs Adler covered us with the pistol. She spoke to Adler in German, so I had no idea what was said, but he nodded at me.

'PC Dexter, please go and move the black car it seems to be blocking our escape,' Mrs Adler snarled. 'Do not try to alert your driver or I will personally kill your Detective Inspector,' she added.

'I'm sorry, I can't drive,' I lied.

'Then you had better learn very quickly,' she said and held the gun to the DI's head.

'Okay… okay!' I agreed.

'Move it past the front door up to the hedge, then get your driver to bring your car in alongside it and tell the driver to follow you in. If I even suspect that you try to alert him, I will shoot your Inspector, then these two men, followed by you and your driver. Erik also has a pistol and will assist in the task,' Mrs Adler grinned, and Adler slapped the bulging pocket of his jacket.

'Why are you doing this Mrs Adler? All we wanted was the answer to a few questions about a chap called Bloor, who we think you know,' I said vainly hoping to get a reprieve.

'Which, we would have answered; however as you see these two men – we thought they were you, but they are in fact members of your military intelligence arrived half an hour ago, accusing us of spying. Fortunately, they underestimated our readiness! Your arrival complicates matters. Your police driver remaining outside causes a further problem,' Mrs Adler shrugged. 'Now, DC Dexter, if you would be so kind?' she added waving the gun about menacingly. I nodded.

She followed me to the front door and stood looking out smiling another *welcome* smile as I moved the Morris then walked over to where our driver could see me and waved him into the space Mrs Adler had suggested. Once he had parked, I used the usual beckoning finger to invite him into the cottage. The poor chap came in without the least suspicion that anything was wrong.

'Here, what's this?' PC Goldman said as he realised the situation and made a lunge for Mrs Adler's pistol. He was swift but she was swifter. As he grabbed the gun, she snatched it away and it went off, either as a result of the tussle or because she deliberately pulled the trigger. Either way it went off and the bullet went through Goldman's upper chest and shoulder, splattering

206

blood and bits of bone over the seated men, and embedding itself into the wall, narrowly missing the chap on the right. Goldman staggered for a moment then sank slowly to the floor with wide-eyed groan. Blood began to seep onto the grey carpet of the office.

'Our escape is now clear, Erik! Tie up DC Dexter and let us be on our way,' Mrs Alder snapped.

'Let me see what I can do for Constable Goldman,' I yelled, moving towards him.

'Stay where you are,' she snapped, waving the pistol menacingly.

'We should kill them all,' Adler suggested, placing his pistol on the floor within reach of his wife and moving me to the side of the other chair.

'I suppose so,' she said and felt in her pocket for a neat, screw-on silencer. 'We have spare petrol, we can simply burn the place!' she laughed.

'Don't move, Mrs Adler, drop the gun,' said Mrs Tooley, appearing silently on shoe-less feet behind Mrs Adler. Mrs Adler gave a sudden jerk, and the look of surprise on her face proved she could feel a gun against her ribs.

'Don't move please Mr Adler I am as willing to use this as you would be. DC Dexter collect Mr Adler's gun please,' she said, nodding to the one on the floor. 'Er… Mrs Adler, hand your gun, butt first to DC Dexter. Pass it to me please DC Dexter,' she nodded and I did as she demanded.

'That feels much more effective than the handle of a wooden spoon,' she said, dropping the kitchen spoon to the floor.

'Bloody hell,' the DI said, Adler snarled something in German and Mrs Adler gave the housekeeper a look of sheer hatred.

'Mr Adler, tie your wife up please,' Mrs Tooley said.

With Mrs Adler, looking very sorry for herself tied hand and foot, and sitting on the floor, I took PC Goldman's handcuffs and secured Adler's hands behind his back, and tied his feet. Then I went to give PC Goldman what assistance I could. As I turned him onto his uninjured side, I could see the extent of his injuries. There seemed to be a blood pumping and I was at a loss to know what to do. Thankfully with the Adler's out of action, Mrs Tooley had rushed to the office cupboard found a first-aid kit and begun to deal with him as best she could.

As I untied DI Brierly, PC Goldman began to stir. The two chair bound hostages began to mumble their displeasure at being left until last.

'I'm Detective Inspector Brierly, and these people hold vital information in my murder enquiry. Who the hell are you?' the DI asked, as I passed him the pistol that Mrs Tooley had given me when she knelt by PC Goldman.

'About bloody time,' said the first one as his gag was removed, 'I am not prepared to divulge our names, however we are agents of MI5!'

'I'm afraid I must push you to prove your identity,' the DI shrugged. 'We as you see, seem to be holding all of the cards,' he added nodding towards the pistols we both held.

'Very well, but to you alone Inspector,' he said and pulled a small business type card from his pocket and held it for the DI to inspect. Whatever the card contained, it definitely impressed him, as did the second chap's card once he had also been released.

'As you can see Inspector, we outrank you and since we were here to question Mr and Mrs Adler, though that of course is not their real names, on a charge of military spying I think our aims also outrank yours. However, it saddens me to have to admit, that I have no power of arrest since the establishment of Special Branch. They, rather than assisting us in our work, seem to see us as a rival to be thwarted. They were supposed to assist us in this matter but unfortunately seem to have failed to materialise. I must therefore ask you to carry out that task for me, Inspector.'

'That will not be necessary, Inspector,' Mrs Tooley said. 'I am a member of Special Branch and have been here for the last six years. Although a minor operative of the branch, I do hold powers of arrest,' she grinned.

'Before you make your arrest, would it be possible for me to question them with regard to what they know about the death of Richard Sidney Bloor?'

'I had that man in my sights for ages. He's been coming here regularly over the past six years, passing first rate information to these two. Since his information is vital to their work, I would doubt if Bloor's death has anything to do with them. Very soon, I had enough information on them to have made an arrest, but my masters were interested in their other espionage activities and decided to let them continue, whilst I gathered more information. Unfortunately, the death of Mr Bloor complicated matters somewhat. When I showed them the piece in the paper from my *sister,* they went into a huddle in here damning the man's stupidity. In German of course, thinking I wouldn't understand. So ask your

questions by all means inspector,' Mrs Tooley, or whoever she was, said.

'Mr Adler what can you tell me about the man
we've just mentioned?' the DI asked.

'I cannot see any reason why I should provide
you with any answers that might help to put me behind
bars,' Adler said.

'We already know that the person in question
was passing information to you on a regular basis, he
admitted as much to his brother, adding to the information we already had from another source. We also
believe that the information he was bringing to you was
as good as useless and that you killed him in revenge for
making you look a fool in front of your masters!' the DI
said, bluffing on what we actually knew.

'The fat fool, Bloor?'

'Yes, I understand you made contact with him
after a trade visit to Rolls Royce?'

'He took no, er, persuading. The offer of two
hundred pounds every time he brought me useful information made it simple. The fool did not even try to bar-
gain haggle, as you say,' Adler sneered.

'He agreed to help, just for the cash?' the DI
asked.

'You English are fools, showing us around your
factories, allowing us to ask questions: open and friendly
fools. You think that everyone will play the game the
English way, play by the rules. Yet do you not also have
a saying "Rules are made to be broken"?'

'What part did you play in his killing?'

'Why would I kill him? He laid the golden egg
for my masters, but for me also. I was authorised to pay
him three hundred and fifty pound but the fool settled for

two hundred. In any case the man died in a picture house, fifteen miles from here, it said so in the newspaper!'

'That's right, he did.'

'And as for his information it was first class, my masters in the Fatherland were more than happy with it,' he sneered.

'Are you saying you pocketed the other hundred and fifty pounds?' the DI asked.

'There you go again Inspector, the Englishman playing by the rules. My masters would not even begin to worry where the money went, the secrets of a world class company are worth many thousands.' He said, as I telephoned for an ambulance.

'Were you aware that Mr Bloor was a diabetic?'

'That I did know; he showed me the syringe and all of the other equipment he had to carry, the size of a woman's handbag. I informed my masters and they provided the latest German equipment, able to fit in his jacket pocket, also a supply of insulin. Further proving, I think that keeping him alive was vital to our work,' he grinned. 'Also I was able to suggest, from information received from the manufacturers, how to adjust the insulin measure to suit his eating. One of the rules he put on his participation was that we provided him with a midday meal. It seems his wife was very strict with his food. We met his needs, of course,' the German grinned.

'Did he ever inject himself, when he was here?' I asked.

'No, never here. Are you suggesting that the fat fool forgot to inject himself with insulin?'

'Something like that, yes,' I said and the DI nodded.

'Then, the man killed himself by his own stupidity,' Adler said contemptuously.

'Mrs Tooley, could you provide us with a sample of tap water, please?' I asked.

'I can, but why?' she asked, and I explained.

'You're wasting your time, when the quarry was being excavated they came across a natural spring, I understand the water has fed the cottage ever since.'

'There's no connection to the mains?'

'None, the water here is as good, perhaps better than the supply to the village.'

'Could I have one, so we can eliminate it?'

'Of course if it will help, I'll find you a bottle,' she said and led me to the kitchen.

With the Adler's arrested, no doubt making them available should we need to ask any more questions, and PC Goldman on his way to Crammingdon General, our work there seemed to be done.

'Ah, Dexter, we have a car and no driver.'

'Yes, sir,' I agreed.

'You can drive,' he grinned.

'Yes.'

'I need to learn.'

'Ah.'

'What's so difficult? You know how – teach me.'

'Before I can do that, I'll need to get used to a powerful patrol car. The last time I drove a fast car I ended up with a smashed up car and an injured passenger.'

'Ah! Then *you* drive, I'll just watch. Bloody slowly, Dexter!'

'Yes, sir.'

The car was surprisingly easy to drive. Mike, Mr Cox's mechanic had created a car that was smooth, with a sweet clutch and gear-change action, steered exactly where you placed it on the road, and I quickly fell in love with it.

'Okay Dexter, pull over and let me have a go,' the DI said. It seemed I had impressed him, and since it was a direct order, what else could I do?

'This is a main road, perhaps it might be wiser if I pulled off into the next side-road, sir?'

'No. This is a nice wide, straight bit, stop here.'

'Right, sir!' I reluctantly agreed and eased the car to a stop well into the side of the road.

With the DI in the driving seat, I explained the principles of getting the car moving, and more importantly, how to stop it.

'So now you can gently increase the engine speed and slowly bring up your clutch pedal, sir!' I said, ready for the worst. The car lurched a couple of feet and stalled.

'What happened?' he asked.

'You didn't give the engine enough revs, sir!'

Over the next twenty minutes, he created all of the faults that I had managed when learning, plus a few new ones, all his very own.

'I'm never going to get the hang of this, Dexter.'

'You will, sir. But I think it might be wise to let Mr Cox's showroom manager teach you, he got me into it in a couple of hours,' I said as we swopped places again.

'Mm, perhaps you are right. We've wasted enough time. Get us back to Whitecross Yard, and we'll

213

get another driver to take us back to Bloor's house.

The Assistant Chief Constable called DI Brierly into his office the instant we arrived at Whitecross Yard. I went up to the office, to find a message on the DI's desk. Wondering if it was something I could deal with in his absence I unfolded it. It was a note from the Desk Sergeant informing us that, whilst we were out, there had been a message from Codnor police station to the effect that the nosey neighbour across the road from the Bloor's had reported that she had again seen the car outside the house. It included a registration number and I set a search in motion with the Vehicle Taxation Departments in Derbyshire and Nottinghamshire.

The DI returned to the office just on half past four.

'That didn't go too well,' he said and slumped into his chair. Taking the hint, I put the kettle on and rinsed the mugs.

'Not happy about PC Goldman being injured, sir?'

'He asked for a full written report on his desk first thing in the morning.'

'You were in there a long time, sir. He must have been pretty unhappy!'

'He was unhappy that an officer had been shot in the line of duty, of course. However, we had a lengthy discussion on many aspects of policing. He has some interesting ideas on the way forward as he puts it. Mr Cox will be a happy chappy, one of the suggestions is an increase in the motorised fleet. I suggested that we needed a replacement driver for our visit to the Bloor home this afternoon but he said the CID cars would be in the yard first thing in the morning and you could perform as my driver until I have gained sufficient skill.'

'Leaving it until tomorrow, now then, sir?' I said as he picked up the note.

'Have you seen this note, Dexter?'

'Yes, sir. I've started a search on the number plate, stressing that it could be important in a murder enquiry. I hope I've done right, sir!'

'Any idea when we are likely to get an answer?'

'Both Derbyshire and Nottinghamshire agreed to try to get back to us today, sir!'

'Good work, Dexter.'

'Thank you, sir.'

'Any thoughts, about who was calling on Mrs Bloor, in her husband's absence?'

'Still calling on her, now that she's a widow, sir.'

'Indeed. That number trace should prove interesting, Dexter.

'Yes, sir,' I said as the kettle came to the boil.

'Are the Assistant Chief's ideas anything you can share with me, sir?' I asked as we sat with our tea mugs.

'Surprisingly enough one of his most interesting ideas is a way to reduce the amount of paperwork we have to fill in every day. I will certainly welcome that with open arms, if it ever happens of course.'

'A move in the right direction, certainly, sir.'

'His other idea that caught my interest was motorcycle patrols, replacing pedal cycles where possible, but that will have to wait until the funding is available.'

'That seems a good idea.' I said. As the DI made to leave the office the phone on his desk rang.

'You get that, Dexter. I need a pee.'

215

'Right, sir,' I picked up the phone and introduced myself, explaining that the DI wasn't available.

'Armstrong, here, I've another puzzle for you and your boss,' he tittered.

'I'm sure that will please him, Dr Armstrong,' I smiled.

'Your tramp, Norfolk Jimmy, isn't!'

'Isn't? Isn't, what?'

'Isn't a tramp. The first thing we do is to wash the corpse. Normally in the case of er… gentlemen of the road, it is no easy task, dirt and bodily functions are ingrained in the skin, almost tanning it. However not in this case; on removing his clothing, I found a well-cared-for body, clean and free from the usual fleas and lice I would have expected to see. Yes, those areas that are visible, hands, face, hair, give a very good impression of neglect, but that's just it, an impression. I didn't think to analyse what the colourant was, my assistant had washed it off and of course it drained away, but my guess would be some sort of non-greasy stage make-up.'

'He was pretending to be a tramp?' I suggested.

'Most definitely, I can't see why, but then that's your problem. I'll put it all in a report; you'll have it in the morning.'

'Thank you Dr Armstrong,' I said.

DS Whittington, with the DI in overall control, was actually processing Norfolk Jimmy's case, so I gave the DI Dr Armstrong's message as soon as he returned.

'That certainly adds to what Whittington had come up with. I think it's time to look at that suitcase! Where did he put it?'

'I thought he was going to put it under your desk, sir.'

'So he was. I wonder where the hell it is.'

There was a knock on the door, and Mr Cox poked his head into the room.

'Your two motors are awaiting your inspection, Detective Inspector,' he smiled.

'Come on Dexter, let's go and take another look.'

We made our way to the back yard, and Mr Cox gave us a few suggestions on using them; daily checks and not letting the fuel tank run too low.

'I can't see what you gain by providing these vehicles practically for nothing,' the DI said.

'That's easy! Firstly, my insurance on the garage only allows me to keep fifty vehicles there at any one time. I like to keep about half a dozen less than that, so that I have a bit of emergency space. These two have been hanging around unsold for three or four months, like I said, and I need the room,' he said pointing to the neat little saloon's we had already seen. 'But, if I'm really honest, it's a sprat to catch a mackerel, I know the Chief Constable is considering extending his fleet, and I want the business!' he grinned, as the driver of the Ford handed me the sets of keys.

'I can't fault that!' the DI nodded. 'I've chosen the Singer and Dexter is going to be my driver.'

'A good choice, but they are both reliable motors, I don't think you'll be disappointed.'

'Your salesman taught Dexter here to drive, could he do the same for me?' the DI asked.

'I don't see why not! Doesn't Mr Dexter fancy the job?' he smiled.

'He hasn't driven a lot since he learned, and your chap is used to teaching your customers!'

217

'True, leave it to me, I'll get it arranged. I assume evenings would suit you the best?' Cox asked and the DI nodded.

A large Daimler saloon wafted silently into the yard and turned around.

'That's our lift back. Enjoy your newfound mobility!' Cox grinned, as the car drove off.

'Perhaps we should give it a trial run, sir?' I suggested.

'Tomorrow will be soon enough, we need to find that suitcase.'

'DS Whittington suggested that Norfolk Jimmy is, was, well known for carrying out confidence trickery. Why has he never been caught?' I asked.

'I admit I was wondering that. Perhaps Whittington can shed a bit of light on it, and tell us where that bloody suitcase is.'

Alice had made another steak and kidney pie, the mouth-watering smell drifted down the entry as I pushed my bike from the road. The day had again been warm, and she had taken the boys and Nelly's two girls up to Edmund's Seat, a flattened area on the hill overlooking our part of Crammingdon. There's a seat, as the name suggests, several in fact, and a lovely safe area where the kids of the neighbourhood can play, whilst the mothers   chat.

'It was lovely up there this afternoon, all the kids played hide and seek. The boys are worn out and ready for bed,' she smiled, giving me a peck of a kiss.

'You can tell we've been married a couple of years. Is that all I get after a hard day at work?'

'You'll have to wait and see,' she winked.

'Fair enough!' I grinned. 'Now where's that steak and kidney pie?'

There was a knock at the door and after a moment Nelly let herself in. I'm not certain that I like that part of the local folklore, being a police officer I am often called on to advise people on personal security matters, but it was the norm in the area, so I let it go.

'Evening, Nelly. What can we do for you?' I asked.

'Oh, thank goodness you're home. Dick is hopping mad about what's happened, could you pop down and have a word with him?' she replied.

'Go on, but don't be long, the potatoes will be done in five minutes,' Alice said.

Dick sat in his fireside chair, not that there was a fire on such a hot evening, with a face that Dad always said looked like "someone who has lost a pound and found a penny".

'Evening, Dick. Why the glum face?' I asked.

'This came in the afternoon post,' he said handing me an official looking letter. 'It's from the company whose van knocked me off my bike.'

'Ah, are they refusing to pay out?' I asked as I unfolded it.

'They are trying to make out that it was my fault. Reckoned I rode out in front of the van without looking properly,' he shrugged, and I have to admit it wondered at the time if Dick had perhaps been partially to blame. I read the letter. 'According to this, not only are they not prepared to pay you anything in the way of compensation, they are claiming damages from you for repairs to their van and disruption to their delivery schedule,' I said.

'That's how I read it, too. Cheeky buggers!'

'I think it's a try-on, Dick. Their driver admitted to me at the time that he was looking down at is delivery sheet and didn't see you.'

'That should be good enough then if you tell them that.'

'Mm, there might be a problem, Dick I was off duty at the time hadn't signed on yet that morning.'

'You took charge of the situation, Nelly said so.'

'It's one of those strange situations, I'm a police officer, I'm expected to give assistance and guidance, even when I'm off duty, but not actually official until I've signed in for my shift.'

'So what he told you carries no more weight that if he'd told the grocers cat.'

'Well, as much weight as if he'd told any other neighbour. There's another problem, if it ever came to court it would come out that our two families are friends,' I pointed out.

'Oh, bloody hell. I was banking on getting a bit of cash to repair my bike and pay for the rent and food and stuff.'

'I've got a couple of suggestions that might help your case. You said that the driver of the van visited you in hospital.'

'That he did. All apologetic, said he hadn't seen me until too late.'

'You said that he had told you that his employer had given him a reprimand for disobeying company rules.'

'That's right, lucky not to have lost his job, he admitted.'

'Did anyone hear him say that, a nurse or a doctor or anyone?' I asked.

'No, but the chap in the next bed heard it all, said I was lucky he hadn't killed me, when the chap had gone.'

'Did he give you his name?'

'The driver or the chap in the next bed?'

'The chap in the next bed.'

'He did but I can't remember it.'

'Well I suggest you get your brain into gear and try, because he's an independent witness, and could swing the thing for you,' I said though, I wasn't absolutely sure his testimony would count.

'Mm, you said two suggestions!'

'Are you a union member?'

'Yes, though the company don't recognise the union, we have no rep in the factory.'

'Go directly to your union, and see if they will take on the case. Alternatively, go and see your employer and show them this letter, they could well make a counter claim for loss of your time and expertise.'

'Time and expertise, bloody hell, that's a good one,' he grinned.

'Fire with fire, Dick, that's the best I can offer. Now I've a steak and kidney pie needing my attention.'

'I think I'll have the best chance with my employer, they're pretty fair. Thanks Will.'

Nelly came in just as I was leaving.

'You'll have to make do with mashed potatoes they were starting to go into the water,' Alice said, as I came through the back door. 'Nelly says that Dick isn't going to get any compensation for his accident.'

'I've suggested a couple of things that might…'

10

DS Whittington was in the office when I arrived next morning, looking at the suitcase in question.

'Morning Sarge. The DI was looking for that last night,' I said nodding at the case.

'I thought it would be in the way under his desk, so I moved it down to the front desk, much to the desk sergeant's annoyance,' he grinned. 'I've just staggered back up with it, it weights a ton.'

'What's in it?' I asked.

'I haven't managed to open it yet, but I've brought this from home,' he said, holding up a large screwdriver. 'If the DI agrees I'll give it a bit of brute force.'

'That sounds like him now,' I nodded, as his familiar footfall sounded on the stairs.

'Morning, my merry men. Ah, the suitcase,' he said as we both wished him good morning. DS Whittington explained where it had been and produced the screwdriver.

'You are sure that this belongs to Norfolk Jimmy?' the DI asked.

'In his railway locker, sir.'

'Good enough. Open it, sergeant.'

'It's a very nice case, it's a shame to damage the

locks,' I said.

'Have you got a better idea, Dexter?'

'I could carefully drill the rivets out, sir.'

'How long would that take?'

'About twenty minutes, sir. Once I've borrowed a hand drill.'

'Twenty minutes! Give it some screwdriver, Whittington.'

'Right, sir,' he said and in a couple of seconds the lid was open and the case as good as destroyed.

'Well, who'd have thought that?' the DI said, with a shake of his head.

The case contained beautifully laundered shirts, trousers and underwear and as DS Whittington carefully lifted them out, he found a thin leather briefcase hidden among the clothes.

'Better have a look in there, don't you think Detective Sergeant?'

'Oh yes, I think so, sir,' he said unbuckling the securing straps and tipping the contents on to our shared desk.

For the second time in as many days, we found ourselves looking at a little stack of five-pound notes.

'Some tramp,' the DI exclaimed.

'It rather adds to the belief that he was a confidence trickster,' Whittington nodded.

'I wonder what's in there?' I asked, pointing to a leather pouch that had been rather overshadowed by the cash find.

'Not a bad little haul,' the DI said, picking it up and tipping out two good quality gold pocket watches, a gold wristwatch and strap, and several gold and silver rings. More importantly from the point of view of deciding the man's real name, was a Lloyds Bank savings book in the name of Sylvester Barclay, with a total of four hundred and fifty one pounds entered on the last page.

'I wonder who that is, sir?' I asked pointing to a paper label pasted into the lid of the case.

'Mm, Mrs Mable Bretton. Not him then.'

Below the name was an address in Towcester, Northamptonshire and a telephone number.

'I wonder what she can tell us about how Norfolk Jimmy came to have possession of her suitcase,' the DI said. 'Give her a call Whittington and get on to Lloyds Bank to find out what they can tell us.

Come on Dexter, we need to call on the widow Bloor.'

DS Whittington picked up the phone as we headed downstairs to try out the Singer saloon. As we crossed the yard to the car Tom Greatorix, reporter for the *Argus* our local newspaper, was leaning against the bicycle shed.

'Good morning, Detective Inspector.'

'Morning, Tom! You're about bright and early.'

'I just thought I'd refresh your memory, we had, if I remember correctly, an agreement. You asked for my help identifying an unknown man who died in the local fleapit. I arranged for our staff artist to do a line drawing of the man from a visit to the local morgue; the chap's not been the same since, I hasten to add. I believe the front page picture created the desired effect, is that right, Tom?'

'It did, and thank you.'

'Our agreement was that you'd keep me up to date with developments in the case, am I right?'

'As soon as there is anything I am able to release, you'll be the first to know.'

'You had several responses to the picture, so did we. I happen to know that the person in question in one Richard Sidney Bloor, a retired engineer with a highly prestigious local company. Would you care to comment Detective Inspector?'

'Your information is correct. However, at the moment that information is part of an ongoing investigation. As soon as I am able to give you a further bit of information rest assured that I will,' the DI blustered.

'Mm, sources tell me that Mr R S Bloor was in regular contact with a German couple, a Mr and Mrs… er…' He referred to his notebook 'Adler. Is that correct?'

'I can't comment on that,' the DI said.

'Ah – then I'm right. I have a young reporter, trainee you know, a bright lad. He happened to be at the "Royal" yesterday, visiting a sick aunt, when in rushes an ambulance carrying an injured police office er…' Again, he looked at his notebook. '…a PC Goldman, with gunshot injuries. Like I said he's a smart lad, he interviewed the ambulance crew and low and behold, he found out that you and DC Dexter here were at the Adler's cottage, and that they, the Adler's were taken into custody. Am I right so far?'

'Tom, this is an ongoing investigation. You know I can't comment on it until it is more conclusive.'

'They were, as I said, arrested. However, they are not here at the nick. Where are they then I thought, my enquiries came upon a brick wall. No one knows where they are or what has happened to them. My newshound nose started twitching as you might imagine. So, I

225

went to see Mr Bloor's wife. Who should be there but her brother-in-law, a window cleaner; he said you two have been sniffing around and confiscated some photos. Sniff, sniff, ferret, ferret – put two and two together and come up with a story.'

'Bloody hell, Tom. Don't bugger my case up, this is big. I'll tell you this, but it's not for print, yet.

'Understood!'

'The Adler's were arrested by Special Branch. They were taken away from under our noses, even though we are treating Bloor's death as murder.'

'Mm, the window cleaner reckons that his brother was passing on information about a new engine that is being developed, to this Adler couple, assisting in their commercial spying. The Adler's realise, that the authorities Special Branch, MI5 or whoever, are closing in and they kill Bloor to cover their tracks. That's the basis of my story. However I'll shelve it, for the moment at least. Don't wait too long before you let me in on the reality, the national dailies are beginning to get interested.'

'Alright, again this is not for print yet.'

'Agreed.'

'A Special Branch arrest, isn't like a copper nicking a burglar. They can whisk a suspect away, and er... take whatever steps they think necessary to effect an exchange of information.'

'Bloody hell, are you talking torture?'

'I wouldn't go that far but, intensive interrogation,' the DI said.

'So you don't know where they've been taken?'

'I do not. And I'll tell you something else, I don't bloody want to know! Contrary to what your little

226

imagined story suggests, I don't now think that the Adler's were responsible for Bloor's death. That being the case, the least I know about Special bloody Branch the better I like it.'

'Oh. I see. In that case I've got to rethink it,' the news hound said, with a scratch of his chin. 'Bugger!'

'I will leave you with a small clue,' the DI grinned.

'Go on then.'

'Tap water!' the DI chuckled.

'You what?'

'Tap water, Tom. You know, the stuff we drink and wash in; although in your case, I'll give the second part of that statement the benefit of doubt. Good morning, happy news gathering,' he grinned.

'I bloody hate you Detective Inspector Thomas Brierly!' he said with a shake of his head.

'Mutual, I'm sure. See you in "The Nags" tomorrow lunchtime, I might well have something to interest you by then.'

'If I've not already worked it out myself.'

'Good luck with that.'

''Ere, what's the car about?' he said nodding at the little Singer as we each opened a door,

'Ah, now there's a news item that I can help you with. Have a word with Mr Cox, Cox's Garage, he can tell you a nice little front-page story. You might even tweak an advert out of him. Got to go, Tom,' the DI nodded.

The little car ran as sweetly as I expected, Mr Cox's mechanic, he'd called him an engineer and he was right, had magic in his fingertips.

227

'It's a nice little motor, Dexter,' the DI said as we pulled up at Mrs Bloor's house.

'It certainly is, sir.'

Mrs Bloor opened the door at the second knock.

'You again! You were here yesterday. What do you want now?'

'I realise that this is a painful subject but we have a few more questions regarding your husband's death. Can we come in please?'

'I suppose so,' she said and stepped aside. 'I suppose you'd better sit down,' she said showing us through into the front room.

'As I told you yesterday, we are treating your husband's death as either suicide, or more likely, murder.'

'I doubt it would be suicide, Ricky was too much of a coward. Once in a while he would trap or cut a finger at work, you'd have thought he'd chopped it off the amount of fuss he made about it. So, if it's anything other than natural causes, I'd say it's murder,' she shrugged.

'You say your husband was a bit timid. Did you ever give him his insulin injections?' the DI asked.

'When he first found out, I always did it for him, then suddenly, he started doing it himself, he'd been given a new little kit from somewhere, said it didn't hurt and he'd see to it, to save me the bother.'

'You didn't do it again after that?'

'No, never again after that, can't say I was all that bothered, I hate needles, even stickin' 'em into him.'

'Forgive me Mrs Bloor, you don't seem to be all that upset by your husband's death.'

'When we first met, he was quite an athlete,

"eleven stone, wet-through!" my Dad used to call him. A runner he was, used to run three or four miles every day. A real athlete, in more ways than one.'

'As part of our investigation, we looked into your husband's background. You were married in 1922 I believe?'

'January the fifteenth 1922, chucked it down with rain all day! Some sort of omen I suppose that was.'

'How long had you known him before that?'

'We both started at Rolls Royce about the same time, in the middle of 1919. He was an engineer, I was a secretary, we met in the main canteen. Real handsome he was then, tall and athletic, like I said; all the girls were after him. To stand a real chance a girl had to offer more than just friendship, you understand?'

'You felt that you had to buy your way into his affections?' the DI suggested.

'You could put it that way, but he'd never, you know, I was his first and there was real love both ways. He was a real husband, even before we married. My Dad was disgusted when he realised that we were "living in sin", but I didn't care, all I wanted was Ricky.'

'Your husband weighed twenty-six stone when he died. In ten years, how did that come about?'

'Like I said he was a runner, decided he wanted to run a cross-country, he normally ran on the track, you see. Well, he ran a couple and got really hooked on it. I didn't mind, he was tired out when he'd done but he always had a bit in reserve, if you get my meaning? Then he takes a tumble crossing a brook, twisted his knee. Bad it was, had to be strapped up for five weeks, so no running and very limited other activities!'

'That still doesn't explain the huge gain in

weight.'

'Athletes use a huge amount of energy, especially runners, they need stamina, it's not just little spurts of energy like some sports, it's sustained for a couple of hours, more sometimes. That means big meals, they get used to big meals, even when they are laid up like Ricky was.'

'I see. Did he never run again then, Mrs Bloor?'

'In the five or six weeks that he was laid up and then three or four months when he was not doing much running, he put on two and a half stone, none of his clothes would fit him, he had to get new everything. He ran a couple of half-mile track events, felt okay with his knee and went for another cross-country. He put his knee out again, and this time it was the end. No more running, but still he couldn't give up the big meals. I tried to limit his intake, for my sake as well as his. I tried to get him to fill up with more healthy stuff, salads and fruit, "rabbit food" he called it.'

'You were here when your brother-in-law suggested that your husband was passing information to a German couple. Were you aware that was the case before he spoke out?' the DI asked.

'I knew he was up to something. Always out in his workshop, doing his photography,' she said.

'Do you know of a Mr Charles Barton, your husband's department manager at Rolls Royce?'

'I knew him back then, lost touch when I married. He made a play for me before I got Ricky interested. I was quite a 'flapper' in them days. Not just him; I could have had my pick but Ricky was different, more er… aloof, harder to crack and a better prize, at least that's what I thought. Funny, how things turn out, don't you think, Inspector?'

'After you husband retired, did he keep in touch with Mr Barton, do you know, Mrs Bloor?'

'After you'd gone yesterday, Tommy, my brother-in-law and me, had a long chat about what Ricky had told him in the pub that day. We put two and two together and reckoned it was someone in his old department that was passing information to him, I should think that Chas Barton, could be a likely candidate, he'd be in the know about everything that was going on,' she shrugged.

'That's true he's certainly one of the people we are investigating. Changing the subject slightly, when we found your husband in the cinema, he had consumed two large chocolate-coated bars, his stomach contents also showed a large meal, roast beef, I believe. From what you have suggested, that was unlikely to be something you would have prepared for him, Mrs Bloor?'

'On a Sunday, a Sunday roast, his treat for being good the rest of the week, ha! Some bloody hopes. No will power you see, no self-control. If it's considered to be food, even salad in small measures, he'd stuff it away. He even used to eat them French things, "escargot" he used to call them to disguise the fact that they were snails; bloody snails, I ask you! Turns my stomach just talking about them, but he'd stuff 'em down him by the plateful.'

The DI gave me the nod to continue the questions.

'On that day, what time did your husband go out, Mrs Bloor?' I asked.

'It was one of his early days. Normally he'd go out about one o'clock, before we had the midday meal, said he was eating out with a friend. He'd be picked up in a car, and brought back the same way. On his early

231

days, he'd go out about eleven, picked up the same way, but come back by taxi about five o'clock.'

'We believe he ate early with the Adler's on those days and the Adler's dropped him in Codnor and he was taxied to Crammingdon to the Magnificent Cinema As you know that was where he was found,' I pointed out.

'I suspected that was where he went, he loved all them comedy films, Laurel & Hardy, Harold Lloyd, Buster Keaton, bloody silly if you ask me but he like 'em.

If he was eating chocolate fudge and stuff, like you said he'd have to juggle with the amount of insulin he injected. That's it! That's why he started injecting himself, so I wouldn't know what he was doing. The stupid, stupid man!' she said and bit her top lip to control her tears.

'You told me a few moments ago that your husband was brought back by taxi, is that correct?' I asked.

'Oh, it didn't drop him outside the house, just at the end of the road.'

'According to the statement we had from a taxi driver, he picked your husband up on Crammingdon market place, but dropped him on Ripley market place, not at the end of your road. How do your account for that, Mrs Bloor?' I asked.

'He must have got another taxi.'

'Why would he do that?'

'I gave up trying to fathom Ricky's mind years ago, so sorry I haven't a clue,' she said with a shake of her head.

'Mrs Bloor did you, on the day your husband died, exchange his insulin for tap water?' the DI asked.

The question unexpectedly like that, shocked even me. That she was thrown off guard for a second or two was clear. Her eyes darted around the room, unable to look at us directly. Then she snapped.

'That's what you think is it? That's why you are here, you've got me down as the wicked, murdering wife!'

'A simple question, Mrs Bloor, we happen to know that your husbands insulin had been changed for ordinary tap water, did you or did you not, change your husbands insulin for tap water?' the DI persisted.

'No. I did not!'

'Thank you Mrs Bloor, that's all for now, please don't leave the area, we could well need to speak again,' the DI replied and stood for us to leave.

'How dare you come here accusing me of murdering my husband?' she yelled as we left.

'Well, what did you make of that, Dexter?' he asked as we settled ourselves back in the Singer.

'I think it was very well rehearsed, sir.'

'She was trying to edge us away all the time, making us look in another direction. I've been too long in this game to fall for obvious diversions like that.'

'Is she guilty then, sir?' I asked.

'I'm not sure if she actually changed the stuff, but I'm pretty bloody sure she knows who did.'

'Protecting someone, you think?'

'That's my guess, but who?'

'How do you think we should play it now then sir?' I ask, at a loss to see the best way forward.

'There's an old saying Dexter. "Give 'em enough rope and let 'em hang themselves!" Mm, it'll be

233

nice to see,' he grinned.

DS Whittington was on the phone at his desk when we arrived back at the office and we all nodded hello.

'How are you getting on with the Norfolk Jimmy case?' the DI asked as he replaced the phone.

'That was Lloyds Bank, as usual they refuse to answer any questions about a customer's account, even though I pointed out that the man had been murdered and the account could well be relevant. I've left it at that for the moment sir.'

'We can always get a warrant if we need to, so that's fair enough. Have you managed to speak to the woman in Towcester?' the DI asked.

'Yes, she seems to be a strange old bird, reckons she met a "down and out" man at a sort of soup kitchen. She works there helping out clearing tables, washing up, that sort of thing. By her own admission, she gets talking to the "customers" especially the men. She stressed that it was just to see if she could help, no other motive, just try to make a difference to their lives, she said.'

'A do-good busy-body,' the DI suggested with a smile.

'Maybe, but I think it's genuine concern, sir. Anyway, she gets talking to Norfolk Jimmy and is impressed by his cultured voice. He gives her the big sob-story, how he had a well-paid job in a manufacturing company. A friend, or someone he thought was a friend, persuaded him to make some investments that went wrong and left him penniless. He lost his house, and his wife left him taking his two children. Anyway Mrs Bretton takes him into her house. He takes a bath and she provides him with a suit of clothes that was her late husbands. He smartened himself up and stayed with her for about a week or so, and "reluctantly" tells her he needs to approach the bank to see if they will make him a loan to tide him over whilst he gets on his feet again.'

'He comes back and tells her that they refused, so she gives him some money to be going on with.' the DI said, shaking his head.

'Not exactly a new story is it, sir?'

'Did she say how much?'

'Two hundred and fifty pounds, sir,' Whittington shrugged.

'He could buy another house with that, how did he get her to part with that much?'

'She was adamant he didn't ask, she offered it of her own free will, at least that's what she believes. The man is a confidence trickster; he accidentally let his tale of woe come out, or let her drag it from him, you know how it works, sir.'

'I bet she hasn't even begun to press charges.'

'Why should she, he had promised to return the money, and she was convinced that he was coming back.'

'What did she say when you told her he was dead?' I asked.

'She burst into tears, I think she had become rather attached to the stinker,' the DS said shaking his head.

'I assume you suggested it was murder?' DI Brierly said.

'That made it worse. I could hear her sobbing and sniffing over the phone.'

'What about the suitcase?' I asked.

'She gave it to him, together with a dollop of her husband's suits, shirts and underwear.'

'Blimey, how long were you on the phone?' asked the DI.

'The girl called the "three minutes", just as I was thanking Mrs Bretton, sir.'

'She told you all that in three minutes?'

'Yes, sir. I also asked if she had any idea who might have murdered him,'

'I guess she hadn't?'

'Not a clue sir, but I gave her our number and she agreed to ring if anything occurred to her,' the DS shrugged.

'So we are no further forward?'

'No sir, sorry.'

'The ball is still in our court, the murder was on our patch – my patch. Keep looking. I can't close it just yet. Have you no other leads?'

'There's still the tramp in custody in Derby, sir. I'm going to interview him again, now the local lads reckon he's sobered up.'

'They've still got him?'

'Yes, sir. Apparently he socked one of the local lads on the schnozzle and tried to escape, it seems they've put him back in his cell and thrown away the key, sir,' Whittington grinned.

'Not the actions of an innocent man!'

'No sir, I'm still waiting for a match on the blood on his shirt. They say it's more difficult once it's dried, and on a dirty shirt as well, doesn't help. The sergeant in charge has tried to hurry things along, he wants the cell freed up but he said the Derby pathologist won't be rushed. At the moment, I can't prove he was under the archway. Both Doug, and Golden Lily were so far gone they wouldn't have known their own names.'

'Do you have a name for him?'

'Not yet, sir.'

'Can't Doug or this woman Diamond Lily identify him?'

'It's Golden Lily, actually, sir. They reckon not, but I think she knows him but won't or daren't say sir.'

'Like I said keep with it, if we can place this chap in Crammingdon we're half way there.'

'I intend to, sir,' Whittington nodded.

'There was a phone call just before you came in, sir. Derbyshire motor licence office, they've matched the number on the car Mrs Rogers, the nosey-neighbour gave us. It's a black Austin Twelve registered to a Mr Charles Barton, 62 Ashworth Hill, Crammingdon, sir.'

'Charles Barton?'

'That's who they said, sir.'

'Mm, we thought she was hanging back on something, didn't we Dexter?'

'Yes, sir.'

'She admitted having known Charles Barton years ago but said she had lost touch, once she married.'

'That's what I've written in my notebook, sir.'

'Time for another word with Mr Barton, you've got his work phone number, I think Dexter?'

'Oh yes, sir,' I said finding the page in my notebook and passing it over to him.

'I'm off to interview my bloody-shirted tramp, sir,' Whittington said and nodded to us both. 'I'm looking forward to going there under my own steam!' he added jangling the keys between his thumb and finger and grinning broadly.

'Okay, let's hope we can tie that one down this time.' The DI nodded. 'Hey, don't smash the bloody thing up!'

'I'll put the kettle on, sir?'

'You're getting the hang of this Dexter,' he grinned as he raised the phone.

I looked at the milk in the bottle by our little sink, only an inch or so remained, about enough for our two cups but when I sniffed it, I decided perhaps a fresh one would be preferable. I rinsed the bottle and went down to the front office to exchange it. By the time I was back the DI had made his call.

'Mr Barton is not at work again today,' he said.

'I wonder where he is, sir.'

'I wonder if he's the one who's been passing information to Bloor, and now he's done a runner.'

'That's what I was thinking, sir.'

'Let's go and see if he's at home.'

We galloped down the stair and out to the little Singer.

Sixty-two Ashworth Hill turned out to be quite a modest little detached house. It had all the signs of being lived in, a bottle of milk stood in a shaded area of the front porch, the morning newspaper was poking out of the letterbox and washing was on a clothesline at the back. We rang the doorbell several times but without anyone answering.

'Can't have gone far, the washing is still out, sir.'

'Go and feel it, see if it's dry.'

'Right, sir,' I agreed and walked down the garden path, 'Bone dry, sir. All of it.'

'Looks like he's already gone, Dexter.'

'Leaving his washing, sir?' I said, and felt stupid as soon as I had said it.

'Just a smoke-screen, Dexter – just a smoke-screen.'

As we got back in the car, a man turned up on a cycle with a little trailer attached. In the trailer were some for sale notices. He stopped at the gate and selected one of the notices, already attached to an eight-foot post, and started to nail it to the gatepost.

'Is this house for sale?' the DI asked.

'Who wants to know?'

'I do,' the DI said taking out his warrant card.

'Oh, er... it's for sale or rent. The chap rang the office yesterday to say he was leavin' so it's back on sale again.'

'Was the house his or was he renting?'

'Just rentin', a pain in the arse they are, them what rents. Generally they just do a moonlight, days, weeks sometimes before we know they've gone.'

'Moonlight?' we both said together.

'Moonlight flit, disappeared, buggered off! At least this bloke was paid up and let us know he was off. short notice though.'

'His washing is still outside,' I said.

'I don't deal with laundry – just for sale signs,' he said knocking in the last nail.

'Come on Dexter, no point hanging around here the man's gone but where to?'

'Are you thinking we should go back to base, sir?'

'Might as well why, what are you thinking?'

'What if our man has gone to the Bloor house, if he had been seeing Mrs Bloor behind Sidney's back, the two of them might be "flitting" together!'

'After she as good as pointed the finger at him? Come on Dexter we never did get that cuppa.'

Nelly was just collecting her girls as I cycled down the entry that night.

'Hello Nelly, how's Dick today?'

'A damned sight happier than he was yesterday. He went to see his boss this morning and showed him the letter from the delivery company. His boss got on the phone to them whilst Dick was there, gave 'em a real dressing down. They've agreed to repair his bike and pay him his full wages until he's back at work,' she grinned.

'That's not bad, so he didn't press for some sort of compensation?'

'Dick's boss advised him to take the offer, like he said, if it went to court it could be ages before there's a settlement and that didn't help either of them.'

'That's true. I've some news for him, as I left this evening the duty sergeant told me the van driver is facing a charge of driving without due care and attention. I'll pop down and tell him all about it once I've had a wash and put the boys to bed,' I said.

That wasn't the only piece of news of the day. Gordon Hemmings, the escaping burglar who had stabbed DC Harrington had appeared in court accused of six robberies, resisting arrest and causing grievous bodily harm to a police officer, had pleaded guilty and gone down for five years.

Next morning, DS Whittington was sitting at the desk we shared, looking a bit glum.

'Morning Sarge, got a problem?' I asked.

'Mm. My nice little case has just turned to dust. The knife the kids found on Parsons Rec. is too blunt to have killed Jimmy, the kids had destroyed any worth-while fingerprints anyway. The Derby force, still haven't got a name for the blood soaked tramp, but it doesn't really seem to matter. It's not Norfolk Jimmy's blood, unless he's had a massive transfusion of stag's blood.'

'Not him then?'

'No, so no result. Except, they've charged him with poaching and assaulting a police officer; socked one of 'em on the beak, if you remember,' Whittington grinned.

'Mm,' I nodded. 'No other leads?'

'Dead end, I reckon it'll be one of those cases that'll remain unsolved, pity it's got my name on it,' he shrugged.

The DI arrived a few moments later, grinning from ear to ear.

'Good morning my merry band of thief takers,' he chirruped. 'I had my first lesson with Mr Cox's chap last night, he reckons I'm a born natural,' he added as we both said good morning.

'Doing well then, sir?' I asked.

'He seemed to think so. Er… what's wrong?' he asked and Whittington gave him the story he'd given me a few minutes earlier.

'Don't get too down hearted, you can't win 'em all and who knows something could turn up. Just let it jog along in the back of your mind.'

'Yes, sir.'

The first teacups of the day had been washed,

when the phone rang and DI Brierly picked up the receiver.

'Thank you, we're on our way,' he said as he replaced it.

'Seems you were right, Dexter. That was Codnor Police, Mrs Rogers had just reported the black car outside Mrs Bloor's house,' he smiled.

It's about a half hour drive to the Bloor's house, but I coaxed the Singer into making it in just over twenty minutes. As we turned into the end of the road a car, a large black saloon, was just pulling away from the gate.

'Is that them? What number did the motor office give us?'

'RC, er… something ending four-seven, it's in my notebook but I can't reach it, sir,' I said, struggling to get at the thing and still keep control of the car.

'No matter, it's Barton's car alright.'

'It looks as though we are just about it time, Dexter. She is with him, I can see her, she just turned to look.'

'Don't know if I can get them to stop, sir.'

'Blow your horn and flash the headlights,' the DI said, putting his arm out of the window and signalling for them to stop.

It was clear that they had seen us and didn't intend to stop. With a puff of blue smoke the black car sped off, turning right at the end of the road, with the tyres squealing and headed off into the countryside.

'They're off. The buggers are trying to get away. We can't have that, can we Dexter?'

'No, sir.'

'What's the chance of catching 'em?'

'If Mr Cox's mechanic has done his job properly, that shouldn't be a problem, sir,' I nodded dropping
down a gear and putting the accelerator to the floor-
boards. The engine roared and the car gave us a jolt in
the back. Jimmy, Mr Cox's salesman had taught me to
drive and his words came instantly back to me. "One day
you'll be driving one of these beauties," he had said,
pointing to the three brand new patrol cars ready for delivery, "There's nothing wrong with speed, provided it is
used intelligently." He had then gone on throughout the
lessons explaining where and how to look, how to judge
the actions of others, and probably the most important
point of all, how to judge the correct entry speed for any
bend.

'Steady on Dexter, this thing's like a bloody
stallion!'

'I could easily catch him sir. but I think that
might spook him into doing something silly, he doesn't
seem to be a very skilled, sir.'

'And *you* are?'

'I know not to brake on a bend the way he did
just now,' I said. 'He's already driving beyond his ability.'

'So speaks the great oracle of driving; how
many times have you driven on your own, Dexter?'

'About half a dozen sir, but Jimmy, Mr Cox's
salesman taught me and he had driven the 1926 Monte
Carlo Rally as mechanic to Mr Cox. He explained the
things that every driver should know, sir.'

'Oh, I stand corrected, Dexter. Just don't smash
my new car, that's all.'

I held back from the big Austin, running about a
hundred yards behind him as he careered along country

lanes barely wide enough for his car in places and making every mistake in the book. At every bend he braked too late and had to fight the steering to stay on the road. Thankfully there was been a dry spell in the weather making the roads dry and free from muddy deposits. At one point he forced a cyclist coming the other way into the ditch at the side of the road. By the time we reached him, he was standing up again, shaking his fist and shouting at the rapidly disappearing car.

'I think this isn't going to end well, Dexter!'

'I'm trying to keep with him, without being too threatening. I don't want to force him to drive more erratically than he already is, sir.'

'I don't know this road, is there anywhere we can safely overtake and stop him?'

'No idea sir, I'm on totally new ground.'

'What's your plan?'

'I don't really have a plan, I'm just hoping he runs out of fuel before we do, sir,' I grinned.

'How much petrol have we got, Dexter?'

'Not a clue sir, the gauge say's half a tank, but I've no idea how accurate it is, or how much the tank holds.'

'Bloody hell!'

'Sorry, sir.'

The road began to run along with a canal on the left hand side, sometimes along the edge of the towpath sometimes veering a few yards away, following a series of gentle bends. Bends, I was able to drive with gentle pressures and releases of the accelerator. That Barton was making very heavy going, braking and speeding up sharply at every change of direction. Disaster, I felt could only be a moment away.

'He's going to end in the canal the way he's going, Dexter.'

'I wonder if he's seen that lorry, sir?'

'What lorry?'

'That one, sir,' I said nodding towards a point a few bends ahead, where the road crossed the canal via a hump-backed bridge. Beyond the bridge on the other side of the canal a heavily laden small lorry was about to start a slow speed climb of the hump.

'Bloody hell, I hadn't seen that,' the DI exclaimed.

'Neither has Barton, sir,' I replied as the lorry appeared at the brow of the bridge just as Barton was making the left hand turn onto the bridge. Instinctively he swerved away, his left wing clipped the right hand wall of the bridge, spinning the car around as it crossed the towpath and plunged into the canal. The car ended up on its side, with the driver's side in about four feet of water. I stopped at the foot of the bridge and we both climbed out. The lorry driver had stopped on the brow of the bridge, and was just able to get out by walking along the parapet wall until he was in front of his vehicle and could drop to the surface of the bridge.

The passenger door of the car was above the water and Mrs Bloor was struggling to open it. I jumped into the water and my feet instantly sank into five or six inches of soft silt, before feeling a firm surface. With the water just below my armpits, I tried to help her open the door.

'Get me out, get me out, I can't swim!' she yelled, though her head was well clear of the water.

'You're okay, don't worry, I'll get you out, once I can get the door open.'

'Hurry, hurry up, I'm drowning,' she yelled, though she was well out of the water, standing on something – Barton I guessed.

The door was large and heavy, and I couldn't get it to go all the way forward so that I didn't need to keep hold of it. A heavy leather check strap restricted how far it could open, to prevent it fouling the bodywork in normal conditions.

'I'll have to close the door again whilst I get my penknife to cut this strap, I'll wind the window down so that you can put your head through.

'Don't close it, don't close it, I'll drown! I admit it I swapped his insulin for water, just get me out,' she yelled. Loud enough for the lorry driver, a totally independent witness, to hear.

I had no choice but to close the door and with her head through the now open window, she repeated her admission as I struggled to get my knife out. I opened the door again holding it with my left hand whilst sawing at the leather strap with my right. With the strap cut through I was able to swing the door forward and out of the way, giving a clear opening. I helped Mrs Bloor out and carried her to the DI and the lorry driver on the bank. Of Barton, there was no sign. I climbed onto the side of the car and stretched down into the muddy water as far as I could touching what seemed to be a shoulder. I grasped the material of his jacket and tugged. Yanking for all I was worth I managed to raise his head above water. By this time the poor chap had been under for four, perhaps five minutes and I was sure he was beyond help. The lorry driver had dropped into the water and gave me a hand getting Barton back to the road. DI Brierly, the only one in the company still dry, had put his

246

coat around Mrs Bloor's shoulders and sat her in the sun on a grassy bank. Taking it in turns we tried to resuscitate Barton but to no avail. I had suspected the chap had died, held down by being stood on by his ladylove.

A car came up behind the Singer.

'What's gone off?' the newcomer asked, though it was reasonably easy to see.

'I need a phone,' the DI said, showing his card.

'Phone at my farm a mile or so back,' he said.

'I need to get this woman somewhere dry.'

'Here get this round her,' he said, handing the DI a blanket that exuded a distinctly rural smell. 'Is he a goner?' he continued nodding towards the body of Barton, still on the roadway.

'No sign of life,' the DI nodded and Mrs Bloor burst into tears as the DI helped her into the newcomer's car.

'Thank you, I'd never have got him out on my own,' I said, shaking the lorry driver's hand.

'No trouble, it's lucky you were following him, I'd never have got either of them out by myself,' he answered. 'What was she on about, swapping insulin or something?'

'It's a long story, but she just admitted murdering her husband,' I said.

'Drowned him surely?'

'That's not her husband!' I said.

'Just as dead as if he was.'

'True,' I agreed.

The DI was chauffeured back by the farmer and told us that a doctor and an undertaker were on the way, as was a patrol car to take Mrs Bloor into custody.

'You heard the woman admit changing her husband's insulin for water Mr...?' the DI asked, the lorry driver

'Hotchkiss, Norman Hotchkiss, and yes I did.'

'Take Mr Hotchkiss's statement, Dexter.'

'I can't, my notebook is rather wet, sir!'

'Then I'll do it,' the DI grinned.

As he took out his notebook, there was a loud "twang".

'Oh, bloody hell, me handbrake's gone again!'

As though in slow motion, we watched the lorry roll down the bridge towards us, gathering speed. We leapt out of the way just in time, however, the little Singer wasn't quite so agile!

'What the bloody hell are you smirking at, Dexter?'

The post mortem on Mr Barton, concluded that he was already dead by the time the car settled in the water, proved by the absence of water in his lungs. His neck was broken, probably in the impact with the bridge, and the sudden spinning of the car.

The *Argus* ran a front-page story about Marco Tizzoni; and Crammingdon's much loved market musician was swamped with offers to donate a replacement accordion.

PC Goldman, the officer injured at Stone Haven Cottage, is making a slow recovery, though his injuries mean he is unlikely to be able to continue in his present position with the force.

Three weeks later, the Adler's were charged with espionage, a story Tom Greatorix was pleased to share with the national dailies having had the initial scoop in his name.

DC Harrington returned to work, and on the day I exchanged plain clothes for my uniform, Tom had another scoop when Mrs Bloor was charged with murdering her husband, a charge she strenuously denied despite her confession in front of the lorry driver.

Thomas Brierly (Detective Inspector) was heartbroken that he never drove his little Singer saloon. The lorry insurance paid out and Mr Cox supplied a rather ugly Morris Cowley saloon as a replacement, much to the DI's disgust.

PC (64) William Dexter
12th October 1932

Perhaps you missed the first in the
Whitecross Yard Murders.

The Killing of Cristobel
Tranter

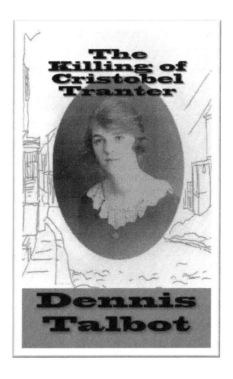

*Young police officer Will Dexter finds the body of a
20year old girl in the entry to a yard of slum houses.
The local CID investigate the case, and Will returns to
normal police duties. A chance car crash weeks later
starts a chain of events that sees him involved in the
crux of the investigation and deep in the blood-soaked
ending.*

Coming Soon

Too Many Wrong Notes

Finally, amid a personal trauma, Will Dexter finds a permanent place on Crammingdon's tiny CID team.

Local author Edna Worsley, creator of animal stories for children, is involved in a massive donation to a local church, but it's not what it seems. The notes are all counterfeit. Does she know they're fake?

When the majority of evidence suggests that the notes are actually being produced locally; just how involved is she?

The final showdown comes in an upstairs room of a derelict farmhouse, with the blood drenched cash, real, fake, who cares? Certainly, not Superintendent Barker!

Also from Dennis Talbot

Three humorous novels introducing Josh Tolson, the son of Walter Tolson the car manufacturer. He's an amiable enough young man though perhaps not the sharpest knife in the box. Some years ago, Walter found his son a manservant, Ellingham, to steer him through his inevitable self-inflicted problems. Josh tells the stories in his own amusing way, You'll smile, chuckle, perhaps even laugh out loud at the way he perceives life!

If you love the great P G Wodehouse, these three humorous novels from Dennis could be for you!

"A Small Price to Pay, Sir!"

(ISBN 978-1848-9738-79)

Josh agrees, much against his better judgement to assist Jane, his ex-fiancée, in a risky enterprise. Ellingham is unhappy with the situation but reluctantly goes along with things. When Liz, then Ramona arrive on the scene, Ellingham decides that it is time to extricate his young master. However, Josh has other ideas!

("A Small Price to Pay, Sir" reached the final of the People's Book Prize 2016)

"Best Foot Forward, Ellingham"

(ISBN 978-1848-9761-84)

His friend Spotty persuades Josh into investing in a risky enterprise in the USA. Whilst starting up the new venture his old friend Chas, asks him to be his best man at his wedding to Jane, Josh's old flame!

With help from Ellingham, Josh must work his way through miserable mother's-in-law, financial crisis and unruly children, all whilst realising he may have found the love of his life. Can Ellingham come up with all of the answers this time?

"Look Lively, Ellingham"

(ISBN 978-1848-9780-96)

In this the third book in the series, Josh has no alternative but to take nine year old Angelica (hooligan in ankle socks) to the zoo. When catastrophe and mayhem gets them thrown out, he hopes that's the last he will see of her for a long while.

Then Aunt E asks Ellingham to rid her of a tiresome guest, but when his efforts only seem to make things worse, she decides to take matters into her own hands and invite Angelica to stay, despite Josh's warnings of disaster! What's more, Ellingham seems to have lost the plot!

Made in the USA
Columbia, SC
18 September 2018